## "Go down to the wharfs myself?"

Ananiah asked incredulously. "You know a lady could never do that, Captain Colburn."

"But a *lady* can come crawling over garden walls like a cat, begging passage to England with a man she knows nothing about, then face down a pack of Admiralty lords for her rascally old father?" Sam laughed. "A *lady!*"

"I never begged." Impulsively Ananiah pulled off her earrings and pressed them into his palm, where the clustered diamonds glittered incongruously against the pattern of a working sailor's scars and calluses.

"Take these as surety. I can sail in a day." Her fingers scarcely brushed against his, but it was enough to make her heart quicken, and she withdrew her hand as if she'd been burned.

Sam tossed the earrings in his palm, lightly, like dice, weighing them against his own misgivings. Baubles to her, yet the pair could make the *Truelove* all his . . . .

"Keep your diamonds, Ananiah Snow," he said softly. "Passage on the *Truelove*'s not for sale, and neither is her master."

Dear Reader,

The holidays are upon us and Harlequin Historicals is celebrating with a quartet of keepers!

First, *New York Times* bestselling author Elizabeth Lowell brings us *Reckless Love*. Janna Wayland is as untamed as the wild horses she trains. But when Ty Mackenzie comes into her life, her unbridled passion forces her to make a painful choice.

Margaret Moore, author of the Warrior series, takes us back to the age of Norsemen in her latest release. *The Viking* is Einar, a warrior whose decision to take Saxon woman Meradyce hostage changes his life forever. Filled with adventure and romance, this is a *must* read.

In *Providence,* Ananiah Snow—a woman with a scandalous past—risks everything when she hires handsome sea captain Sam Colburn to find her missing father. Yet losing her heart to Sam proves the greatest risk of all. Another swashbuckling, romantic tale on the high seas by popular author Miranda Jarrett.

And rounding out December is *Counterfeit Laird* by Erin Yorke. This charming tale about the people in a small Scottish village who trick American businessman Creag Blake into believing he is the long-lost laird is sure to please readers—especially when the sparks begin to fly between Creag and the old laird's granddaughter, Jeanne....

All of us at Harlequin wish you a happy and safe holiday season and best wishes for the new year!

Sincerely,

Tracy Farrell
Senior Editor

# Providence

## MIRANDA JARRETT

*Harlequin Books*

TORONTO • NEW YORK • LONDON
AMSTERDAM • PARIS • SYDNEY • HAMBURG
STOCKHOLM • ATHENS • TOKYO • MILAN
MADRID • WARSAW • BUDAPEST • AUCKLAND

ISBN 0-373-28801-8

PROVIDENCE

Copyright © 1993 by Susan Holloway Scott.

**Books by Miranda Jarrett**

---

## MIRANDA JARRETT

is an award-winning designer and art director whose writing combines her love of history and reading. Her travels always include visits to old houses and historical restorations.

Miranda and her husband, a musician, live near Philadelphia with their two small children and two large cats. She is still trying to figure out how to juggle writing, working and refereeing disputes among preschoolers in the sandbox.

For Tracy Farrell
Perfection as an editor, a joy as a friend

# Chapter One

*Providence, Rhode Island*
*June 1796*

Five minutes. That was all Ananiah Snow guessed she'd have to find the man who could save her father's life. Five minutes of gentlemen staring and ladies gasping behind their fans, of people she once considered her friends pointedly looking away when she walked too close. Five minutes before the servants came to hurry her out the door and away from the respectable society that no longer included her.

She crouched on the top of the brick garden wall, carefully holding her gauzy skirts clear of the damp moss. Laughter from the party drifted through the warm summer night, across the whirring of the katydids in the ivy below and over the nervous thumping of her own heart.

Why did she have to be such a coward? Arriving uninvited through the garden door at Sarah Brown's Wednesday collection was nothing compared to the dangers her father risked at sea with every voyage. But still her hands were clammy and her breath was tight in her chest, and she wondered if she'd remember any of the speech she'd rehearsed to say to Captain Colburn when she found him. *If* she found him.

"Pray come back down, Miss Ananiah!" urged her maid, Letty, in a shrill whisper from the pavement eight feet below. "Lord, but your father will have my head when he learns of this! Mad, I was, to let you tease me into it, and—"

"Hush, Letty, be still, or you'll raise the watch!" With what she hoped was a stern scowl, Ananiah reached down to take the long white gloves that Letty reluctantly held up to her. Captain Snow might well ask for Letty's head, but at the same time, he'd be able to praise his daughter's spirit for once. Too often he'd chided Ananiah for not having enough backbone, and the memory of his lectures gave her the resolve she needed.

"I'll meet you at home as soon as my business is concluded," she said, sitting back on her heels on the wall. "I'll be safe enough on Benefit Street."

"Safe!" said Letty scornfully. "A young lady's never safe on any street in a seafaring town!"

"Letty, this is Providence, not Port Royal. I swear no harm will come to me, or you, either."

"It's not me I'm paid to watch over." Letty sniffed and tugged her shawl over her narrow shoulders. "I'll go, miss, because you wish it, but mind you take care on this business of yours. Even in your blessed Providence, there's plenty of folk who wish you ill."

She turned and stalked away, shaking her head and muttering to herself, and with a long sigh, Ananiah watched her go. Letty was protective, that was all. How could it be otherwise, after what had happened in Martinique?

Shoving the memory away, Ananiah stood upright on the wall, the plumes in her hair brushing gently against the leaves of the trees overhead. When she had been girlhood friends with the Brown daughters, she had often come into their garden this way, over the wall, and she remembered a crab-apple tree at the northwest corner whose branches had been bent to grow against the bricks—an easy path to the ground.

Or at least it had been easy when she was twelve, in linsey-woolsey and darned stockings. At twenty-four, in a French gown of embroidered muslin, the journey was a bit more difficult. Slowly she inched along the moss-covered wall, her arms outstretched, her long kid gloves clutched in one hand and her fan in the other. The moss was thicker and more slippery than she remembered, and she placed each foot as carefully as a market-fair rope dancer.

"I knew well enough I was in Providence," said a man's deep voice from the garden somewhere below her, "but I'd no notion I'd find the place peopled with angels on high."

Ananiah froze, her arms still outstretched, and peered down into the shadows. Now that she'd stopped concentrating so hard on not falling, she could smell the tobacco from the man's pipe, and she cursed the habit that had brought him from the drawing room at this moment. If he called the others, her plan would be over before it had begun.

The man chuckled, still hidden by the darkness. "Take care, angel. Don't fall from grace on my account."

"You can't stop me, you know," she said, stiffening. Either he recognized her, or his jest was only a cruel coincidence.

"What, from breaking your pretty neck?" His footsteps crunched on the path of crushed shells, then turned silent as he walked across the grass towards the wall. "I'll be damned if I'll stand by idle and let you come tumbling down. Even angels can use a hand once in a while."

"I' m not an angel, and I'm in no need of your assistance, thank you." She heard the nine-o'clock bell from the meetinghouse in the distance. If she didn't hurry, she might miss Captain Colburn altogether, and lose her last chance to help her father. Focussing again on the wall, she scurried the last few feet to the crab-apple tree.

As she clutched at the topmost branches with relief, she heard the man swear, and realized he'd come rushing forward to the foot of the tree to catch her if she'd fallen. Purposefully ignoring him to preserve what was left of her dignity, she gathered her skirts in one hand and climbed down the espaliered branches. She smoothed her hair, drew on her gloves, easing the kidskin along each finger, and turned at last to face the man behind her.

With his legs spread wide and his arms folded across his chest, he was larger than she'd expected, much larger, and though she wasn't a small woman herself, the sheer breadth of his chest and shoulders blocked her way. In the faint moonlight that filtered through the trees, she still couldn't make out much of his face beyond the angled planes of his cheekbones and jaw, and his wavy, tousled hair, which needed retying. His dark coat was lost in the shadows, leaving only a white shirtfront, a patterned scarf loosely knotted around his throat, and a white long-stemmed pipe tucked into the top buttonhole of his coat.

"You will let me pass?" she asked, the command she'd intended rising upward into a question. She was wary of the kindness she heard in his teasing. Kindness had become rare in her life, and she couldn't afford to trust in it. With a little shake of her shoulders, she tried to steady herself, and mentally excused the lie she told next. "I'm expected within the house, you see."

Clearly puzzled, the man frowned, his shadowed brows coming together. "Then why come this way, over the wall?"

Ananiah looked down at her fan to avoid his scrutiny, and toyed with the silk tassel looped through the ivory blades. She wondered what the color of his eyes might be, and if by day his hair were dark or fair. She liked his voice, deep and low, and she knew she shouldn't. God preserve her, hadn't she learned anything from Étienne?

"I have no invitation," she said in a small voice. "This—over the wall, I mean—was the only way."

The man chuckled again. "Truth to tell, I don't have one, either. But John Brown seems a welcoming sort of man, and if he opens his doors to every ragtag shipmaster like me in his port, I doubt he'll turn out a lady like you."

He reached out to her, brushing her cheek lightly with the backs of his fingers. Ananiah closed her eyes, almost dizzy from the unexpected gentleness of his touch. Two years had passed since she had been alone with a man, but she knew what would happen next. If she didn't stop him now, he would kiss her, and though she knew he shouldn't, her feet seemed planted to the ground, unable to carry her to safety. His fingers traced along her jaw, the movement too light to be called a caress, but still too sensuous for Ananiah to ignore. He cradled her chin against his thumb, and she wondered if he could feel the wild pounding of her pulse.

Slowly, so slowly, he tipped her head back, and on their own her lips parted expectantly as his mouth lowered towards hers. His other hand curled around her waist to draw her closer, and she swayed back against his forearm. Then his lips found hers, warm and beguiling, and with a breath of a sigh that was lost between them, she let herself yield. He tasted of tobacco and rum, and as his mouth moved over hers she felt the warmth of his kiss spread to her limbs, and her hands crept up around his neck for support. She lost herself in forgotten sensations and nothing else seemed to matter. When had she last felt like this, lost in a world that narrowed to the circle of a man's arms?

*Not since the summer night when she'd turned nineteen, when Étienne de Gramont had brought her to a garden near the sea, a garden filled with parrots and the honeyed scent of scarlet flowers, and asked her to be his wife. Long ago, but not long enough for her to forget the sorrow that had come from Étienne's kisses, and the lies that had torn both her heart and her world apart forever.*

Abruptly Ananiah pulled away. "This isn't right. I can't stay. Forgive me, but I can't." She knew she was barely making sense, but she could no more control her words than the way her heart still beat too rapidly and her body ached to be next to his once again. "I'm here to meet someone. That is, I expect to, if he's there still."

"He?" the stranger repeated softly.

"He. A gentleman."

The stranger sighed and ran his fingers back through his hair. "Ah, well, then I don't dare keep you, do I, angel?"

"Don't call me that again, please," said Ananiah quickly, thankful for the shadows that would hide the glitter of the tears in her eyes. The unexpected note of regret in the man's voice too closely matched her own feelings, and reminded her of other meaningless words she'd heard, in long-ago moonlight. She would be twenty-five years old this autumn, long past her time for garden dalliances, and she ordered herself to think of why she had come here this night, of her father in his prison.

The man shrugged and shook his head, and, with a slight, self-mocking bow, stepped aside to let her pass. "Didn't mean to give offense," he said good-naturedly, almost talking to himself. "But how you looked in that white gown, high on the wall above me —you put me in mind of something fine and pure, like angels."

Ananiah stared down at her gown as the breeze blew her skirts around her legs. Even here in Providence, she still chose to follow the high-waisted French styles because they suited her. But fine and pure, fit for an angel? No. Even new, the gown had never been that.

"All the French ladies on Martinique wear white," she explained swiftly, "and I followed the fashion, too, to please my husband."

"Ah, your husband," said the stranger, and he cleared his throat awkwardly. "On Martinique, you say?"

Ananiah winced, and wondered miserably what had made her speak of Étienne. Of course this man, stranger or not, would know the shameful truth. Why else would he have kissed her? The regret she'd heard in his voice was likely only because she hadn't let him tumble her here on the grass. Everyone in Providence knew about Ananiah Snow and what had become of her. Only her father believed in her innocence.

*Her father...* She'd tarried too long as it was. With her head bowed, Ananiah slipped past the stranger and ran towards the house.

# Chapter Two

Shaking his head, Sam Colburn tugged his pipe out of its buttonhole and felt his pockets for more tobacco. Here the loveliest creature he'd seen in ages had nearly dropped like a plum into his arms, and the best he could do was to mumble some nonsense about angels that had sent her scurrying off before he'd even learned her name. It was more bad luck, pure and simple, the same infernal bad luck that had plagued him like the devil these last six weeks, and he hadn't the first notion of how to shake it.

He looked longingly after the girl as she slipped in the garden door to the house, the candlelight for a moment catching the line of her bare shoulders before she disappeared. Sweet Jesus, but she was pretty, with wide green eyes and pale gold curls tumbling loose over her shoulders. And the way the sheer fabric of her gown clung to her curves made him ache at the memory.

He didn't usually make a practice of kissing young women he hadn't met, at least not well-bred ones with diamond earbobs and kidskin gloves. If he wanted, he could probably blame it on the rum—he'd drunk more than his usual limit tonight, from boredom and despair—but there was something else about the girl that he couldn't quite pinpoint. Though she'd melted into his arms readily enough, it hadn't been from wantonness. There'd been an odd, tentative yearning to her kiss, an unspoken longing that he wasn't sure any man could have fulfilled, but he would have liked the chance to try. And she was unhappy, that was clear enough. What would it take to lift the sadness he'd heard in her voice?

Sam smiled wryly to himself. How conveniently the rum made him overlook the fact that the woman already had a husband, and likely a lover, too. If she was unhappy, it was her own doing. Best to steer clear of waters that were muddied.

But still he couldn't help wishing he was the one she'd been meeting here in the welcoming shadows. Certainly Sophie Crowninshield hadn't wasted any time in finding a new bridegroom to replace *him*. That was where his luck had first gone sour, when Sophie had convinced him to offer for her. Why had he expected it to be otherwise? Deep in his pocket, Sam's fingers again twisted around her last letter, the one that had so formally informed him of her betrothal to Robert Pickering. Though it was written in Sophie's own childish hand, Sam knew her father had dictated it, just as he'd angrily dictated to his fellow merchants in Salem not to ship their cargos with Sam on the *Truelove*.

The other letter in Sam's pocket was from the firm that had lent him the money to buy the *Truelove,* and showed how eagerly merchants from Salem to Boston had sided with Elias Crowninshield against the upstart son of a drunken Dock Street cooper. Sam knew the words by heart: ''Jos. Beltan & Bros. would regret to be forced to foreclose on the brig *Truelove* if Captain Colburn does not honor them directly with another payment." Hell, if he didn't find a cargo here in Providence, he wouldn't have the hard money to pay his crew next week, and then they'd be gone, too, along with his ship and his Sophie and his dreams of being a grand man in Salem.

Combing his hair back haphazardly with his fingers, Sam shoved the unlit pipe into his pocket and headed back to the house. High time he forgot wealthy girls who looked like angels and remembered instead what he'd come here to do. As he stepped back into the crowded room, he plucked another tumbler from a servant's tray, emptied it, and looked about for the next Rhode Island merchant he might try to convince of the *Truelove*'s virtues. Sweet Jesus, he'd rather dive into a cove full of sharks than go hat in hand like this.

But as he scanned the room, his gaze caught and held on the curling ostrich plumes bobbing above the crowd of men's heads and shoulders. Curious to see the man the young woman had chosen over him, he quickly elbowed his way towards the feathers.

She stood alone, to one side of the arched doorway to the hall, fluttering her fan nervously. She, too, was searching about the room, her chin lifted high. Though Martinique ladies might favor sheer muslin cut beguilingly low at the bodice, the ones in Providence clearly didn't, and Sam saw how the other women glared at her with a combination of scorn and jealousy. Not only was his angel the most elegantly gowned woman in the company, she was also hands down the most beautiful, and Sam wondered why the gentlemen, too, chose to keep their distance from her. Perhaps it meant she'd be willing to grant him a second chance.

But before he could join her, a woman in maroon silk and black false curls swept forward and began to whisper furiously in the younger woman's face. The younger woman's cheeks flushed, and her chin dropped as her face went stiff with obvious misery. It seemed to Sam that even the plumes in her hair began to droop beneath the other's whispered attack. Though Sam had limited experience with drawing-room manners, he knew a bully wherever he found one, and for the second time that evening he came to the younger woman's rescue.

"Excuse me, mistress," he said heartily as he cut himself between the two women, "but I've been looking to have a word with this lady all evening."

"'Lady,' indeed!" The older woman almost hissed with scorn as she snapped open her fan. "I can quite imagine, Captain, what sort of *words* you'd wish to have with a hussy like Ananiah Snow!"

Sam tipped his head, one brow cocked as if he couldn't quite believe what she'd said. "Whatever words I choose, ma'am, are bound to be more agreeable than the ones you're using right now. Not that any of them would be your particular business."

Around them conversations dwindled and died as other guests turned to listen. Ananiah stared down at the fan clutched so tightly in her fingers. Her cheeks—no, her entire face and throat—were on fire. This was so much worse than anything she could have imagined. She wished the polished floorboards would open up and swallow her up whole.

But Deborah Collins plainly relished the audience, and her voice rose with self-righteousness. "I spoke but the truth, sir. None here will say otherwise on the strumpet's behalf. Too grand was Miss Ananiah to wed any decent Providence boy! Nay, she'd rather let that rascally father of hers sell her to some filthy island Frenchman—"

"That's enough," ordered Sam curtly. He didn't believe for a minute that the girl was a strumpet, not the way she blushed. He took her hand firmly in his own and led her away, across the hall to the empty dining room. The table had been cleared and the cloth drawn from dinner, but the candles remained lit in the tall branched holders, and Sam closed the heavy paneled door behind them.

"You shouldn't do that," said Ananiah in dismay as she retreated to the far end of the table. Nothing was going the way she'd planned. She hadn't counted on there being so many men here that she didn't recognize, and no way for her to determine which one was Captain Colburn. She'd been caught gawking like a country girl when Mrs. Collins pounced on her, and every one of the woman's spiteful words had struck home. Then finally had come the man from the garden again, sweeping her away from the drawing room like some sort of prize. Worst of all, she had gone with him meekly, letting him take her hand, just as she'd let him kiss her before. Mrs. Collins had every right to call her a strumpet when she behaved like one. Oh, why hadn't she listened to Letty and stayed home where she belonged?

"You really must open the door, sir," she continued, trying to sound reasonable. "I can't be alone with you like this."

Sam grinned. "You were in the garden."

"That was different," said Ananiah quickly. She rubbed her thumb against her middle finger, twisting her ring around and around her finger. "We were there together only by chance. In passing, I mean. And no one knew."

Sam's left brow cocked upwards again as he leaned against the edge of the table, his long legs crossed and his hands thrust deep in his pockets. The candlelight fired the chestnut streaks in his dark hair and softened the angles of his features. Sometime in the past his nose had clearly been broken, and a pale scar curved like a moon over one cheekbone. While his face wasn't regular enough to be called handsome, decided Ananiah, there was more than enough strength and character, and good humor, too, to make him attractive. Horribly, dangerously attractive, because he knew it as well as she did.

"So my company's safe enough," he mused, "so long as no one knows?"

Reluctantly Ananiah nodded, wishing her reasoning didn't sound so foolish coming from him.

"And what about kissing me, eh? That didn't count, either?" He meant to tease her, that was all, but instead of blushing prettily again the way he'd hoped, her cheeks paled.

"You heard what Mrs. Collins called me," she said bitterly. She'd been chaste as a nun since she returned to Providence. How could he know how much her carefully rebuilt self-respect meant to her? "A strumpet and a hussy. Doubtless you heard worse than that about me before."

"Haven't heard a word, and I don't particularly care if I do," declared Sam. "Men go to war over money and honor and politics, but with women it's always the same. One lady dawdles a little too long with another's man, and there you are, at it like cats."

"It's not that simple."

"Never is, when it's your quarrel, Ananiah," said Sam, letting the rippling syllables of her name play across his tongue. An unusual name—complicated, like her. "I'd much rather hear why this rogue you're so determined to meet hasn't done damn-all to defend you."

Ananiah bristled, drawing herself up very straight. Of course she'd heard much worse language from her father, but this man didn't have the right to use it before her, any more than he had the right to use her given name.

"There's nothing to tell you, sir," she said primly. "I can scarcely expect Captain Colburn to defend me when I've yet to meet the gentleman."

"But you have, angel, and I did," said Sam softly, not quite sure what to make of this curious good fortune. "I'm Samuel Colburn, captain of the brig *Truelove*, out of Salem, and though I haven't a notion as to why you've sought me out, I'm at your service."

"You?" she asked with open dismay. She had imagined her savior to be as old as her father, someone trustworthy and venerable. This man was far too near to her own age for comfort, and too cocksure by half to be trusted. *"You?"*

"Aye, me," said Sam defensively. "I've never had cause to be shamed by who I am, and I'll be damned if I'll start now."

"I didn't mean to imply that you should," said Ananiah quickly. "It's only that you were not—not as I expected."

"I 'd say the same of you, angel." She didn't have to spell it out. He could see how she was appraising him beneath her lashes, gauging his worth the way the rich always did, the way they always had with him as far back as he could remember. "Maybe you could begin by explaining why you're so disappointed."

"I said I was surprised, not disappointed." Slowly Ananiah walked around the table towards him, trailing her fingers across the inlaid wood as she tried to recall the formal little speech she'd rehearsed for the imaginary white-haired Captain Colburn. "I had heard that your financial obligations press upon you, and that that is why you have come to Providence."

Damnation, but she was direct! "I'm flat to the wall without a dollar to my name," Sam answered bluntly. "If I don't find something, anything, to carry within the fortnight, I'll lose my brig to the thieving rascals who hold the lien on her. Even a fine lady like yourself might call that 'pressing.'"

"Then perhaps . . ." she said, her voice little more than a whisper. "Perhaps we may be able to help one another." She looked up at him uncertainly. There was no mistaking the antagonism in his face now that she'd blundered so badly and insulted him.

Sam stood in hostile silence, forcing her to explain herself. She owed that to him. He was willing to wait. But the waiting would be easier if she weren't standing so close to him, near enough that he could smell the heady fragrance from her skin, sweet, like lilies.

With a sigh, Ananiah lowered her gaze from his face to the blue scarf around his throat. A coward, that was what she was. A strumpet and a coward, and she couldn't tell which was worse. Mechanically she began to rush through her speech. "My father is captain of the ship *Commerce,* of this port. In January he sailed for Bordeaux. He never arrived, nor have I received any word from him or another to explain how he came to grief."

At once Sam's expression softened. "I'm sorry, Ananiah," he said gently. "To lose your father at sea that way—"

"But he's not dead, Captain Colburn!" she protested. "It's the English. I'm sure they've captured the *Commerce,* and taken my father prisoner. He's always boasting how he taunts the navy ships and how he always refuses to stop and present his papers. He outruns them instead. Not that he has anything to hide, of course. It's the king who has no respect for American trade."

Sam listened and shook his head. He could fill in the rest far better than she could herself. Running the English blockade to trade with France was the one sure way to quick profits for American ships. Without it, Sam himself wouldn't own as much of the *Truelove* as he did. But any kind of risky trading had to balance daring with common sense, and taunting navy ships wasn't something Sam would recommend. The old fool should consider himself fortunate if he'd only been taken prisoner and not blown clean out of the water for his impudence—an opinion, of course, that Sam's own common sense made him keep to himself.

"Desperate I may be, angel," he said, "but I'm not about to go chasing into some English prison after your old man."

"I never expected you to do that!" Ananiah's eyes widened with indignation. "I only wish you to give me passage to London. I'll go to the Admiralty myself, and have my father freed. Passage, that's all I wish from you, and I'll pay whatever you want if you'll take me."

For a long, pleasurable moment, Sam let himself picture her in the *Truelove*'s cabin, curled up willingly on the sheets of his cot. From that single kiss he knew she'd have none of Sophie's virginal skittishness. Her figure was riper, too, made for a man's touch. But how would she be after ten days of rough weather and cold food and no water for washing? Well-bred ladies expected niceties, no matter whose bed they were warming. And then there was her husband...

"I don't take passengers. Never will," he said flatly. "More trouble than they're worth. It's too dangerous, with the English still after us like the war didn't settle anything. I don't want some green-gilled lubber yapping in my ear if I've got a frigate on my tail. And as for ladies on board—ladies bring nothing but bad luck in deep water, and that's the Lord's own truth."

"Even if it means you'll lose your brig to the bankers?" Ananiah had heard this witless argument about women and ships often enough from her father. "Are you superstitious enough for that?"

Sam cleared his throat, scowling. She had him there, no mistake, and he didn't like it. He waved one arm towards the window, and the harbor that lay beyond it. "You've got a score of shipmasters out there. Why pick on me?"

"Because they all turned me down," she said, her desperation creeping into her voice. "You're my last chance, Captain Colburn."

"So I'm your last chance, am I?" His scowl deepened to a black frown that made Ananiah's hopes falter. "A pretty way you have of trimming a man's pride, sweetheart."

"I've little enough pride of my own left, Captain," she said sadly. "Though I love my father, I know his faults. He's a brash man who has prospered where others have failed, and he likes to make a show of his success in a way that many think unseemly. While my mother lived, she could smooth over his squabbles with our neighbors, but now there are precious few in Providence who'd call him friend. The ones who might still help him answer first to their wives, and none would risk having me on board his ship. I had hoped that because you were from Salem, none of that would matter to you."

Her words trailed off forlornly. Around her throat was a long gold chain, and she unconsciously swung the sapphire locket that hung from it back and forth between her fingers, sending little blue reflections from the stones across the curves of her breasts. Sam swallowed hard and forced himself to look away. She'd tempt a saint to stray, doing little things like that, but worse was the way he wanted to help her. He'd been an outcast too long himself not to want to, but God in heaven, the grief she could bring him! With Sophie, he'd already run afoul of a possessive father. He didn't want to consider what trouble he'd find with a jealous husband on his tail.

"If it's only passage you want, then why didn't you come down to where we're moored?" he asked. Restlessly he ran his fingers through his hair as impulse warred with his instincts. "Why gamble that I'd be here tonight at all?"

Her neat brows drew together. "Go down to the wharfs myself?" she asked incredulously. "You know a lady could never do that, Captain Colburn."

"But a *lady* can come crawling over garden walls like a cat, beg passage to England with a man she knows nothing about, then face down a pack of Admiralty lords for her rascally old father, who knew full well what he was about, and now must pay the king's piper?" Sam laughed. He couldn't help it. "A *lady*, for all love!"

"I never begged," she said stubbornly, ignoring his other objections. Lord knows if she began thinking about them too much, she'd lose her nerve altogether. Impulsively she reached up and pulled off her earrings. She took Sam's hand in hers and pressed the earrings into his palm, where the clustered diamonds glittered incongruously against the thick pattern of scars and calluses.

"Here, take these as surety," she said. "You may have a draft for the balance whenever you wish. I can be ready to sail in a day." Her fingers scarcely brushed against his, but it was enough to make Ananiah's heart quicken again, and she withdrew her hand as quickly as if she'd been burned. Two months in close quarters with him at sea: she'd been fool enough to kiss him in the garden, but she'd never guessed the punishment would be this high.

Sam tossed the earrings in his palm, lightly, like dice, weighing them against his own misgivings. Baubles to her, yet the pair could make the *Truelove* all his. "What surety do you have that your father's even alive?"

"If my father were dead, I would know it," said Ananiah simply. "He's always come when I needed him. I can't fail him now, when he needs me."

While part of him didn't want to know, Sam still had to ask. "Why not go to your husband?"

He was surprised by the way she seemed to fade into herself at the mention of her husband. "I would never ask Étienne, and he wouldn't offer. Besides, I believe my father would refuse his help even if he did."

She searched his face for the answer she needed. He must agree, she prayed to herself, he must, he *must*. "Please, Captain Colburn. I would give all my father's fortune to have him back."

Sam knew that if he kissed her again this time she wouldn't run, and again he imagined her in the *Truelove*'s cabin, her pale eyes cloudy with passion and her hair loose and silky across his pillow. She would be soft and eager beneath him, and in the time it took to reach England he would make her forget all her sorrow, just as now he was willing to forget she was married to another man.

She and her offer were both tempting, very tempting. He wished his conscience would let him accept. With his fingers, he gently brushed her long curls back from her face and replaced her earrings.

"Keep your diamonds, Ananiah Snow," he said softly. "Passage on the *Truelove*'s not for sale, and neither is her master."

# Chapter Three

"I wouldn't be expecting any grand welcome, miss," said Letty with a sniff as Ananiah leaned eagerly out the window of the hired carriage. "Like as not that man's going to pitch you overboard when he learns what you've done to him."

"I've told you before, Letty, Captain Colburn's not like that," said Ananiah. Even when he'd refused her offer at the Browns' house, he'd been kind to her. The memory was comforting, and without it, she wouldn't have had the courage to be here today. And, too, kindness was much easier to accept and explain than what she'd felt when he kissed her. "He seemed a reasonable enough man."

"No man's reasonable when he's been tricked into doing something he don't want to do. Especially if it's a lady doing the tricking."

Ananiah sighed impatiently, wondering just how many more times she and Letty would have this same conversation. In the seven years since Letty had become her lady's maid, they'd never argued as much as they had this last week, and Ananiah hadn't even mentioned what had happened in the garden. Even so, from the stiff-backed way Letty sat on the edge of the seat, her plump face shining from the heat and the warmth of the new wool gown she'd chosen for traveling, Ananiah didn't doubt the little woman had plenty more to say. Letty always did.

"Oh, he might be a bit cross-tempered at first, Letty," she began as she retied the wide ribbons of her hat under her chin.

"That bow was fine as it was, miss!" said Letty indignantly. "You'll only crease the silk with your fiddling about like that."

Again Ananiah sighed as Letty reached forward to pluck at the bow. "I said, Letty, that Captain Colburn might be cross-tempered at first, but I expect he'll soon see that what I've done is all for the best. Mr. Morrow said Captain Colburn's been patience itself this past week."

This time Letty only muttered to herself, and gladly Ananiah turned back to the open window. Though she wouldn't have admitted it to Letty, she knew herself that what she'd done *was* trickery, the same kind that Étienne had used on her. But she hadn't lied, the way her husband had. She'd rather die than do that. She'd made sure that Mr. Morrow, her father's oldest and most trusted clerk, understood her reasons and wishes. If Captain Colburn had assumed certain things about his new cargo, that was his own fault, not hers. Uneasily she twisted her ring beneath her glove, wishing she were already on board and in her cabin. She told herself her conscience was clear, but somehow she doubted that the *Truelove*'s master was going to agree.

They were almost to the docks now, the driver slowing the horse as he picked his way through carters and sailors, apprentices on errands and farmers come to market, all crowded together because of the business that had brought them to North Main. Ananiah had lived nearly all her life within sight of the river, but she was certain she'd never seen the water so bright in the morning sun or the sky so blue overhead, the white gulls wheeling and diving among the tall masts and spars of the ships in port. How angry could any captain be, with a day like this for sailing?

The carriage stopped and swayed as the driver climbed heavily from the top. Outside the window Ananiah could see the weathered brick warehouse and the shop that had belonged first to her grandfather and then her father, and the blue-and-gold sign of the compass rose that hadn't changed since before the revolution. Beyond the carriage's other window would be her family's dock, and tied to it would be the *Truelove*. Without waiting for the driver, Ananiah unlatched the door herself and clambered down into the street. Holding her skirts above the dust, she slowly circled in front of the horse and gazed at the ship before her.

The *Truelove* was smaller than she'd expected, at least twenty feet shorter than her father's ship. She was plainer than the *Commerce*, too, without any of the fancy woodwork and bright paint that her father favored. The *Truelove*'s sides were dull green trimmed with black, and the sails hung out limply to dry were stained and patched like old quilts. Ananiah remembered her owner-captain's poverty, and wished she'd told Mr. Morrow to authorize funds for refitting too. But humble though the little brig was, the *Truelove* was lovingly tended, with every line coiled in perfect loops and her decks as clean as a drawing-room floor. A trim little vessel, thought Ananiah, hearing the words in her father's bluff voice. She imagined him standing on the wharf beside her, his bristling white brows drawn together as he appraised the brig. Lord, she missed him. She'd weather the wrath of a dozen

Captain Colburns if it meant she'd have her father back.

The last of the water casks for the voyage was being lowered through the hatch, the task supervised by the mate. There was no sign of Captain Colburn. So much the better, decided Ananiah. She'd rather he learned about her plans in private. At least if they spoke in his cabin, he couldn't toss her overboard the way Letty had predicted.

She crossed the street resolutely and marched up the plank onto the brig, the scarlet ribbons of her hat streaming out over her shoulders. As she stepped onto the deck, her skirt snagged on the rail, and when she had pulled it free she turned back to find every man on the deck frozen in place and staring at her as if she'd risen from the dead.

"Good afternoon," she began, and when none of them replied, she repeated it. "Good afternoon!"

Finally a boy stepped forward, tugging off his knitted cap. "Do you be lost, miss?" he asked, his voice breaking and sqeaking upwards uncontrollably. "This here be the brig *Truelove*."

Far below, in the hold, Sam shaded his eyes with his hand and looked up at the bright square of blue sky framed by the hatch, and the barrel that hung suspended on the rope. What the devil had happened now? He had been working since before dawn, readying the brig to sail with the late tide, and he was hot and hungry and his patience had vanished hours ago.

"Th' line must've fouled again, Cap'n," muttered Lawson, wiping his shirtsleeve across his brow as he straightened to look at Sam. "Happened thrice yesterday."

"Then the double-blasted lubbers should know better than to do it again!" Furious, Sam charged up the companionway, his oaths growing louder with every step. He'd given his word to Morrow that they'd sail this evening, and he wasn't about to let some fumble-fingered crewmen make him miss the tide. As he reached the deck, he saw the men standing idle around the hatch and the dangling barrel. No, they were worse than idle, they were preening and smoothing their hair and grinning like idiots, and Sam's temper snapped.

"What the high holy hellfire do you men—"

In unison the men all turned to face him, their expressions a mixture of guilt and surprise at being caught gawking. But Sam spared only a moment for them before his gaze found the woman near the gangway. She wore white again, this time sprinkled with red flowers all over, and a short red jacket buttoned snugly beneath her breasts. On her head was a wide straw hat with a turned-back brim and and a great looped bow of red silk ribbons on the crown, and more ribbons tied beneath her chin. He'd never seen anything like it before on his deck, and he didn't want to now.

"Good day, Captain Colburn," she said, and smiled tremulously, the same way she had that night in the garden, when he'd kissed her. Sam didn't need any more reminders. He swore again, under his breath, but still loud enough for her to hear. Although she blushed, she held her ground, and he grudgingly gave her credit for that. "It seems a lovely day to set your sails, doesn't it?"

"Aye, ma'am, and that's why you must leave now," he said irritably. Though his crew had the sense to keep their faces impassive, he could still feel their curiosity as clearly as if they were openly winking and guffawing. "We're outward bound with the next tide, and we've no time for idling."

"Then pray go about your business, Captain. I've no wish to keep you from your tide." She couldn't help wishing he'd call her "Ananiah" again, instead of this stiff, proper "ma'am," though it was probably best he didn't. In evening clothes he'd been somehow contained, but now, with him dressed in an open, grimy shirt and close-fitting breeches, she was all too aware of his physical presence as a man, of the width of his shoulders, and of the damp curls on his broad chest. On his own deck he seemed infinitely more powerful, more imposing than she remembered, his copper-streaked hair bright in the sunlight. "But when you can grant me a moment of your time—"

"I can't, ma'am, and that's the Lord's own truth." Impatiently he swept his damp hair back from his forehead. Her immaculate gown made him painfully aware of his own filthy shirt, plastered to his back and arms with sweat.

"Surely one minute—"

"Nay, ma'am, not one, not one hundred." He shook his head, trying not to notice how the breeze off the water was blowing her gown tight over her hips and legs. She followed the French fashion for few petticoats and no stays, and clearly she had the figure to wear it. "I must ask you to leave."

Ananiah swallowed, forcing the bright smile to stay on her face. There was no postponing the truth any longer. "Then I won't trouble you, Captain. If one of your men might show me to the supercargo's cabin—"

"So that's it, then? You've come to see that lad off?" Sam's eyebrows rose with his question. Her interest in some young supercargo disappointed him, though he should have expected it. They'd be of a piece, gently bred and unused to work, though God only knew what her poor husband made of it. "I've a mind to see the milk-fed puppy myself. Morrow insisted he have every comfort he'd find in his mama's parlor, and space for his man as well, yet the whelp's not bothered to show his face on board. Fearful of dirtying his ladylike hands, I'll wager. Gentleman or not, he'll find out soon enough there's no idlers on the *Truelove*."

The hands laughed appreciatively, for the unknown supercargo had been the object of scorn and countless jests among them all week. Sam saw how the girl's smile faded. Well, it wouldn't hurt to let her know how the men felt about her beau, he told himself doggedly, but deeper down he wished he hadn't been outspoken enough to hurt her.

"If you'll just show me to the cabin—"

"Nay, ma'am, I won't," Sam declared roundly. He could see from the way the ribbons on the top of her hat quivered that she was angry now, not hurt. He liked that better, her plump little mouth set in a determined line that was quite charming. If he hadn't been so blasted busy this week, he might have called on her after all, husband or no. "You can say your farewells on the dock. I can't have you languishing below."

"Captain Colburn," she began sternly. "Captain Colburn. If you can cease your deluge of wit long enough to listen to me, you'll learn that there is no supercargo. Mr. Morrow was to tell you that the cabin was for a representative of Thomas Jenkes and Son, the company for whom you are sailing today."

"Aye, he did." Sam shrugged carelessly, more interested in enjoying the fire that anger brought to her green eyes than in her words. "Who else would that be, beyond a supercargo to oversee the sale of the goods when we land?"

Ananiah had had enough of his teasing at her expense, and of his crude suggestions that she'd had an intrigue with a supercargo. A supercargo, of all things! Next he'd have her in bed with dry old Mr. Morrow. She'd had more than enough. It was high time Samuel Colburn learned who had saved his precious brig from his creditors.

Then suddenly, unexpectedly, he grinned at her, the smile reaching clear to his eyes and making every teasing word he'd spoken a secret between them alone. She felt the anger that had given her courage vanish and the words themselves disappear, and she could do nothing more than gape openmouthed for endless moments like some half-witted fool.

And then in those same moments Sam realized the truth. She meant to claim that tiny cabin for herself. Slowly he began to shake his head as every bit of his teasing good humor disappeared. "Off my deck, ma'am. There's no place on any vessel of mine for a woman. I told you that before. No wheedling or whining's going to change my mind, so the sooner you take yourself away, the better for us all."

Ananiah gasped indignantly. "I'll thank you, sir, not to speak to me like that!"

"And I'll thank you to leave my men to their work." Sam glared around at his crew, who hastily returned to lowering the water cask into the hold. But beyond them he saw a porter bent beneath a great trunk covered in horsehair, and a stout, bustling young woman with a ruddy face leading him up the gangplank, her own hands clutching a wicker hamper.

"Belay that!" he roared. The porter was familiar enough with irritable captains to stop at once and slide the trunk from his shoulders to the gangplank. But the young woman continued, her cheeks puffed out from the climb, forcing Sam to step forward and block her way. "You can just turn about the way you came, lass, and take your mistress with you."

"No, Letty, you come on board directly," Ananiah said, interrupting Sam. Then she turned once again towards him. "How dare you speak to my servant that way!"

"Because on *my* brig my word is law, and I say you leave, or I'll have you carried off!"

"And if you do, I'll see *my* cargo's drawn from your hold, and you arrested for breaking your contract!"

Stunned, Sam stared at her. She was still the same pretty creature in a foolish hat with red ribbons, with the same soft, yielding body he'd held in his arms and the same full lips he'd kissed once and wanted to kiss again. But all he saw now was the trap she'd just sprung on him. Because he was poor and she was rich, she thought she owned him. If what she was saying about the cargo was true, then she as much as did. God, what a fool he'd been!

"You've put on quite a show for everyone, Mistress Snow." He caught her roughly by the arm and pulled her across the deck to the companionway. "But we'd best go below and finish this between us alone."

"Let me go, Captain!" demanded Ananiah. Though she twisted and fought him, his hold remained firm on her arm, and she had no choice but to follow, her slippers skidding across the polished planks. "Release me at once!"

"'Tis a pity you didn't fight for yourself this way with that other lady at Brown's party," said Sam, his jaw tight as he half dragged her down the steep steps. "Then I wouldn't have come plunging in like a damned fool to save your honor, and would have been spared the trouble of your acquaintance."

He threw open his cabin door and shoved her inside before following and bolting the door after them. Too angry to be afraid, Ananiah waited in the center of the cabin, her arms folded defiantly across her chest.

Pointedly Sam set the cabin's single armchair in front of her with a thump. Ananiah lifted her chin higher and disdainfully shook her head, and he shoved the chair back under the desk. "Then be mulish and stand, ma'am, 'tis no matter to me," he growled. "But you will explain yourself, and now."

"I told you before that I must travel to London to see my father freed—"

"And I told you I wouldn't take you." Sam folded his own arms across his chest, partly to mock her stance and partly to keep himself from throttling her. "So instead you've found some way to bribe Morrow, to coax yourself passage with me?"

"No!" cried Ananiah hotly. With an exasperated sound, she turned sharply on her heel, tangling the ribbons on the crown of her hat in the low beams overhead. She yanked the hat from her head, scattering hairpins and leaving her hair disheveled and half-down over her shoulders. She shoved a loose curl back from her eyes with a muttered oath of her own, and swung around again to face him. "I've done this as fairly as I could. Any honest man would see that!"

He snorted derisively. "Oh, aye, so I'm dishonest now, too?"

"Oh, just hush!" She knew he was purposefully provoking her, but she couldn't stop herself from spitting fire back at him, and she couldn't remember when she'd lost her temper so completely. She realized how she should have brought Mr. Morrow with her to explain. "Hush, and mark what I say! You've been paid to carry a cargo on account from my father's firm."

God in Heaven, this was worse than he'd suspected. "Your father is Thomas Jenkes?"

"That's my grandfather. My father never bothered changing the firm's name to his own." She lowered her eyes to his folded arms, finally unable to meet his gaze when she spoke directly of what she'd done. His shirt was open low at the throat, and the sleeves were carelessly rolled above his elbows. In the sunlight that reflected from the water through the row of curving windows along the stern, the hair on his forearms glinted like dark red gold. The only time Étienne had revealed that much of his bare arms was in the few seconds when his valet would exchange his dressing gown for his shirt.

But Samuel Colburn wasn't a gentleman like Étienne. Far from it. She swallowed hard, trying to forget him, and instead to concentrate on what she was saying. "If the amount Mr. Morrow has paid you isn't sufficient—"

"Nay, 'twas more than handsome, and well you know it." Sam's anger settled into a cold, dark fury. He'd been trapped again, led by his empty pockets and a pretty face the same way as he'd been by Sophie. No, it went back further than that, back to when he'd been a starving boy begging for a man's work from the fat shipowners along Wharf Street. He'd worked from dawn to nightfall, yet still they'd cheated him, paying him half wages on account of his age, and sometimes nothing at all. He shook his head and shook away the past. "But fair or not, it doesn't matter. I'm ending this devil's bargain right now."

"You can't," said Ananiah, still avoiding his face. She couldn't look at him and see the hatred she knew she'd find. Hearing the anger and humiliation in his voice was bad enough. She'd gone over the details with Mr. Morrow to make sure Captain Colburn would have no choice, but she hadn't realized he'd react like this. "You've signed a contract, and you cashed the draft for your payment the day you received it. But you saved your ship, didn't you? She's yours, free and clear, as long as you deliver the cargo as promised. Can't you see that we'll both benefit from this?"

"Nay, ma'am, I cannot." All he could see was how she'd tricked him into getting her own way.

The terse denial slashed at Ananiah's conscience like a knife. He'd spoken before about his pride, but in her own urgency she'd ignored it. Now she realized how much pride meant to the man, and, worse, how little she'd left him. He would never understand what she'd done, and he would never forgive her. The brief warmth of his kindness was irretrievably lost. She told herself that it didn't matter, that her passage to England and her father was what counted most.

At last she let herself glance up at him. His face was hard and implacable, his mouth a grim, set line. She found it impossible to reconcile this Sam Colburn with the one who had laughed and teased her and called her his angel. And kissed her. She couldn't forget that, even if he chose to. Lord knew they'd never do it again.

If only he would smile at her one more time.

"It's not so difficult to understand," she said softly, the fight gone from her now, "if only you wouldn't insist on being so—so bullheaded about this."

"The way you've just gelded me, my head's about all I still can claim as my own." His voice had grown deceptively low, almost thoughtful, in a way that she didn't find at all reassuring. "You and Morrow were

most thorough together, weren't you? You've granted
me no quarter at all. You'll have your cabin and your
passage to England and my joy once I set you down
and see your back for the last time.''

His smoky blue eyes narrowed as he studied her, her
hair tumbled over her shoulders, her cheeks still
flushed with anger, and the brim of that ridiculous hat
crushed between her fingers. Deep down he wondered if things might have been different between
them.

Before she'd shown her true nature, he'd liked her,
and he still desired her. But at heart she was no different from Sophie or her father or the rest of them in the
big houses, and he couldn't forget it. He searched her
face for any gloating sign of triumph, any pleasure in
her victory, and found instead eyes that were unreadable behind spiky dark lashes. Only the rapid rise and
fall of her breasts beneath the red jacket betrayed any
emotion at all.

Damn her, she'd won. She'd gotten her way. Was he
worth so little, then, that she couldn't bother to take
pleasure in her victory? Slowly he reached out and
twisted his fingers in the long, loose strands of her
hair, drawing her closer as he wrapped the hair around
his knuckles.

''No,'' she murmured, looking away as she shook
her head. Her hair pulled taut against his fingers.
''No, please don't.''

As she turned away, the same locket she'd worn before slipped from her bodice and swung against the
back of Sam's hand. Diamonds and sapphires in
heavy gold worked in the shape of a heart, a potent
reminder that the gap between their stations was as
wide as the Atlantic. Abruptly he released her and
turned towards the windows, away from her.

"You and your maid will keep to your cabin except with my permission, ma'am." He clenched his hands behind his back and stared, unseeing, at the river. "You will take your meals alone together, and you will not speak to or distract my men. You will in no way interfere with my command or with the progress of the vessel, or I shall see that your cabin is locked from the outside, with you within. I trust, ma'am, that I have made myself clear."

Sam heard her sigh—with dismay or relief or weariness, he couldn't have said—and then he heard the soft *shush* of her skirts as she left the cabin and closed the door after her. She had no right to leave the captain's cabin until he'd dismissed her. But she would learn he was the master on board. Aye, she'd learn, and learn it well, for he would teach her.

For the sake of his sanity, he prayed the crossing would be swift.

# Chapter Four

Ananiah slept little that first night on the *Truelove*. She'd kept to her cabin and out of Captain Colburn's path the way he'd ordered, but still her thoughts had replayed that awful conversation with him, and long after dark she'd tried to imagine other words, better words, she might have said instead. Below her, Letty had already succumbed to queasiness, clinging to her woolen mattress and moaning so piteously that Ananiah hadn't the heart to tell her that they'd yet to leave the river.

And so Ananiah lay awake, listening to the water along the brig's sides, the creaking of her timbers, and the calls and cries of the men on watch overhead. She had sailed three times with her father, and the familiar sounds were comforting, reminding her of him and the *Commerce*. Their tiny cabin was aft, near the captain's, and she could clearly hear him speaking to the pilot who was guiding them through the twists and shallows of the river and the islands of Narragansett Bay, and heard him, too, when at last he left the deck for his cabin, shortly before dawn. He'd been with the pilot at the wheel all night, and Ananiah figured he'd have to sleep at least for an hour or two. She dressed herself hastily, glanced back at Letty, who was dozing fitfully, and climbed up the narrow companionway to the deck.

The horizon had only just begun to pale, and the few men on watch paid her scant attention. She pulled her shawl more tightly over her shoulders; July or not, the early-morning air was chilly. Standing close to the larboard railing, she let the tangy breeze from the water play across her face as she looked east into the coming dawn.

The shore was still no more than a dark silhouette, but because she knew where to look, she could make out the steep gables of a house's roof, and the larger shadow of a barn beside it. She had been born there, on her grandfather's farm, and she wondered wistfully if the wild plums by the stone wall would be ripe yet.

"I thought, ma'am, that I'd told you to keep below."

Ananiah's spirits sank. From the severity in the captain's voice and that hateful "ma'am" she knew she would be banished again to the stuffy cabin. She let herself look hungrily at the farm a moment longer before she turned to face him.

She reminded Sam of a guilty child caught with her hand in the sweetmeats, her blue eyes very round with apprehension, while her chin remained defiantly set. Her dress made her look younger, too. This morning she wore a simple wool gown with a patterned yellow shawl tied over her shoulders, and in place of the arranged curls, her hair was brushed back over her ears and braided haphazardly in a single uneven plait. The wind had pulled several strands loose, making soft wisps around her face that he longed to touch and brush back from her cheeks.

"I haven't forgotten your orders, Captain," she said, "but I'd hoped you wouldn't begrudge me my last sight of Rhode Island."

"You'd hoped, too, that I wouldn't catch you at it," he said gruffly. Still, it was impossible to deny such a request. "Go ahead, look your fill. Once we clear Aquidneck, there's nothing but ocean and sky."

"Thank you." Yet she didn't turn back to the shoreline. Instead, she watched him as long as she dared. He wore his dark blue jacket carelessly open, the polished brass buttons winking in the dawn light. Even so, she could see how its simple lines had been tailored to fit his broad shoulders, and that the quality of the wool was too fine for a man who claimed poverty. She wondered if he had a mistress he sought to please by such things, or a wife who tended them for him and she wondered, too, why it mattered to her. She sighed and turned back to the rail, leaning her elbows on the painted wood, and to her surprise he came to stand beside her.

That he'd done it surprised him, too. He'd meant to send her back to her cabin for disobeying his orders, but instead he'd been disarmed by the simplicty of her request, and by the sight of that long, uneven braid flopping between her shoulders in the wind.

Longing for a way to break the uneasy silence, she twisted her hands in the ends of her shawl. Why didn't he just leave her alone? She felt he was testing her, waiting for her to blunder so that he could pounce on her again, and she couldn't begin to guess which answers would be the right ones and which wrong.

"Was it hard for you to leave Salem?" she asked finally, deciding the question was safe enough. "My father says that farewells are worse for sailors than any storm."

"Aye, once it was." Fleetingly Sam remembered watching his mother and his two sisters waving from the dock, their figures blurring as he'd tried manfully to keep back an eight-year-old's tears. "But now there's nothing left to hold me there."

"There's nothing left to hold me to that farm, either, now that my grandmother's dead," said Ananiah. "It's all let to tenants who wouldn't recognize me beyond my name. But I was born in that house, there, while my father was in Surinam."

Until now, he hadn't realized that there'd been no one to see her off in Providence, none of the family or friends he would have expected her to have. He glanced down at her small-boned hands clasped over the rail. "I can't picture you on a farm."

His disbelief was so complete that Ananiah laughed. "My mother would have agreed with you. She fled back to Providence within a fortnight of my birth. Oh, the house and the farm, and the whole island with it, have been ours since Adam—or at least Roger Williams—but we're town folk now, through and through."

Sam stared out at the farm as it slipped behind in their wake. So her family owned all of Patience Island. Why did he care, anyway? It was only the diamond earrings all over again.

Abruptly he pushed himself away from the rail. "It's just as well you've risen early, ma'am," he said curtly. "We'll make Newport soon, and I expect you to come ashore to the customhouse there with me."

He saw the question in her face and continued brusquely. "You are the representative for Thomas Jenkes and Son, aren't you?"

Ananiah shook her head, bewildered both by his question and by the sudden shift in his manner. "But

I believed that Mr. Morrow had cleared everything through the customhouse in Providence.''

"After what you two have done to me, I can't trust the ink you've set to paper. I want those manifests and clearances read by someone without any interest in the matter. Likely your family owns the customhouse, along with every other damned thing in this state.''

She nodded again, then bowed her head. He was right not to trust her. How could he, after what she'd done?

Damnation, why didn't she fight back? To see her crumple like that made Sam feel mean-spirited and small, and yet though he hated himself for baiting her he couldn't stop. Had she ever considered his feelings, his pride?

He stared down at the pale, vulnerable curve of her nape, at the little loop where she'd missed fastening the top button on the back of her gown. There was nothing at all wrong with the manifests. Whatever else Morrow might be, he was the kind of clerk who'd sooner put a knife to his own throat than make a false accounting. Didn't Ananiah know enough to trust her own man?

*Ananiah.* Sweet Jesus, he could call her "ma'am" to her face every time, but in his thoughts she was still Ananiah.

And this time he was the one who fled.

Long before the *Truelove* had tacked around Goat Island into the curving arms of Newport's harbor, Ananiah stood waiting nervously in the shadow of the mainmast. Beside her stood Letty, pale and miserable from the ship's motion, but unwilling to let her mistress wait alone.

"Your hat, Miss Ananiah, your hat!'' she said, disdainfully holding up the plain chip bonnet that

Ananiah had insisted would be most appropriate for a customhouse. "This sun will burn you brown as a savage, and I won't be to blame."

But Ananiah didn't hear her, listening instead to the first mate call his orders. She knew enough about sailing to see the ship's progress slow, and as the anchor was dropped into the water she began to hope that perhaps the captain had changed his mind about their trip to Newport. They were barely inside the harbor, and far from any of the docks.

"Well, are we going to this town or not?" demanded Letty crossly. With the hat still in her hands, she trailed after the mate on unsteady legs. "You there! My lady can't go walking across the water!"

The mate turned and grinned as he grasped Letty's arm to steady her. He had a round, good-natured face framed by curling ginger hair, and tattooed on his forearm was a circle of five stars. "No one's 'specting her to, lamb," he said, winking broadly. "Amos Howard knows how to treat a lady, no mistake. Your mistress will go gentle as a basket o' eggs to market."

Letty sputtered indignantly, but Ananiah noticed she didn't pull away, and she thought unhappily that she'd have to speak to her maid before the captain did. Letty wasn't by nature a flirt, but still, the last thing Ananiah wanted to hear was more reasons why women didn't belong at sea.

"Amos Howard, is it?" Her seasickness forgotten, Letty tossed her head coyly. "Well, don't you be getting saucy with me, Amos Howard, or I'll—"

"Let the woman go, Howard!" roared Sam as he came on deck. Letty scurried back to Ananiah's side, while Howard jerked stiffly upright, his eyes focussed somewhere to the left of Sam's angry face. "God in heaven, you'd think this was a floating bagnio!"

"It wasn't how it looked, Cap'n—" began Howard, his face flushed turkey red beneath his tan, but Sam quickly cut him off.

"You knew my orders, Howard," he snapped, his resentment at the women who'd disrupted his ship's order bubbling over again.

"But nothing happened, sir! Ask any man here, or the lady herself!"

"I'll trust my own eyes, Howard. You'll be watch on watch until Sunday, and so will anyone else who can't keep his hands out from under the petticoats." He glared at Howard, wishing it had been one of the others instead. Howard was a new man, taken on at Providence, and though he'd come with the best of recommendations from his last master, Sam would rather have had some old acquaintance for his mate, someone he knew well enough to trust and confide in. Still, the man had worked the long hours before they sailed without grumbling, and he could hardly be blamed for trying to take what that fat little baggage of a maid offered him. "Is the boat ready?"

"Aye, sir," said Howard promptly, but with a new edginess that Sam couldn't miss. "Ready an' waiting."

Sam swung his hat up and settled it on his head. In a flat leather pocketbook under his arm he had the bills of lading and the other papers for the customhouse. Remembering the unnecessary errand he was beginning only irritated him further.

Glowering, he turned towards Ananiah. "Are you ready, ma'am?"

"Of course I'm ready." Hastily Ananiah took her hat from Letty and tied it beneath her chin, hoping he couldn't see how her fingers shook. He'd buttoned his coat and tied a pale blue scarf under his shirt collar with an elegant flourish, but beneath the black brim of his hat, his face was cold, and his brows were drawn sternly together as he watched her.

She had only the vaguest idea of what happened in a customhouse, and she doubted he'd offer any clues, but she told herself it would be good practice for dealing with the officials in London. No admiral in the Royal Navy could be any more daunting than Captain Colburn, and she was determined not to let her anxiety show.

"Letty, you are to stay in the cabin with the bolt drawn." She'd deal with that problem later, and she knew from Letty's sullen, pinched expression that it wouldn't be pleasant, either. Ananiah sighed softly to herself, and stepped forward with her hand outstretched towards Sam.

"We're going ashore, ma'am, not leading a quadrille," said Sam in disgust, and Ananiah jerked her hand back to her side. "Over the side with you now, and into the boat."

Her cheeks flaming with humiliation, Ananiah hurried to the break in the railing beside him. A gentleman would have taken her hand and assisted her and not have made her feel like a fool for expecting such a tiny courtesy.

She stared over the gently bowed side. She'd never considered how one left a ship that wasn't tied up safely to a dock. Far below her, a longboat bobbed and bounced against the brig's sides, the faces of the four seamen at the oars turned expectantly upwards.

"You prance about on walls well enough, I recall," said Sam dryly. The untidy braid she'd worn earlier had been replaced by an artfully careless arrangement of ringlets and sleek loops, no doubt the work of her maid. That lopsided plait had been the best her own fingers could manage, and he had an oddly touching image of her trying to divide and brush her hair herself.

Ananiah looked at the insubstantial rope ladder, the rungs no more than slippery sticks, and at the dark green water beneath it. She could imagine herself dropping down into it, could feel the waves clutching at her skirts and dragging her under. Of course, she couldn't swim. She was a lady, not a fish.

"I cannot," she whispered, fear tightening her throat. "You must go without me. I can't do it."

"Aye, ma'am, you can and you shall," said Sam firmly, "if I must carry you myself."

Ananiah closed her eyes, wondering which fate would be worse. "You go first."

Sam saw how she fought against her panic. He had spent so many years clambering up ratlines and over crosstrees that he gave no thought to a simple rope ladder. His frown deepened; he was unhappy with his own thoughtlessness. He hadn't meant to terrify her. He'd just opened his mouth to tell her to stay when she opened her eyes with a little shake of her shoulders. "You go first, Captain Colburn," she said, with a resolve that he hadn't expected. "You go first, and I shall follow."

Captains never went first, but this time Sam forgot ceremony. Once in the boat, he took off his hat and shaded his eyes with his hand as he looked up at her frightened face at the rail. Damnation, she didn't have to do this. It was her own choice, not his.

"It's not right, miss," said Letty, appalled. "It isn't decent. Your father—"

"Hush, Letty!" snapped Ananiah. "Just hush!"

Quickly, before she lost her nerve, she sat on the rail and swung one leg over the side. Her foot searched in the air for the first rung, found it, and with a deep breath and a wordless prayer she turned and gingerly let her other foot down to the next rung. One, two, three rungs; her fingers were white as she clutched at each, the toes of her slippers bumping against the ship's side as they groped for each new footing. Four, five; she must be almost to the boat by now, though she didn't dare look.

"Handsomely now, lass, steady as you go," murmured Sam unconsciously. His gaze briefly swept over the men at the oars. "And eyes down, you gaping sods!"

In unison, four heads dipped low, but Sam's turned upwards. He would not let her fall, not after he'd driven her so hard. A gust of wind tugged and caught at her skirts, swirling her petticoats upwards. Her slippers were red with silk tassels, her stockings had lacework clocks at the ankles, and she tied her garters below the knee. Above the ribbon the skin of the back of her knee was creamy pale, perfect, and he felt his whole body tense at all it suggested.

Ananiah felt the chill of the breeze on her legs, bare above her stockings. Too late she realized the wind from the water had betrayed her. She thought of the men below her, and forgot both her fear and her precarious hold. With one hand she reached out and grabbed at the billowing skirts, trying to bunch them more modestly about her legs. As she did, the brig rose and dipped with a swell, and with Ananiah clinging to its lowest rungs, the ladder swung outwards like a pendulum. She scrambled to recover her balance, felt her fingernails scrape on the brig's planking instead of the ladder, and then she was falling towards the water, and the gap between the brig and the boat.

From where Sam stood, he could see that she hadn't been in any real danger at all. She'd slipped, and he'd caught her as she fell, then pulled her back into the boat. But though she hadn't flailed about or screamed as most women would, her fear was real enough. As he held her in his arms, her back pressed against his chest, he could feel her trembling, and the pounding of her heart against his wrist. His insistence had done this to her, and he hated himself for it. Yet how to apologize or explain in a way that meant anything, when he himself didn't know why he'd done it?

Waiting for words that didn't come, he held her longer than he intended, long enough to become aware of how the soft underside of her breast was pressed against his arm and her legs lay across his own. He let the scent of lilies, her scent, fill his senses, and he thought again of the shadowy garden where he'd kissed her, before she'd tricked him and ruined everything before it began.

She was safe, she had not fallen, she hadn't drowned; yet even as Ananiah felt her fear give way to giddy relief, she recognized the moment when the shelter she'd found in his arms changed to an embrace she didn't welcome. She felt trapped, pinned against the hard wall of his chest, the buttons on his coat digging into her back. She wondered how much of her ankles he'd seen when she'd fallen, and to her humiliation she realized that now her legs were wantonly straddling his, and her skirt was still bunched over one of his knees. With a little cry of shame, she tried to wriggle free, and as quickly as he'd caught her, he now let her go, and she plopped down hard on the bench in the stern sheets of the boat.

Unable to meet the eyes of the oarsmen facing her, she stared down at her lap, smoothing her skirts over her knees. From beneath her lashes she saw Sam drop down on the seat beside her and jam his hat back on his head. His thigh brushed against hers, and she jumped away from him on the narrow seat, choosing to cling to the side and be dappled by spray rather than risk being touched by him again. Perhaps she'd imagined it. Why should he want to caress her, when he so clearly despised her? No, she must have imagined everything after he'd pulled her into the boat.

Beside her, Sam had no such doubts. He could still feel the gentle curve from her waist to her hip from when his fingers had spread along her body, and the scent of lilies beneath his nose. Touching her at all had been a foolish mistake. But it wasn't until Sam turned to glance back at the brig and met Howard's gaze that he realized that he'd made a dangerous one, as well.

"The clerks will all be at their dinners now," said Sam as he glanced up at the clock on the front of the old colony house. "No sense in going to customs until half-past."

"We could wait for them in their office," suggested Ananiah timidly beside him. It was the first time he'd spoken to her since they'd left the brig, and since they'd left the four seamen to wait with the boat she'd felt even more unsure of what he expected of her. The July sun was hot here on Thames Street, the afternoon still and dusty even near the docks, and she longed to sit anywhere that would be in the shade. "It's not so very long to wait."

"Too long for me. I don't cool my heels waiting on any clerk's belly." He looked down the street, pointedly over her head. "I remember a passable tavern along here somewhere, something with a hound in the

name. The Red Hound, or the Spotted Hound, or
some such. Come, I'll find it soon enough.''

Glad to be included, Ananiah hurried to match her
stride to his. Her slippers weren't made for walking—
the soles were so thin, she felt every pebble—and she
hoped the tavern wasn't far. The woolen gown that
had seemed just right on the water was beginning to
stick damply to the small of her back with the heat.
She slipped her shawl from her shoulders to the crooks
of her arms.

Without looking at her outright, Sam knew she was
scurrying to keep to his pace. He knew he should slow
his steps, but he didn't trust himself to be alone with
her any more than he had to. The sooner they reached
the tavern, the better. He glanced down to see perspiration glistening on the pale skin between her shoulder blades, and a single stray ringlet clinging moistly
to the nape of her neck. He knew there, near the
heartbeat at her throat, the scent of lilies would be
strongest.

''Newport's not the town it was since the war,'' he
said abruptly, striving to turn his thoughts away from
the woman beside him. He waved his hand at an
abandoned house they were passing. Boarded up by
owners who had fled the British occupation twenty
years before and never returned, the house was
scarcely more than a shell. The fence had long ago
been torn down, and the shutters ripped off by the
army for firewood. The window glass had been shattered by vandals, and the roof shingles torn away by
storms. Fat bees hovered lazily in the honeysuckle
vines that threaded through the empty casements.

''My mother said when she was young, Newport
was the finest town in Rhode Island, and she laughed
when my father predicted that some day it would be

Providence instead," said Ananiah sadly. There was little of the elegant town her mother had described in this shabby, drowsy seaport of empty lots and gray houses in need of paint. "How could she know what the war would do?"

Sam looked at her sharply, marveling how she could make even a ramshackle house widen the distance between them. "The war did far worse than knock down a few old houses."

"I'm not that great a fool," she answered defensively. She'd left her fan on the brig, and without it she now fluttered her fingers rapidly beside her cheek to cool it. "I know as well as you do what the war did."

"Snug in your fine house in Providence, I'll reckon you didn't," said Sam, his voice distant. He reached out and yanked off a branch of a weedy bush, stripping away the leaves one by one. "But I went to sea when I was eight, to war on a privateer when I was fourteen, and to prison in the Old Mill three years after that. True, I didn't see much more of the fighting, but by then I'd had my fill. Enough to be a judge, anyway."

He tossed the stick away, already regretting that he'd told her that much about himself. Of course she wouldn't understand, and he'd be wasting his wind to try. "The Wicked Hound," he said, looking ahead to the tavern's painted signboard. "How could I have forgotten that?"

The tavern door was propped open in the heat, and a brindled dog with a grizzled muzzle lay asleep in the sun beside the step. Sam drew off his hat and ducked to clear the door's frame, and Ananiah followed warily, imagining what her father would say to see her enter a waterfront tavern.

Once her eyes accustomed themselves after the bright afternoon sun, she could see that the front room was only half-filled with men who sprawled across the benches and leaned on the tables with tankards. Paid-off sailors between voyages, she guessed, both from their clothing and from the way they looked as if they'd been in their places all morning and intended to be there all afternoon and all night as well. In the half-light that filtered through the grimy casements and the haze of tobacco smoke, they seemed wild and rough, and every one of them turned to stare at her with a common hunger that made her feel like a mouse confronted by a pack of especially desperate tomcats. The tired-looking barmaid was the only other woman in the room, and Ananiah shrank closer to Sam's side.

The owner bustled towards them, wiping his hands on his apron. "G'day to ye, Cap'n," he said, grinning too widely as his gaze slid up and down Ananiah. "Doubtless you'll be wanting a private room fer ye an' yer lady, aye?"

"Doubtless, nay," answered Sam, returning the grin wickedly as he smoothed back his hair with his fingers. "I don't take private rooms with married ladies. 'Tis not the best place to meet their husbands, eh?"

The keep guffawed loudly, joined by the others within hearing, while Ananiah, mortified and staring at the floor, considered all the ways she could slowly, painfully, kill Sam. Wicked hound, indeed; he should have it painted on his forehead.

"I'll take that table there, in the corner, to show I've nothing to hide," he continued, wondering why he wasn't enjoying her discomfort more. The Lord knew she'd done it often enough to him. "Rum for me, tea for the lady, and whatever your cook has in his pot for dinner for us both."

In the corner he'd chosen, Ananiah sat in a wobbly chair with her back to the wall and her hands in her lap, trying to consider neither the pattern of old grease that marked the top of the table nor the men who still openly watched her. Her tea, when it came, was weak and stale, the saucer and cup were unmatched, and there was no sign of a cup plate or spoon. Sighing, she balanced the saucer between her spread fingers and swirled the tea without drinking it. None of this was bringing her any closer to London or her father.

"You didn't have to say that about my husband," she said quietly without lifting her eyes from the tea. "I told you before he wouldn't trouble you."

Frowning, Sam ran his fingers up and down the battered side of the pewter tankard. He could just make out her reflection in the pewter, the green of her gown and the yellow straw of her hat. "You've told me a good many things, ma'am, and I've learned through hard experience it's best not to trust you."

"Ah." She tipped the saucer of undrinkable tea back into the cup and slid them both across the table, away from her, saying nothing more than that single breathy syllable. "Ah."

"Sam Colburn, by all that's holy!" bellowed a man behind them as he pounded Sam affectionately on the back. The man was nearly as tall as Sam but thin as a spar, and he wore a red kerchief tied low across one side of his face to cover the empty socket of a lost eye. The one that remained was as black as the brow above it, and to Ananiah's dismay it now winked boldly at her. "Justin Forbes, lovey, Justin Forbes's the man you've been waiting for. You forget this old rascal

Colburn here and come with me, and I'll treat you like a lady queen, damn me if I don't!''

Sam rose quickly to his feet, his chair toppling to the floor with a crack that silenced the rest of the room. "Clear off, Justin. This one's already a lady, and she needs nothing from you to prove it."

"So that's how it lies, Sam, does it?" Forbes turned his head to look at Sam, that single brow curling downwards. "Here I come over to offer my congratulations about Miss Sophie, but already you've found another plump chick to take her place away from home. Filling her nest, too, are you, Sam? You know you never was one to share."

Sam moved so fast that Ananiah wasn't certain just what happened next. She saw the startled look on Forbes's face as Sam's fist struck his jaw, saw how the thin man toppled over backwards and crashed into another table, saw the other men jostling closer for a better view as they shouted and offered advice. Then she felt Sam's fingers closing around her wrist as he pulled her from her chair and through the crowd and the open door and into the street and past the barking, brindled dog that had given the tavern its name.

"You're not hurt, are you?" he demanded, searching her face anxiously as they stopped at the end of the street. Her eyes were bright with excitement, her cheeks were flushed from running, and for the first time since he'd known her, she actually looked happy. He couldn't begin to figure it, so he didn't try.

She shook her head, stunned that he had struck another man in her defense. He still held her hand firmly in his own, and she wondered if he'd merely forgotten to let it go. She hoped he hadn't.

"You were frightened, though."

Again she nodded, keeping her chin low. "I can't help it. I'm a terrible coward."

"That's not the same thing, Ananiah." Gently he slipped his fingers beneath her chin and held her face up towards his so that she couldn't look away and hide beneath the brim of her hat. His eyes were serious, but not grim, and the dark hair falling over his forehead gave him an air of rakish carelessness. "Everyone's scared of something one time or another. If you can hide it, then the world calls you brave. If you can't, well then, you're a coward. A lady who scrambles down the tumblehome of a blue-water ship hides it very well indeed."

She blushed with pleasure at the compliment. She still didn't believe she was the least bit brave, but she was glad he'd said it anyway. "Were you frightened of that man Mr. Forbes?"

"What, of Justin?" Sam laughed out loud. "Nay, I've tussled with Justin Forbes for years beyond counting. We're both Essex County lads, y'see, accustomed to scraping and scrapping in rumshops, and neither of us means much by it."

Ananiah didn't see much beyond his smile, and once again she thought of a wicked hound—but one whose company she rather liked. "But you hit him hard enough to knock him onto the floor."

His smile faded. He deserved a thrashing as much as Justin for bringing her into that place to begin with. "I had reason enough, lass. He'd no right to go tangling your name with mine like that."

Her pleasure shattered. He'd been protecting his own good name, not hers. Justin Forbes had mentioned some other woman—Sophie, that was it—and then congratulations. If Sam Colburn was newly wed, then of course he didn't want word of Ananiah Snow reaching his Sophie's ears. Not again, she thought unhappily. Dear God, not again!

She quickly pulled her hand free of his, and turned her face as if to retie her hat, and his fingers slid from beneath her chin. She couldn't meet his eyes, not now, not after she'd been so foolishly wrong, and not with her own shame and disappointment written as if on a banner across her face.

He looked at her questioningly, then stuffed his hands in his pockets. Maybe she hadn't heard what Justin had said. Maybe she was only now realizing what had been implied. Was just the suggestion of it that repulsive to her?

"Come along," he said stiffly, turning away from her. "It's high time we went to the customhouse."

# Chapter Five

Of course, the *Truelove*'s papers were in order, as Sam had known they'd be. The elderly clerk had barely glanced at the words and figures once he saw the name of the house in the heading, and Sam had waited for Ananiah, standing silently beside him before the tall desk, to pounce on his suspicions in triumph. But she hadn't, her neat profile remaining unchanged inside the curving brim of her hat, and Sam wondered why not. He certainly would have, given the same opportunity. She said nothing to the clerk, and nothing beyond a faint handful of thank-yous to the sailors who helped her into the boat back to the brig. He'd never known a woman who could close herself off so completely. It was as if she'd shut and barred some secret door against him, and it bothered him.

They were scarcely over the *Truelove*'s side and back on her deck before Amos Howard came hurrying towards them, his face drawn with concern. "We've a guest on board, Captain Colburn, sir."

Sam shook his head as he glanced back over the side. He'd been too caught up in his own thoughts to notice the other boat tied to the *Truelove*'s moorings. Ten score of pirates might have boarded while he was gone, and he wasn't certain he would have noticed. Lord, would this day never end? "No visitors when I'm ashore, Howard. Not a one, mind?"

"But he said his business was most urgent, sir," persisted Howard. "Came right up alongside us and demanded to see the lady directly. I couldn't see how I could turn him away."

"Saying it went against my orders would have done well enough, Howard," said Sam, but his irritation was lost on the other man.

"He's a gentleman, sir," he said earnestly. "I knows him from Providence, and my brother sails in one of his ships. I took the liberty o' putting him in your cabin, sir, and had Jeremy bring him a neat glass of sherry."

"Howard..." began Sam sternly, then stopped, working hard to control his temper as he pictured his tiny stock of sherry being guzzled by some fat-bellied gentleman sitting in *his* chair in *his* cabin. New man or no, what the devil had Howard been thinking of, anyway?

Ananiah was listening with growing uneasiness. "You say this gentleman wishes to speak to me?" she asked Howard doubtfully. "It's not Mr. Morrow, is it?"

"Ananiah Snow!" thundered a voice behind them, and she spun around to find a man with a florid, square-jawed face glowering at her as he climbed the ladder to the deck. "What's this all about, my girl? Here I come back from Boston and find you've run off like a gypsy, shaming your poor father all over again!"

"You've no right to judge me, Captain Gill," Ananiah said. The man was large, the seams of his coat straining across his back, but Ananiah met his eyes

without flinching, her chin high. She remembered
what Sam had told her earlier about hiding her fear,
and if she had ever needed to seem brave, it was now,
in a fight against a wicked, clever man like George
Gill. "I'll thank you to stop meddling in my affairs,
and leave me alone!'

Gill snorted contemptuously. "It's talk like that that
ruined you, Ananiah, and near broke your father's
heart. You'll send him to his grave for certain when he
hears about this."

"How dare you pretend to care about my father!
You'd sooner see him rot in that British prison than
risk a penny of your own to help him!" She was barely
aware of how Sam and the sailors on the deck had all
stopped their work to listen, how the ship itself had
grown strangely quiet.

But Sam had heard enough, and now he stepped
between them and turned to Gill. "I'm Sam Colburn,
and this is my ship. You'd do well to explain yourself
before I put you off."

Gill grunted, his eyes never leaving Ananiah. He
plucked at the incongruous lace ruffles on his shirtfront. "George Gill, merchant and master of the ship
*Lion,* of Providence. John Snow's my partner—"

"On two ventures only, Captain Gill, and twenty
years ago at that!" cried Ananiah indignantly.
"Shares, and that was all! He doesn't trust you any
more than I do!"

"John Snow's *partner,*" repeated Gill emphati-
cally, "and his old and dear friend besides. On his behalf I've come to take this daughter of his back home
where she belongs."

"You won't take me anywhere," declared Ananiah. Though she held her arms steady at her sides, her
thumb, hidden in the folds of her skirt, worked ner-

vously against her palm, twisting her ring. "I won't return to Providence until I bring my father with me."

"A pretty threat, that one." Gill laughed, a short, unpleasant bark. He stepped around Sam and beckoned to Ananiah to join him. "I've two men in London now looking into your father's case, and I swore to you I'd go there myself next voyage. That's how these things are done, girl, with bribes and threats from lawyers, not dainty handwringing and wailing from young women."

Ananiah shook her head. "Do you think I'd be here now if I believed you, Captain Gill?"

Gill still held his hand out to her, flicking his upturned fingers impatiently for her to join him. "Foolish chit. Don't you realize that it's your fault the British hold him? There's nothing the British hate more than a Frenchman, and if they've learned about you and Étienne de Gramont, well then, your father will be the one to pay."

Sam laid his hand on Gill's shoulder. When he spoke, his voice was calm and low, but the threat in his tone was unmistakable. "Stop right there, Gill, before I knock your foul words back down your throat."

Gill shoved Sam's hand away. "Defend her, will you?" he said scornfully. "There's plenty that say John Snow sold his daughter for the plantation and two hundred Africans, but I know John, just as I know this sorry creature that is his daughter. Settlement or no, she was willing enough to go to the Frenchman's bed."

Sam lunged forward and seized Gill by the front of his coat, dragging him off his feet. The older man struggled and swore, swinging his fist up to try to catch Sam's jaw. Sam jerked his head clear and slammed Gill back hard against the mainmast. The man grunted at the impact but struggled still, and again Sam struck him back against the hard pine.

"Sam, don't!" shrieked Ananiah as she rushed forward and grabbed Sam's arm with both of her hands. "Stop now, or you'll kill him!"

Breathing hard, Sam half turned with Gill's coat still bunched in his fist, and stared down at her fingers on his sleeve. "You heard him, what he said about you!"

"It's not worth it, Sam," she pleaded. "Let him go back to his boat, and we'll sail, and that will be an end to it."

"You'd want that?" asked Sam incredulously.

"What I want doesn't matter." She released his arm, too conscious of having touched him. "This isn't another tavern brawl. George Gill's a powerful man, and he'll make trouble for you."

"Do you wish to go with him?" Earlier Sam would have rejoiced to be rid of her, but now, strangely, he had no wish at all for her to leave.

"No." Her smile was swift, brilliant, and gone in an instant. "Oh, no."

Sam dropped Gill back to his feet, still holding him tight to keep the man from staggering. He led him to the side and whistled to the hired boatman, then motioned for two of his own crewmen to help ease him down.

"If Mistress Snow hadn't spoken up for you, you'd be swimming back to shore," said Sam. "You remember that, and keep clear of her, like she says."

With an unsteady attempt at dignity, Gill pushed himself free of Sam's grasp. He shook his head to clear it, and put one hand over the back of his neck, rubbing beneath his collar.

"Aye, *mistress* is the proper word for what she's done, Colburn, and merrily, too, from the twenty-dollar-gold-piece look of her," he said thickly. "I hope you'll find she's worth the sorrow she's bound to bring you. She's a damned unlucky chit, make no mistake."

It was all Sam could do not to kick the man overboard. As it was, he didn't wait for the boat to push off before giving orders to raise the anchor and make sail. As the hands ran to swift the capstan, he saw Howard linger too long at the side, his gaze turned towards Gill's departing boat.

"Mind which master you're bound to serve, Howard," he roared, "else you'll wind up over the side with the fat bastard yet!"

Howard's head snapped around towards Sam. His face carefully impassive, he nodded curtly and rejoined the others. Trouble there, thought Sam wearily, trouble for sure, and he almost wished the mate had left with Gill. He'd sooner do without the man entirely than have him serve against his will.

With a sigh, Sam lifted his hat long enough to smooth back his hair, and turned to look for Ananiah. But the place where she'd stood was empty now, and he realized she'd run away again. Blast her, he thought angrily as he charged down the ladder, she'd no right to vanish like that. He needed answers from her, not some conjurer's disappearing act.

"Letty, it's me," called Ananiah, rattling the locked door of her cabin. For once her maid had done what she'd been bidden, and was doubtless deep asleep as well. But Ananiah didn't care. She needed to be alone, or at least alone with Letty, who knew all her secrets already, and she was desperate for the small sanctuary that the cabin could grant.

Sam had told her he didn't care about her past, and she had wanted to believe him. But after all that Gill had said about her, everything would have changed. She couldn't face Sam, not just yet. He was a man, not a saint, and he wouldn't understand any more than the others did. She needed time to let the old shame lessen again, time alone, time to let the pain of Gill's accusations fade away.

She heard Sam shouting overhead, heard his footsteps crossing the deck, and again she rapped her knuckles frantically on the door, trying to wake Letty. When he came down the ladder, his body blocked the sunlight from the hatch, and with a little gasp deep in her throat, she spun round to face him.

"You're always running off, and I'm tired of it," he said abruptly. "You owe me some answers, Ananiah Snow, and I'm willing to wait until I get them."

He was right. She *was* always running away.

*She remembered the long road to Beau Coteau, the mud from the autumn rains that sucked at her shoes, the parrots that chattered, mocking her from the bougainvillea, and the air so heavy she could hardly breathe as she ran from the house and from Étienne and from the truth, ran until she was sure her heart must burst from grief and shame.*

"Answers, lass," Sam was saying. "I want the truth."

The truth? Ananiah stared at him mutely. This time there was nowhere to run. He loomed over her, his shoulders bowed to clear the low beams of the companionway, and she could feel the louvered slats of the door pressing into her back as she leaned against it for support.

*There had been nothing to anchor her on Martinique. She had lost everything she loved most, and with the pain that had torn at her body she had prayed for death, and nearly found it.*

Sam frowned. Her eyes were huge and blank, and her breath was so rapid as to be almost panting. Gently he took her by the shoulders. Beneath his palms, her skin felt clammy and chilled.

"Ananiah?" he asked tentatively. "Ananiah, lass, tell me what's wrong."

He'd seen this empty look before, long ago, during the war, in men whose souls had broken and fled from seeing too much slaughter. But in a sheltered young woman who had never wanted for anything, such emptiness was inexplicable. What had happened to her to bring her to this?

He slid his hands from her shoulders to her arms, his fingers spreading to warm the blood beneath her pale skin. His thumbs worked harder into the soft flesh of her upper arms as he tried to rouse her from wherever she'd retreated inside herself. He sifted through every word Gill had said, searching in vain for the ones that could have wounded her this badly. As ugly as his accusations had been, alone they couldn't have done this to her. More questions, he thought unhappily, more answers he didn't have.

He drew her close, his arms circling protectively around her, and with her cheek pressed against his chest, he gently stroked her hair. There, in the half-light of the companionway, it seemed right to hold her, seemed the only answer he had to offer.

"Poor little angel," he whispered into the top of her hair. "What shall I do with you, eh?"

He knew the exact moment she came back. He felt a shudder pass through her, and the tiny gasp when she realized where she was. He let his arms slip away when she pushed herself back and stared at him, her eyes now focussed and wary. She bent to gather the shawl that she'd dropped, and wrapped it tightly over her shoulders and across her breast.

"I'm not afraid of you, Captain Colburn," she said quickly. She wasn't, either; it was herself that she feared.

"I didn't say you were," he said gently. "Do you know where we are, Ananiah?"

"Of course I do," she said uneasily. He had been angry with her, and now he wasn't, and she didn't know what had happened to change his temper, any more than she knew how she'd come to be in his embrace. "We're in your brig, the *Truelove,* and I should hope we've cleared Newport harbor."

Sam nodded, encouraged. "Do you remember George Gill coming aboard? How he wanted you to come with him back to Providence?"

Panic flickered in her eyes. "You won't make me go with him, will you?"

"I will not." He ached to hold her again, to reassure her, but he sensed her wariness and kept back. "But I need to know if there are any others like him that may try to stop us. I'll have trouble enough with the English."

Ananiah shook her head. She noticed the white slash of his linen shirt where the sleeve of his coat had been torn, and how, this late in the afternoon, his jaw was stubbled. "No others. But Captain Gill's enough, isn't he? Though it was wrong of you to hurt him like that, he's a bad, wicked man, and I don't know why my father counts him a friend."

"Then he deserved far worse than he got from me," said Sam with finality. "You can't let fools like that tell lies about you, Ananiah."

She looked down at the deck, unable to meet those blue eyes that so loved truth. "He can call me a green-haired donkey's dam for all it should matter to you."

"He called you a sight worse than that," he said, with more bitterness than he realized, "and aye, it does matter to me."

The *Truelove* heeled over neatly on a new tack. Sam automatically braced himself with his arms against the beams overhead, but Ananiah, lacking his instincts, was thrown down the sloping deck against his chest. This time Sam didn't try to hold her, and he saw how quick she was to scramble away from him. The fragile, wounded girl he'd taken into his arms was once again buried deep inside, and now that she had her wits about her, she made it clear enough she wanted no comfort from him.

Ananiah watched his jaw tighten and saw the angry way he shoved hair back from his forehead. She knew what he would ask next, but knowing wouldn't make the answer any easier to give. Her hands twisted in the corners of her shawl.

"You told me you were married, Ananiah Snow," he said slowly. "Why do you choose to go by your father's name instead of your husband's?"

She forced herself to meet his eye, raising her chin to do it. "Because in the eyes of God and the world I no longer have any right to claim it."

His eyes narrowed skeptically. "You're talking in riddles, Ananiah. Either you're a man's wife or his widow, or you're not. Simple enough."

"What I am, or am not, is of no consequence to you, Captain Colburn." It had to be like this between them, stiff and formal. He belonged to another woman, and she would never make that mistake twice. "You have been engaged to carry a cargo for my family's house to London, and to take me as a passenger with it. Nothing more. The—the details of my life are not your concern, nor am I.''

With angry frustration, he struck his fist against the bulkhead. ''The hell you're not!''

The door behind her opened enough for Letty, sleepy and disheveled, to peer out cautiously. She looked first at Ananiah, then at Sam, and with her lips pressed tightly together she opened the door wider and gently took Ananiah by the hand to draw her within.

But Ananiah hesitated, her eyes at last bright with tears. ''You're right, Captain Colburn,'' she whispered. ''I'm not, and I never will be.''

Sam sat high in the maintop with his spyglass in his hand, his long legs curled before him and his back braced against the mainmast. After five days of the crosscutting winds and rough seas that had followed them since they left Narragansett Bay, the storm seemed finally to have blown itself out. The sea had calmed to a heavy swell, and there, far to the northeast, the sky on the horizon showed pink beneath the gray clouds.

''Looks like that's an end to it, Cap'n,'' said Lawson, who was perched comfortably beside Sam, ''an' the *Truelove* brung us through like a queen.''

''Aye, that she did.'' Sam reached out and patted the mainmast affectionately, as if the ship were a living thing deserving praise, and he almost believed she was, after weathering a blow like this one. He grinned at the older seaman. ''Now all that's left is to see how far we've been tossed off course.''

''Ah, not far, Cap'n, not far, with your gift fer reckoning.'' Lawson's mouth twitched upward beneath five days' growth of gray-streaked beard. He'd shipped with Sam since the days when Sam, too, was a foremast jack, where they'd both liked and respected each other. Since he'd no aspirations to rise higher himself, Bob Lawson had chosen to follow Sam from ship to ship, and Sam couldn't imagine sailing without his shy, weathered face on board. "Once Mr. Howard sets th' yards to square again, well then, won't be nothing 'twixt us an' King George, the devil take his wicked soul."

Sam leaned sideways to watch Howard and his work party on the yards below, repairing the only damage the brig had suffered in the storm. "The men like Howard, do they?"

"Oh, aye, Cap'n, there's no point worryin' over Mr. Howard," said Lawson easily. "He's eager an' fair without being lax, an' he's wonderful quick with a jest, for all he's yer mate. He's put that trouble with that saucy baggage right behind him, no mistake. Hasn't given her 'nother thought, has he."

Slinging his spyglass on its leather strap around his neck again, Sam wished he could say the same about the saucy baggage's mistress. No matter how bad the storm, Ananiah had never been far from his own thoughts. He couldn't forget the bleak, empty look in her eyes when he'd found her in the passageway, or the curious way she'd spoken of her husband. The more Sam considered it, the more certain he was that her husband was somehow to blame for the pain she so clearly suffered. But what could a man have done to his wife to scar her soul that way and force her to leave him?

As the brig had fought her way up the crest of one wave and then crashed down into the valley of another, Sam had pictured her huddled in her bunk, her face pale with fear as she clung to the sides, and in his mind he'd formed the kind words he'd have said to comfort her if he'd had the time to knock on her cabin door. And hold her. Oh, aye, he'd wanted to hold her again, too, and tell her the thunder was only empty noise as he stroked her hair.

But Lawson's version was far less romantic. "'Course, it's easy enough to forget a woman when she's moanin' and retchin'," he said with satisfaction. "Jeremy says the pair of 'em has been sick as dogs since the blow began. No suppers, thank ye, says Jeremy, nothing but water left by their door. You was right as rain about them, Cap'n. Women don't have no place in a vessel. Don't have the constitutions for it."

Sam only frowned to himself, saying nothing. He hoped she hadn't let herself become too weak. There hadn't been much of her to spare before.

Holding fast with one hand, Lawson leaned forward, scratching his chin as he peered down at the deck below. "Seems like the weather's turned nice enough for a lady after all. Look, Cap'n, there she is, to the larboard."

A bright patch of green silk against the silver-gray planking, Ananiah walked slowly across the slanted deck, her face turned into the wind and her unbound hair blowing back from her face. She briefly held her arms outstretched, letting the wind billow out her shawl like a sail behind her body as she shook back her hair with such an obviously sensual pleasure that, far above her, Sam knew he'd never seen a woman he thought more unconsciously beautiful, or one he desired more.

"Pretty little creature," admitted Lawson. "She surely don't seem sickly now, do she?"

Watching Ananiah, Sam only half heard the frantic cries of warning from the men below. But there was no missing the long black crossjack as it sliced through the air, the remaining blocks and lines twisting and straining to support the unbalanced weight. Down the crossjack plummeted, tangling and ripping though the standing rigging as it crashed down towards the deck, and down towards the startled, upturned face of Ananiah Snow.

## Chapter Six

At first she didn't realize that she'd been jerked clear of the falling wreckage. The yard and the tangled, torn rigging struck the deck so near to where she stood that lines caught and pulled away her shawl, and the force of the impact threw her back against the seaman who'd saved her.

"Here now, miss, you're not hurt, are you?" His name was Israel Martin, and because he had a large family and a pious wife in Marblehead, he waited only until Ananiah shook her head before he set her firmly back on her own feet and crossed his arms over his chest for good measure. Yet still he smiled at her tentatively, sniffing with awkward embarrassment. "You sure you're all t' rights? Almost pressed flat as a beetle, you was, and it feared me t' watch."

"I'm quite well, and I thank you for your—your concern." Pressing her palms to her cheeks, Ananiah stared down at the litter of rope and wood before her, realizing that without Martin she would have been buried beneath it. She turned back to thank him more warmly, but he'd already joined the other men beginning to clear away the wreckage. She'd seen his kind of shy uneasiness before, and she wondered how bad the stories about her in the forecastle must be to have made him that nervous. Not that the bare truth needed much embellishment. With a sigh, she knelt down to untangle her shawl from where it lay pinned to the deck, one corner fluttering bravely in the wind.

She'd just managed to work it free when she saw the boots come stand before her: well-worn, salt-stained, very large boots that only one man on the *Truelove* would fill.

"What the the hell do you think you're doing here?" demanded Sam, his anger at the carelessness that had caused the accident spilling over onto her. He could see for himself that she was uninjured, more concerned for her cashmere shawl than for her own neck, but he still couldn't shake the image of her up-turned face beneath the falling spar. "I recall ordering you to keep below, and instead you come topside, where you nearly get yourself killed!"

Ananiah scrambled to her feet, the shawl stretched tightly between her clenched hands. Though the storm had passed, he seemed to have somehow kept some of its fury for himself, his expression dark and ominous. On another day she would have kept her distance, but now she couldn't.

"You would have this all be my fault?" she asked incredulously.

"You were where you didn't belong," he said firmly. "No one else put you there excepting yourself, did they?"

"I can't believe you'd say such a thing!" Furious, Ananiah flung back her hair away from her face. Shy Mr. Martin had showed her far more concern than his captain, and she wondered that she'd ever thought Sam Colburn kind. "No, now that I reconsider, I can well believe that you could be so—so hateful! You'd rather I died from want of air down in that wretched little closet you deem a cabin than sully your precious deck!''

"I warned you the *Truelove*'s not meant for ladies' travel—'' began Sam, but Ananiah's indignation raced over him.

"For days and days I've stayed below with poor sick Letty,'' she continued heatedly, "and now the first time she's been well enough to do without me, I'm to be cursed for wishing for no more than a bit of air!''

Sam tried to imagine her as a nurse, but couldn't, not with her pale gold hair dancing around her face and her cheeks flushed with anger. The green silk of her gown whipped tight against the curves of her body in the wind—Lord help him, no petticoats again, no stays, nothing but silk against her flesh—and she held the shawl so tightly between her two hands that he half expected her to throttle him.

"You're overwrought, ma'am,'' he said stiffly. Hell, he was the one who was overwrought. With her so close, he could see the little flecks of green in her eyes, green as the silk. "You'd best go below and rest.''

She flung the shawl over her shoulders. "I don't see what good *resting* would do, not when it's the ineptitude of your own people that caused the accident!''

Over her head Sam spotted Howard making his way towards him, and at once his temper snapped.

"'Ineptitude,' for all love!'' he thundered. Though his words were meant for Howard, he was still turned towards Ananiah, and only her presence kept him from the profanity he'd usually have used. "That's a fine, fancy, lady word for plain, ham-handed clumsiness! Flattening you, ma'am, would have been the least of it! If that crossjack had tipped five degrees more, it would have gone straight as an arrow through this deck and the two below it before it plugged our sides, and we're a precious long ways away from Nantucket for swimming. God deliver us from *ineptitude,* or the devil take our souls!''

Ignoring Howard, Sam joined the others clearing the deck, and Ananiah watched him, saw the long muscles in his back and arms clear through his shirt as he lifted and hauled beside his men. Now that the rush of the accident's excitement was fading, she realized how close she'd come to being killed. No, flattened— that was how Sam had described it. Flattened. And would he have cared at all? Most likely he'd have ordered her broken body sewn up in a hammock and tossed into the ocean, like that of anyone else who died at sea, with a handful of prayers said over the waves, and good-riddance in his thoughts.

She pressed one hand over her mouth and swallowed convulsively, fighting back the inexplicable tears that burned behind her eyes. In the long days of the storm, she had promised herself that she didn't care what Sam Colburn said or thought or did. She wouldn't let him anger her, and she wouldn't run away again when he tried to provoke her. But the promises gave her no comfort now; instead, they only added to the emptiness she always felt inside.

She drew the shawl higher over her shoulders, and with her head bowed to hide her tears, she headed for the hatch. From the steps she glanced down the passageway towards her cabin, but after a week of confinement, she balked at returning there, to Letty and the tiny, airless compartment. Yet where else could she go? Ahead of her were the quarters of the seamen, behind her only the captain's cabin. She continued down the next, narrower set of steps, down deep into the shadows of the *Truelove*'s hold. On the last step, she sat, her knees drawn up and her arms hugging her legs, and with a single muffled sob she closed her eyes and rested her cheek on her knees.

Sam and George Gill were right. She had no place on a ship like the *Truelove*. But she didn't belong in Providence, either, any more than she belonged at Beau Coteau with Étienne. The sad truth was that she didn't belong anywhere. If she had been killed, there would have been no one left to find her father. She'd come so close to death today. But, miserably, she wished it was Sam, not Israel Martin, who'd saved her.

Dear Lord, would she never learn?

In the hold she was below the waterline, and the sounds of the waves against the brig's sides were clearer, the timbers creaking and groaning as the vessel cut through the water. Farther away, behind stacked crates and hogsheads and tuns, she heard the rustling and squeaks of the rats that were the *Truelove*'s other passengers. But there was another sound, too, and, frowning, Ananiah raised her head to listen. A snuffling sound, almost like crying.

"Hello?" she called tentatively, her voice echoing off the ship's curved sides. "Who's there?"

Abruptly the snuffling stopped. From behind one of the tuns Ananiah caught the flicker of a shaded light, and then Jeremy, the ship's only boy, scrambled out.

"I didn't scare you, ma'am, did I?" he asked anxiously, his eyes so round that it was clear to Ananiah that she'd been scaring *him*. In one hand he held an improvised lantern, a bit of murky tallow floating in a battered cup, and in the other a crumpled sheet of paper. "I didn't mean to, I swear to it."

"And you didn't scare me at all, so no more apologies." Ananiah had heard someone say the boy was ten, but even in this uneven light she would have guessed him closer to eight, and small for his age at that. She wondered how his mother could have parted with him so soon, and, for that matter, why Sam had taken him on. Beneath his eyes were smudged damp places that explained the snuffling noises she'd heard and the forlorn way his thin shoulders drooped. "I expect you came here for the same reason I did—to be alone."

"Aye, ma'am," he said halfheartedly. "But you have a cabin all to yourself."

"It's a very tiny cabin that I share with my maid, and she's been seasick since we cleared Newport."

He wrinkled his nose. "I know. I carried the buckets from your door. I was sick the first time out, with my brother Ben, but now I got my sailing-legs, an' I never puke. Well, hardly ever." He scowled down at the paper in his hand, then up at Ananiah from beneath his thatch of yellow-blond hair. "Can you read? My ma can't, but you being a fine lady, I 'spect you might."

Surprised, Ananiah nodded, and he thrust the dog-eared paper into her hands.

"Then, if you please, ma'am, would you tell me what words these be?" he asked, so quickly that the words tumbled out in a rush. "This be a letter from Ben, ma'am, an' though me an' him always sailed with Cap'n Colburn before, now he's second mate to Cap'n Lawrence on th' *Eliza Jane,* but she's a slaver, an' our pa says a slaver's no place for me, so Ben be there, an' I be here with Cap'n Colburn again."

Ananiah nodded seriously. "Your father's right. Slaving's not a decent trade for any Christian." Too vividly she remembered the misery of the slaves at Beau Coteau, and the callous way Étienne and the other plantation owners had regarded the Africans as property, not people. "I'm surprised your brother finds it to his taste."

Jeremy wrinkled his nose again, and wiped it across his sleeve for good measure. "He don't. But he's been courting Sara Webb, an' she won't take him 'less he can give her a household of her own, an' Ben'll earn double with Cap'n Lawrence. I warrant he's writ to me to tell me how things be, but he don't know I never learned my letters, leastways not for words. I tried, ma'am, I tried an' tried, but I can't make it out, an' the others'd call me a lackwit if I asked them." He paused for breath, his eyes pleading. "Please, ma'am, the letter?"

Ananiah smoothed the page with her fingers, thinking. How much she would have given as a child to have a brother or sister to worship and love the way Jeremy did Ben! "I can read it to you, Jeremy, if that's what you wish, but wouldn't you rather be able to read it for yourself, and then write back to Ben whenever you wished?"

Jeremy shook his head fiercely. "Oh, aye, ma'am, I'd like it fine, but I don't got time to waste on schooling. I'm aimin' to be a mate like Ben, not some clerk stuck in warehouse."

"You could be a captain if you could read and write," said Ananiah promptly. "You don't think Captain Colburn would've been content to stay bound to a tall stool in a countinghouse, do you?"

She saw him wavering, and played her winning card.

"And if I teach you," she said, leaning forward to whisper in confidence, "none of the other men in the fo'c'sle need know."

He grinned, and as she made room for him on the step beside her, he set his improvised lantern on the

deck at their feet. By its flickering light, Ananiah
helped him begin to make out his brother's letter—no
easy task in itself, for Ananiah quickly saw from the
penmanship that Ben's schooling, too, had been scattershot. Eagerly, the boy leaned over her arm, and
their heads nearly touched as they bent over the page.
Jeremy's little chuckles of excitement when he could
recognize and find a word again gave Ananiah far
more pleasure than she could have expected.

She slipped her arm across his shoulders affectionately, and without thinking he shifted closer to her.
For all his brash talk, he was still just a lonely child,
and she welcomed his company. Jeremy was the one
person on the *Truelove* who wouldn't, or couldn't,
judge her, and she was able to give him freely something no one else was willing to share. Neither of them
heard the footsteps coming down the companionway
until suddenly Sam was there, his enormous shadow
waving unsteadily over them.

"Jeremy Tate," he began with an ominous calm,
and the boy jumped to his feet. "If I hadn't sworn to
your pa that I'd watch over your worthless little hide,
I'd flail it from your scrawny backside right now and
nail it to the mainmast. What the hell do you think
you're doing, bringing an open flame down into the
hold like that?"

The boy stared miserably down at his bare feet, not
even trying to defend himself. Ananiah rose quickly
beside him, Ben Tate's letter still in her hand. "How
do you know I didn't bring it?"

"Because you, ma'am, wouldn't know the first
thing about floating a wick in old tallow, would you?
Spermaceti candles in silver, that's what I'd believe
from you." He came down the steps heavily, one by
one, until he stood directly above them. The single

beam of sun that filtered down through the hatch turned his hair dark copper. "But you, Jeremy, you know better. Now douse that quick, and then take yourself off until I decide what I'll do with you. Go!"

Swiftly the boy blew out the flame and then flew up the steps, squeezing himself past Sam.

"Jeremy, wait, you forgot your brother's letter!" called Ananiah after him. She tried to follow, but there was no way she could pass Sam on the narrow stairway. He reached down and plucked the letter from her, then glanced at the scrawled handwriting before refolding it and tucking it in his shirt.

"That's not yours, you know," said Ananiah, frowning at the bulge in his shirt where the letter lay against his chest. With him on the step above her, it was nearly at her eye-level. She knew he'd put it there knowing she wouldn't try to retrieve it, and he was right. But the letter was precious to Jeremy, and she owed it to him to ask for it back. "It's a letter from his brother, and we were reading it together. He was doing quite well, too."

He wondered if she'd try to take the letter from his shirt, tantalizing himself with the image of her little hands against his bare chest. "He should be working, not sitting all cozy and sweet with ladies."

"For God's sake, he's only a child!"

"He's ten years old, and he's got a father with one leg and a crippled arm, and four other young ones at home to feed," said Sam, his voice hard. He'd been standing not a yard away from Jeremy's father when the ball from the British cannon maimed him. Taking first Ben and then Jeremy and training them to be seamen was the best Sam could do for him. Besides, Sam liked the boys and treated them well, far better than boys on other ships, and it irritated him that Ananiah thought Jeremy mistreated. "They count on Jeremy's wages, and I already pay him more than he's worth."

"Nonetheless, he should be home with his family," said Ananiah staunchly, "learning to read and write, instead of out here with only grown men for company."

Her condemnation struck him far harder than she could know. "Not all of us have a choice, ma'am. I don't recall anyone asking me if I'd rather grow up rich or poor."

"Well, no one asked me, either," said Ananiah. If her father hadn't been so successful, she would have stayed in Providence and wed some boy she'd known all her life. She wouldn't have sailed to Martinique, and she wouldn't have caught Étienne's fancy, and none of what followed would ever have happened. "You have this notion that a pocketful of gold coins can solve any problem that life presents!"

"Seems to me most times it does."

"Well, it doesn't, Captain Colburn! Most times it just—it just doesn't." She shoved back her hair, wondering how once again they'd come back to arguing over things that could never be changed. "Now please give me the letter so I can return it to Jeremy."

She held out her hand, but instead of giving the letter to her he crossed his arms over his chest. "I'll see that he gets it. And I'll thank you, ma'am, to keep your distance from the rest of my crew as well. I've thirty-two men on board this brig, and I wouldn't vouch for them all if they found you anywhere alone." Truth was, he couldn't even vouch for himself if she didn't leave him soon. Lilies, always the fragrance of lilies around her, teasing him with the promise of an intimacy she'd never grant him. "Stay in your cabin, where you belong."

"Then why don't you just lock me in to be sure?"

"If I thought it would keep you there, I likely would." Abruptly he stepped aside to let her pass. "Keep to yourself until we reach England, ma'am, and I guarantee we'll have no more trouble."

"Trouble from you, not trouble from me. You're a mean-spirited man, Sam Colburn, and I can't believe I ever thought otherwise of you."

*Mean-spirited.* Sam couldn't put the words out of his mind, and with an exasperated grunt he tossed the London newspaper he'd been trying to read across the table. It was old news anyway, three months, time enough for anything and everything to have changed in the war between England and France. He turned instead towards the open windows across the *True-love*'s stern, watching the moonlight play across the froth of the brig's wake.

No woman had ever called him mean-spirited before, not even Sophie, and she had known him better than any other. Hell, she'd been willing to marry him—no, more than willing, she'd practically chased him into the church. She wouldn't have done that if he was truly mean-spirited, would she? And Sophie Crowninshield and Ananiah Snow were certainly two of a kind, both pretty and pampered and accustomed to having their own way. He'd thought that about Ananiah the first moment he'd seen her perched up on that wall, fancy plumes in her hair and diamonds in her ears.

But the more he tried to picture the two women side by side, the more the comparison began to slide away from him. For one thing, Ananiah was older, closer to his own age, and she had none of Sophie's irritating girlishness. Good or bad, Ananiah had seen something of the world, and had been changed by it, too. He liked that about her. He remembered how she'd scarcely flinched earlier, when the crossjack had fallen, when most ladies would have swooned or turned hysterical, and how she'd run right along with him after he'd tangled with Justin Forbes in the rum-shop in Newport.

He'd liked the way she'd defended Jeremy Tate, too, even though the little idiot could have blown them clear out of the water with his carelessness. And though he still couldn't accept the way she'd tricked him, he did admire the loyalty and love she must feel for her roguish old father, enough to make her come traipsing clear across the Atlantic to find him. He doubted Sophie would cross Essex Street on a sunny day to help her father. She certainly hadn't proved very faithful as an intended wife.

He now guessed that Sophie hadn't really been in love with him the way she'd claimed. God knows he hadn't been; it had only been the chance to be connected with the Crowninshields, plus knowing he'd still be away at sea ten months out of twelve, that made him go along with it at all. It was high time he had a son or two to take to sea with him, too, and Sophie would have done that as well as any woman.

Oh, Sophie had liked being kissed well enough, as long as it didn't go much further, but what had fascinated her was his upbringing, as if being the son of an indifferent cooper who'd drunk himself to death qualified Sam as a genuine exotic. In her safe little satinwood world, it probably did. Whenever he'd tried to do things to please her—having a new coat made, say, like the ones her other beaux wore—she'd frowned and told him not to change, she liked him as her wild sea captain instead.

But Ananiah, now...Ananiah veered off on another tack altogether, always insisting that they were more alike than he'd admit. Sam smiled wryly, and propped his feet up against the bulkhead beside the window as he thought how very wrong she was. The day after the party, curiosity had made him go see where she lived in Providence. Captain Snow's house was three full stories of brick and carved woodwork and arched windows with sashes, and a maidservant out front to sweep the white marble steps. All that for one sad-eyed lady with tangled golden hair.

Odd that though the way Sophie had jilted him at her father's orders had eaten at his pride, he found he didn't really care that much that he'd lost Sophie herself. Meek and mild he'd been, letting Sophie toss him over for a Pickering, and her father do his best to drive him under. But now here he was fussing and worrying over two angry words from Ananiah Snow like they meant the end of the world. It just didn't make sense.

He was still marveling at it when the knock sounded on his cabin door. Time for Jeremy to bring his evening coffee, and without turning in his chair Sam growled for him to enter. Wouldn't hurt to let the boy stew a bit longer, especially since Sam knew he'd be too softhearted to thrash him the way he deserved.

Ananiah hesitated in the companionway. Clearly Sam's anger hadn't cooled since this afternoon. She could leave now and he'd never know she'd been the one to knock.

She shifted the heavy round bottle from one arm to the other, awkwardly balancing the box of sweet biscuits against her elbow. Unless she made some sort of peace with him, she was doomed to spend the next

month in her cabin. A glass of canary and a pretty
apology had always worked with her father, and with
Étienne, too. She hoped they would with Sam. She
heard him call irritably again for her to enter, and with
her hip she shoved the door open.

He sat with his back to her, as fine as a lord with his
long legs, in loose duck trousers, stretched out beside
the open window, his bare feet crossed comfortably.
In the white linen shirt and an unbuttoned dark blue
waistcoat, his shoulders dwarfed the back of the battered pine armchair. The long plait of his sailor's pigtail hung down across the back of the chair, and she
thought foolishly of how much better he was at braid-
ing his hair than she was with her own.

"Stand there much longer and you can serve the
damned stuff for my breakfast," he grumbled.
"You've kept me waiting long enough."

She set the biscuits and the bottle down on the table with a thump and went back to shut the door. "I
came to apologize," she said tartly, "but hearing you
now, I've half a mind to make you wait even longer."

He turned sharply in the chair, the surprise in his
face quickly turning to something else altogether. She
wore the white muslin dress with the red flowers from
the day they'd sailed, but now, without the jacket, the
full shape of her breasts was clear beneath the soft,
sheer fabric. She wore no jewelry, only a thin red ribbon tied around her throat, the ends curling down over
her white skin, and her hair, too, was simply dressed
in a loose knot on the top of her head.

She recognized that hungry look in his eyes, and
knew it had nothing to do with the biscuits. Even with
his eyes half-closed and shaded in the swinging lantern's light overhead, Sam's gaze was still so intense
she felt it on her skin like a caress. Not since Étienne

had a man watched her this closely, his desire this evident.

"Apologize?" he repeated slowly. "What the devil for?"

"You were right this afternoon. You're the captain, and I'd no business coming between you and one of your crew."

He cocked one eyebrow, surprised by what even he would have to call an apology. "By my crew, I warrant you mean Jeremy. Is it true the boy can't read? He signed his name in my book well enough."

"My guess is that's all he can do. By his age he should know a great deal more."

"I was seventeen before I could do any more than make my mark and pray I wasn't being cheated," he said bluntly. With his father often too ill from drinking to work, earning a shilling for food had been more important to Sam as a boy than spending one on schooling. But though he looked for Ananiah to be shocked or disbelieving, she merely nodded again with an acceptance that he hadn't expected.

"The boy must know his letters if he wishes to prosper," he said gruffly. "I'd be obliged if you helped him. Just choose some place other than the hold."

"Thank you." A rare smile lit her face, and Sam would have signed over the *Truelove* herself if she but asked for it. "You must have thought us plotting mutiny, skulking about down there. My father would have strung us from the yardarm and asked questions later."

Belatedly Sam realized he still sat in the cabin's only chair. He rose quickly and held it out for her. She perched shyly on the edge, her back straight while her hands fluttered briefly like unquiet birds in her lap. From where he stood, he saw a great deal more of her breasts than she likely realized. Restlessly, he ran his fingers back through his hair. Despite the open windows, the cabin seemed almost unbearably warm.

"I was more concerned with the open flame than a mutiny. Most of my—I mean *your*—cargo is Rhode Island rum. Now, fine your rum may be, but you put a spark to it, and it'll go up like a Chinaman's fireworks." He was babbling like an idiot, all hollow heartiness that made him wince inside. Why was it that the more he wanted to make things right between them, the more confused his thoughts and words became? "Blue flames, right pretty. Once I saw a smuggler's sloop blow outside of Boston. Scattered clear over the bay, and nothing left bigger than your finger."

She turned gracefully in the chair to look up at him, the lantern's light gilding the pale curve of her bare throat crossed by the red ribbon. "Then I suppose I should add my thanks to my apologies. It seems that twice today I've been nearly killed."

She liked the way his grin flashed bright for her benefit alone, and she liked the sound of his voice, deep and showing him very sure of himself. The plain truth was that she liked *him*.

One heavy lock of dark chestnut hair had fallen rakishly across his forehead, and he tossed it back. "I thought that angels were immortal."

"I'm not sure I want to risk my mortal life to find out."

"Then I'm glad you didn't." There was a new edge of seriousness beneath his bantering, his voice deeper, and to his own wonderment he realized he was speaking the truth. "If I'd been wrong, I don't think my own life would have been worth living."

Ananiah turned back to the table, forcing herself to break the easy pattern of flirtation they'd so effort-lessly begun. Flirtation was all it was, she told herself fiercely, and she must give him the wine and leave be-fore it became anything more. But her heart had heard otherwise, and she felt a fragile sprig of hope and happiness begin to grow within her.

"I brought my father's favorite wine from Provi-dence to celebrate his release," she said, self-consciously looking down at her hands in her lap, "but I don't think he'd begrudge you a bottle to-night."

Thankful for something to do, Sam found two tumblers in the shuttered cabinet, wishing the heavy glass was the purest crystal. He pulled his sea chest to the table to use as a makeshift chair, and sat across from her, painfully aware of her knees nearly touch-ing his as he cut away the bottle's seal, drew the cork, and began to pour the amber-colored wine.

Quickly she covered her glass with her palm. "Oh, no, none for me. 'Tis all for you."

"And I say drinking alone isn't worth the wine. Come now, lass, drink up." He slipped her hand aside and filled her glass. "Liberty to the French and con-fusion to the British!"

She lifted it to her lips uncertainly, her eyes meet-ing his across the wine. Without looking away, he drank until his glass was empty, then grinned at her as he thumped it down on the bare table. It was another dare, pure and simple, a challenge Ananiah knew she should refuse if she had any sense left at all. Even af-ter following Étienne's preference for wine at every meal, she had never had a head for spirits.

She should put down the tumbler and leave now. Back to her tiny cabin, where Letty would be waiting to fuss at her and lecture her, and later snore while Ananiah lay awake, curled in a tight, lonely ball as she listened to the wind and the waves. With only her self-respect for comfort. With nothing to regret, nothing to explain, and nothing to dream.

He was so close to her now that she could see every line the sun and wind had etched into his face, and the little chip in the corner of one tooth that kept his smile from being perfect.

She tipped the glass back and emptied it in one long swallow.

# Chapter Seven

Sam chuckled, delighted that she'd managed to surprise him again. He saw her eyes widen as the alcohol met her blood, and saw the flush that warmed her cheeks. Clearly one glass was enough for her. He wasn't a man who enjoyed insensible women, and he thought reluctantly that he should see her back to her own cabin soon.

But she reached across to take the bottle herself and refill their glasses. Very deliberately she opened the box of biscuits, folded back the linen napkin around them, and slid the box to the exact center of the table.

"I baked them myself," she declared proudly, taking one. "You see, I'm not as thoroughly useless as you believe."

In all honesty, Sam could think of few things more useless than baking tiny round sweets fit only for a lady's tea table. But he forgot all that as he watched her neatly break the biscuit in half, dip it in her wine, and then laugh, deep in her throat, when it disintegrated halfway to her mouth. The sight alone of her licking the crumbs from her lower lip would have undone him, but coupled with her laugh, rich and husky and full of promise... Lord, it was more than any man could bear. More than he could, anyway. His whole body felt rigid with longing, every muscle tense, in spite of the wine. Did she have any idea of what she was doing to him?

Still smiling with amusement, Ananiah plucked another biscuit from the box and plunged it briefly into the wine.

"Here, Sam, your turn," she said merrily as she held the dripping biscuit out to him. There was such a strange, fixed smile on his face that she almost began laughing again. "I swear it's not poisoned."

But instead of taking the biscuit, he reached across the table and seized her wrist. If she wanted to play teasing games like this, then he would, too. And he'd win. His blue-grey eyes were dark, the pupils dilated, as he drew her hand towards his mouth. He purposefully grazed her fingertips with his teeth as he bit the biscuit from her hand.

Startled, Ananiah's fingers flew open. But, though she tried to pull free, Sam effortlessly held her hand fast in his. She wasn't laughing now, and with his thumb on the blue veins of her wrist he could feel the quickening of her pulse. With deliberate slowness, he ran his lips along the length of each of her slender fingers in turn and licked away the wine-soaked crumbs. Finally he tipped her palm up and kissed it, pressing his lips into the soft, slightly moist skin. Her hands were so delicate, unmarked by any work. The hands of an angel.

"What are you doing, Sam?" Ananiah asked raggedly. She could not believe the havoc he'd created within her simply by kissing her hand. But it hadn't been simple, not the way he'd done it, and her breath caught again as she thought of the sensual play of his tongue between her fingers. If she let him, what would he do to the rest of her? "What do you want?"

"The same thing you do." This time he kissed her wrist, where the fever of passion already sang, and her whole body trembled.

"That's not true," she murmured, knowing it was a lie. Now the hunger in his eyes must be mirrored in her own, and the certainty of her response both frightened and shamed her. "I didn't come here for—for that."

"No?" He grinned at her crookedly, and she felt one more part of her reserve melt away in the fire of attraction. "I'd swear otherwise, Ananiah. You're a woman full grown, not some silly maid, and I'll warrant you have a fair notion of 'that' already."

Awkwardly she struggled to her feet, her hand still trapped in his grasp, her cheeks flaming. "I don't know what stories you've heard about me, or what kind of woman people say I am."

"The devil take what people say, Ananiah. I told you before, I decide my own mind." With his free hand, he reached up to the scarlet ribbon tied around her throat and tugged at one curling end until the bow gave way. Slowly he drew the ribbon towards him, the thin band of silk sliding across her skin another kind of caress across her bare skin, and Ananiah shivered.

"Before, when I was wed to Étienne, I was innocent of what was said of me," she whispered hoarsely, the pain of the past poignantly fresh again in her eyes. "But if I stay with you, Sam, then everything they whisper about me will be true."

He rose abruptly and shoved the table to one side. The half-full bottle crashed to the floor. Ananiah gasped as wine and shards of dark-green glass scattered across the deck at her feet, then gasped again as Sam swung her over the broken bottle and onto the curved lid of the chest. For an endless moment she balanced there, his hands spanning her waist as he steadied her, her own hands braced upon the hard muscles of his upper arms.

She had no reason to lie to him, yet he still could not believe it. She needed him, *him,* Samuel Colburn. In all his life, no one ever had before. "I've always fought for everything I've ever gotten," he said roughly. "Do you truly believe I'd let anyone hurt you again because of me?"

Before she could answer, he pulled her down into his arms. She turned her face up towards his, and his mouth found hers with a rightness that took her breath away, and she knew that if she let him possess her she would belong to him alone. He tasted of the wine, and tobacco, and the saltiness of the sea that forever was a part of him, just the way she remembered from that first night in the shadow of the garden wall.

But this was nothing like that first lighthearted kiss. This was like nothing she'd ever known. His lips were hard and demanding, and she yielded with no thought but to answer, her own yearning a match for his own. Anger gave an edge to his passion, anger not with her, but rather with the world that had hurt her. He had said he would keep her safe, and from the way he kissed her now, she dared to believe him.

Her frail defenses crumbled before the onslaught of his tongue as it plunged savagely into the softest corners of her mouth. Her body rippled with awakening sensation, and her hands slid up his arms to his shoulders, drawing him deeper, closer. In the entire time she had been wed to Étienne, she had never felt the wild exhilaration of desire like this.

Roughly Sam jerked the pins from her hair and let the heavy silken weight of it tumble over her shoulders, around their faces, bringing with it the scent of crushed lilies. His fingers sought the swelling curve beneath her waist, curling into the soft flesh beneath the sheer muslin as he lifted her hips into his, her legs slipping to either side of his thighs as he let her feel the intensity of his desire. She couldn't get near enough to him, though she pressed closer and closer still as he moved her against him. She shuddered and clung to his shoulders, her mouth open and giving to him, as her whole body wished to be.

Her soft cry was lost in his mouth as she tangled her long legs around his, and he felt the ache of his desire, hard and hot, tighten even further. This wasn't what he'd expected at all, thought Sam with the small part of him still able to think, and he tore himself away from her lips with a groan. The game had ended long ago. He wanted her, all of her, and he didn't want to stop until she was his. His lips marked a path across her forehead, her eyelids, the delicious long curve of her throat, and he buried his face in the fragrant tangle of her hair, murmuring her name over and over.

He raised her once again to stand on the chest above him, and her fingers dug into his shoulders for support. By the swinging lantern's light he saw that the pale skin below her throat was already mottled with passion, and with his thumbs he eased her gown from her shoulders, tugging the muslin away to free her breasts. She didn't try to cover herself, but waited, watching him with eyes heavy with desire, trusting him.

So beautiful, he marveled as his palms traced and held the weight of her breasts, and he heard the catch and break in her breathing. His mouth closed over her, the soft peak hardening at once beneath the pressure of his tongue. Gently he tugged at the tender flesh with his teeth until she whimpered with pleasure and drew his head closer, her fingers tangling in his hair. His hands slid down to her hips, cradling her as she swayed against him, lost in the sweet anguish of his mouth at her breast.

*His beautiful angel, his angel Ananiah . . .*

"Cap'n Colburn!" A man thumped on the cabin door loudly. "Cap'n Colburn, sir, Mr. Lawson said to fetch you prompt and tell you there's a sail he don't know, nine points to starboard."

The moment shattered, Sam swore beneath his breath in angry frustration. He knew he had to go. As captain, he had no choice. But, God in heaven, he didn't want to, not now, not when she was so very close to being his in every way that mattered. He closed his eyes and rested his cheek against her breast, listening to the muffled racing beat of her heart. He gently stroked the backs of her thighs. Another moment longer with her, another moment was all he asked.

"Cap'n Colburn, sir?" the man called again, his voice rising uncertainly. Sam knew he wouldn't go away until he had an answer, and reluctantly he eased himself away from Ananiah.

"Tell Lawson I'll be there directly," he called, his hands still holding her. Her face was bewildered, lost, and he hated himself for having to leave her.

"I must go, angel," he said gently, letting his hand linger on the curve of her throat and shoulder as he stepped away from her. "That sail could belong to anyone in these waters, and I have to know who."

Ananiah nodded mutely, and sank down to sit on the chest. Suddenly self-conscious, she pulled her bodice back over her breasts and wrapped her arms tightly around her body, fighting off the ache of unfulfillment. The giddiness from the wine had vanished, and in its place she felt only a hollow uncertainty.

So her body pleased Sam, just as it had Étienne. She knew too well how little that meant. She and Sam had come so close to being lovers, and as she watched him shrug into his coat, she realized it would have been the worst mistake she could have made. She knew so little about him, and he knew less about her. Otherwise, he never would have said what he had. Yet it had all been so easy to believe when he kissed her.

She curled herself tighter and stared down at the broken bottle on the deck, and the blotches the wine had left on the oak planking. Her unpinned hair hung down like a veil on either side of her forehead, hiding her face from him.

"I'll return as soon as I can, Ananiah," he was saying. He paused before her, his boots crunching on a shard of glass. "Likely it's no more than some homebound whaler."

He bent down and tenderly smoothed her hair back from her face. She was so lovely that part of him refused to believe she wasn't a dream, and he shook his head in wonder. Yet something was missing still; he saw an emptiness in her expression that reminded him uneasily of the time in the passageway. If it was in his power, he would make it right for her, and for them. In an unspoken pledge, he pressed his fingertips to her lips, still swollen and ripe from his own.

"I don't know what went wrong between you and your husband," he said softly, "but the man must have been a fool to let you go."

As he closed the door behind him, Ananiah's face crumpled. "And so," she whispered brokenly, "must be your wife."

\* \* \*

Letty closed the cabin door and retreated swiftly to the edge of her bunk, her shawl wrapped tight as a shroud around her night rail. "You've no business to come calling this time of night, Mr. Howard."

"And you've no business letting me in with your mistress away," he said with an offhand shrug.

Letty knew he was right, and she blushed, already wishing she'd ignored his knock. She tried to look disapproving, but it was hard to be stern to a face as round and good-natured as Amos Howard's. And it wasn't as if he were being disrespectful or forward; he simply stood before her and grinned, his arms crossed over his chest and his stocky legs spread against the brig's roll.

"But I'm thankful you did, lamb," he continued. "I've wanted words with you since we cleared Newport."

She self-consciously twisted the end of her braid in her fingers. "I've been ill, you know. I don't have the stomach for long voyages."

"You'd never know it to look at you now." His wide brown eyes were so full of frank admiration that Letty's cheeks grew hot again.

"You're like every other bold-faced sailor-man," she said tartly, tossing her braid back over her shoulder, "crammed full to brimming with pretty words and promises, when you've likely a doxy in every harbor you've ever cleared."

"Don't wrong me now, Letty," he said seriously. "I've no taste for brothels. But where's a Christian man to find a decent woman when he spends most of his days at sea?"

Letty frowned, unsure of herself and of him. "What do you want, Mr. Howard?"

"Nay, it's what you want that concerns me, Letty. I want to know all about you, what you're hoping and what you're dreaming. A lass like yourself can't want to be tied in service for all your days, can you?"

"It's a better lot than most," she answered loyally. "Captain Snow's house is the grandest place on Benefit Street." But in her mind she pictured her sister's shingled saltbox on Weybossett Point, small and crowded with chubby children and a husband who loved her and teased her and made her laugh.

His eyes narrowed, as if he were reading her thoughts. "What kind of lot can it be, trailing after some Frenchman's fancy leavings? It's a bane on us all, having a wanton creature like that one on board. Things was fine between me and the cap'n before she came along, shaking her skirts in his nose."

"Don't you speak of Miss Ananiah that way!" said Letty warmly. "She never lay with M'sieur de Gramont till after they was wed! 'Twas him that played her false, lying through his yellow teeth fit to break her sweet heart!"

"You take her side, but what's she done by you?" demanded Amos. "Ordered you to keep here all lonesome, that's what, while she's aft frolicking with the cap'n!"

Troubled, Letty stared down at her braid, unable to deny what he said. She'd dressed Ananiah's hair herself tonight, and she'd seen bright eagerness in her mistress's eyes for the first time in years. It was wrong, Letty knew that, but Ananiah hadn't listened to reason. She'd stopped listening the moment they began this fool's errand of a voyage. Captain Colburn was the one to blame, not that Ananiah would admit that, either. He wasn't a gentleman, not with his rough-hewn body and manners to match, and he didn't deserve a sweet lady like Ananiah. Captain Snow would have her head when he learned of it.

"Ah, lass, I didn't mean to make you sad." Amos chucked her gently beneath her plump chin, lifting her face to meet his gaze. "You're a fine, fair girl, Letty Landis, fit to be a captain's lady yourself."

"Not for *him*, I wouldn't." Letty sniffed contemptuously. "He's like a great russet ox, and I wouldn't have him even if he asked."

"Nay, wasted you'd be on him. But there's other men not so blind." He stroked his thumb across the curve of her cheek and, breathless, Letty searched his face, praying he believed what he said. None of the boys at home had ever called her pretty, and to hear it now from a man better than the lot of them together was like magic.

"I've prospects, lass," he said proudly. "When I've done this run, George Gill's promised me a schooner of my own for the Indies."

"You're a clever man if you've caught George Gill's eye. Miss Ananiah don't care for him, but her father does, and in matters of trade I'll take his word." She smiled shyly, wondering at her good fortune. "Master of a sugar schooner, you say?"

"Aye, and I swear that's but a start." From the deck overhead came the sound of the bell that marked the end of the watch, and Amos sighed in irritation. Before Letty knew what was happening, he had placed his hands on her shoulders and kissed her swiftly, his lips soft and warm.

"Mark what I say, lamb," he said afterwards, his freckled face as flushed as her own. "Time'll come that neither of us will have to answer to any but ourselves. God take me if it don't. And you let me in again, mind?''

"Oh, aye, I'll mind, Amos," whispered Letty, smiling happily as she touched her fingers to her lips where he'd kissed her. "I'll mind whate'er you say."

The next day was almost ended before Sam saw her again. He was taking this watch at the wheel himself while most of the men were below at supper, and with each hand on a polished spoke he held the brig steady on her course. The setting sun at his back washed the spread of the *Truelove*'s canvas pink, and turned the sea before him a glittering gold. The air still held the last warmth of a summer afternoon, and the standing rigging hummed with the same westerlies that filled the sails.

It was the time of day he loved best, and yet now he could find no pleasure in it. Far to the southeast, so far that only the tip of its mainmast showed above the horizon, rode another ship, the one Lawson had sighted last night.

They came no nearer the *Truelove*, but they didn't run, either, instead matching every change that Sam made in his course. From this distance he couldn't tell if they were English or French, Dutch or American, a curious ally or a navy ship eager for a prize.

Not knowing made him edgy as a cat, and the whole crew had soon learned to keep clear of his temper. It had been a long, tense day for Sam, but finally Ananiah came to walk on the deck, and his battered spirits soared.

She didn't turn his way, though Sam was sure she knew he was there. Instead, she walked forward, towards the bowsprit, ignoring the wind and spray that blew back the wide brim of her hat and made her plump little maid squawk and flutter at her side. Twice today she'd returned unopened the notes he'd sent to her cabin, and in desperation he'd finally sent Jeremy to tell her she was welcome to come topside if she wished. Seeing her from a distance would be better than not seeing her at all.

He'd been disappointed enough when he returned to his cabin last night to find her gone. Disappointed, but not surprised. He'd behaved like any randy rutting jack on shore leave when he had no business being anywhere near a lady like her.

She'd needed and trusted him, and he winced to think of how he'd treated her in return. Yet hadn't she been the one to come to him? She had welcomed his kisses, and her soft cries when he caressed her had been sounds of pleasure, not reproof. He watched her hungrily as the wind swept her skirts around her slim figure, and wished he knew the real reason she'd left.

Letty seized Ananiah by the arm. "I tell you, Miss Ananiah, he's stripping you naked with his eyes!" she said, scandalized. "No decent man would dare look at a lady like *he's* looking at you! Nay, don't turn, miss, don't look! He don't need another mite of encouragement from you, not after what you did with him last night."

"Hush, Letty," said Ananiah sharply, "and let that be an end to it."

"You can't deny it, miss, can you?" Letty couldn't hide the triumph in her voice. "I saw the proof, bold as paint, on your body when you undressed. Think on what your poor father would say!"

"My father would say you'd forgotten your place!"

Letty's lips flattened into a tight line of disapproval, and she withdrew her hand from Ananiah's arm. "Nay, miss, it's you that's forgotten, and you that's blaming me for remembering. I'll be below if you need me."

"Letty, wait, you must not go!" Ananiah turned swiftly, the ribbons of her hat blowing out behind her, but the other woman was already disappearing down the hatchway. Ananiah sighed unhappily, tugging at the streaming ribbons as her gaze met Sam's, not twenty feet away. The setting sun framed him in a fiery glow, and the brass trim on the wheel winked like starlight. He didn't wave or call to her, but Ananiah felt the unspoken pull, and slowly she crossed the deck towards him, her heart pounding. She reasoned she'd be safe enough here in the open, and he couldn't try to touch her with his hands on the wheel.

"So the other ship wasn't English?" she asked, forcing herself to meet his eye. "We were in no danger of capture?"

"You'd know if you'd bothered to read my messages," he said bluntly. He couldn't tell if she was blushing from being near him, or if the color in her cheeks was only from the setting sun behind him. The shadows beneath her eyes were real enough, though, and he was perversely glad she hadn't slept any more than he had. "We're being followed. I can't tell you why or by whom, but it's best you know."

"I thank you for telling me, Captain. I'd much rather know than not." She wondered if he'd meant to frighten her, because, curiously, she wasn't frightened at all. He had a reputation for outrunning anything that chased him, and she had no reason to doubt him now. "Do the winds favor us or them?"

He hadn't bothered to either tie or plait his hair today, and as it blew forward into his face, he impatiently tossed it back, glaring at her. Hell, how could she stand here as cool as ice, when he was burning inside? "Oh, aye, the winds are fair enough for the *Truelove*," he said, "but not for you and me, are they?"

She dropped her chin, unable to meet the question she found in his eyes. "What happened last night was wrong."

"Wrong!" He had meant to apologize, but all he felt was anger and frustration. His voice turned harsh. "The devil take your wrong, Ananiah! I've never felt anything more right than having you in my arms, and I warrant you haven't, either. There's a bond between us that I don't begin to understand, but at least I'm not denying it, the way you are. And I'd only begun to show you all the pleasure I can give you before—"

"No, Sam, don't!" She closed her eyes, but still she saw what he offered her—wanton, unbidden images that shocked her with their intensity, images of them together in the narrow bunk in his cabin, his powerful body bare as it moved over hers, her own pale legs curled over his darker back as she clung to him, as he filled her, as she cried out again and again with pleasure, and she knew she must not let it happen, dear Lord, she must not be so weak again. "I tell you it's wrong!"

His hands tightened on the turned spokes of the wheel. "For God's sake, why?"

She shook her head, unwilling to explain what to her seemed so obvious. Étienne had been the same way, she thought bitterly, with precious little thought for his wife's feelings when he desired another woman. She stared down at the polished oak of the wheel between them, and for the first time noticed the small brass hearts laid into the wood. She reached out to touch one, the polished metal smooth and cold.

"Did you name the *Truelove* for Sophie?" she asked, her fingers still on the inlaid heart.

"For Sophie?" repeated Sam, mystified. "Whyever would I name my ship after her?"

"Because you loved her," answered Ananiah, her voice so soft Sam had to strain to hear it over the sound of the wind and sea.

"I never loved Sophie," he declared. "Not even on the day I asked her father for her hand. I'm not real proud of it now, but when you grow up in Salem, you learn about the fortune that comes with the whole damned lot of Crowninshields, and I guess I was as taken up with them as anyone. And Sophie herself, well, she's fair enough to look upon, but foolish as any woman born. I wouldn't take a hundred of her for one of you, and that's the truth."

"And you believe that that's reason enough for you to lie with me?" she asked sadly, knowing it wasn't enough for her.

"Nay, lass, not to lie with you, but to make love to you, and there's a world of difference between the two."

At first she didn't answer, and Sam held his breath. Hell, he'd just as much as told her he loved her, and all she could do was look at him like she was going to cry.

"As great a difference as love within a marriage, and love that falls without it?"

"Damn it, Ananiah, don't start twisting words around me again!" He struck his fist against the top of the wheel with frustration. "I've told you all there is to know about Sophie. The *Truelove*'s named for, well—named for herself, since I've always loved her above any other thing, at least until now. But you're not even listening to what I'm saying, are you? Maybe you'd be better in a pulpit than with me, so you could preach to the world all your high-and-mighty right and wrong!''

"That's not fair, Sam!''

"Nay, belay that, I've a better notion for your sermon. Why don't you just tell me what the devil happened to your own precious marriage?''

She gasped and drew back as if she'd been struck. "You told me it didn't matter to you.''

"It doesn't. But it matters to you, and if I ever want another chance to kiss you again, I'll have to know the truth, and you'll have to tell me.''

Her eyes were full of silent pleading. "You'll hate me for it, Sam.''

"Nay, angel, I swear I won't,'' he said firmly. "I couldn't.''

She turned away and gazed out over the rail to the water, to the endlessly changing pattern of white foam and dark waves. Wearily she thought that it didn't matter if he heard the story from her or from another. No matter what he claimed, he would never look at her the same way again, and he'd still be married to another woman.

The sun had finally slipped below the horizon, and the low gray clouds to the west were streaked with red, when Ananiah began telling Sam the truth.

# Chapter Eight

"I was nineteen the summer my mother died," she began, her eyes focussed on the past and not the sea before her, "and Father took me with him to Martinique, and introduced me to Étienne de Gramont. Étienne was very handsome and very amusing, and Father liked him because he was wealthy, and because before the revolution—the one in Paris, I mean, not ours—he had been a chevalier to King Louis. Father said I was fortunate to have a man like Étienne court me, and that an alliance with his family would be an honor to the Snows. It wasn't difficult. Étienne was lonely, a widower, and before my father sailed away, I'd married him."

*Étienne had told her she was the most beautiful woman he'd ever known, and she'd thought he was the most handsome gentleman, with his dancing black eyes, and black hair only just touched with white, lace on his shirt and silver embroidery on his peach-colored coat. Each morning he'd brought her white roses from his garden at Beau Coteau, the buds tightly furled and touched with dew.*

Absently she twisted her ring around her finger. "I was happy because I loved him. He indulged me in whatever I wished, and perhaps because I was so much younger, he never expected much of me beyond being gay and pretty and—and compliant. And because I wished to please Étienne, and my father, too, I always was, even if my husband's wishes were not—not always to my taste.''

*In the beginning, her youth had been enough for him, and he had been gentle with her in the tall carved bed shrouded in gauze against mosquitoes. But soon the charm of her innocence had passed, and, unworldly though she was, she'd known what he asked of her then was shameful. The night he tried to bring one of the woman slaves to their bed, she'd locked the door against him. Furious, he'd shouted obscenities at her, demanding that she let him in, until finally he'd shoved the sobbing slave up against the locked door and taken her there, where Ananiah, sickened and shaking on the other side, could hear it all.*

Sam frowned, noting how pale her face had become as she chose her words with painful precision. He could only guess at what she wasn't saying, and what that French bastard had made her do, and he understood now why she'd withdrawn from his own loving. He hated Gramont for how he'd hurt her, for the calculated cruelty with which he'd destroyed her trust and innocence. Lord, what he'd give for the chance to make him suffer for what he'd done to her!

''If I had been older or more clever,'' Ananiah continued softly, ''I think I would have seen what Étienne tried to keep hidden, and asked about the letters and the messengers from Paris. I wouldn't have been as blind, and I wouldn't have been as—as surprised when Hélène arrived at our house from Paris.''

She stopped then, sinking back into her own thoughts, forcing Sam to prompt her. ''Who was Hélène?'' he asked gently. ''His mistress?''

She turned her face to him and smiled bleakly. "Oh, no. *I* was his mistress. Hélène was his wife."

*She'd come back from riding to find Hélène in her drawing room, the house slaves gathered around her chair in wonder. The woman had been frail and gaunt from prison, her shoulders twisted and her face scarred beneath her rouge and powder from beatings by the guards at La Conciergerie. But when Ananiah entered, hatred had given Hélène de Gramont the strength to stand and spit in the face of her rival, and call her a whore. And Ananiah had been powerless to deny it, because she had known Hélène was right.*

Ananiah looked away swiftly, afraid to see the disgust she knew would be on Sam's face, and she spoke hurriedly, rushing to finish before he could interrupt her. "Étienne had told me Hélène had died on the guillotine, but now I think he'd known all along that she lived. He just hadn't expected her to ever be freed to return to Martinique. But even with her in his house again, he didn't want to give me up. He said we could go on as we were until she died, and then he would marry me again."

*He'd struck her when she said she would leave, hit her hard with the flat of his hand, and dragged her to the tall bed one last time. She hadn't let him know how much he hurt her, and she hadn't cried. But that night, as she fled and the others slept, the pains had begun, and she'd wept then, knowing how much he'd taken from her.*

Her voice dropped down to a broken whisper. "But I did leave, Sam. I wouldn't stay. I left. And I'll never marry again."

"My poor angel," Sam said hoarsely. Though she'd said his name, he wasn't even sure she was aware of him before her. "It wasn't your fault, lass, none of it."

Her eyes were still blank and staring, her lips were open and her breathing was shallow, and she'd hunched her shoulders defensively with her head bowed. She seemed so fragile, he wondered that the wind didn't carry her away. Nothing he could say to her would begin to be enough, and learning how she'd been so wounded didn't tell him how he could make her better. What words could possibly reach her?

Without thinking, he left the wheel to take her in his arms, and without his hands for guidance, the brig lurched crazily off course. Immediately, Sam lunged back again to steady the ship. He scanned the deck for anyone he could give the steering over to, but the only other crewmen were high in the rigging. Desperately he looked back to where she waited. It was almost dark now, and her white dress fluttered in the quarter-moon's light as she turned away to leave him.

"Ananiah, sweet, promise me you'll come to me tonight," he called hurriedly. "I swear I won't touch you if you don't wish it, but I can't let you go after this. We need each other, Ananiah. Ananiah!"

"No, Sam, I won't," she said, her voice curiously emotionless. "I won't make the same mistake twice."

"Damn it, Ananiah, it wasn't your mistake, and I'm not Étienne. For God's sake, don't you know by now that I'd never hurt you? What do I have to say to make you believe me? Damn it, lass, don't run away again!"

That stopped her. Her back was still towards him, but at least she was listening. He took a deep breath, determined to keep her attention now that he had it.

"You promised to help Jeremy with his letters. Tomorrow morning, in my cabin. He'll be there for you."

The wide brim of her hat dipped twice as she nodded, and then she was gone, easing past Lawson in the companionway. The older man watched her go, then came over to Sam. Lawson's brows were raised in a question that he clearly thought the better of asking once he saw the black look on Sam's face.

"So I hear we've lost our friends t' the south, Cap'n," he said amiably, cocking his head in that direction. "Matty Ralph says we lost 'em the middle o' the last watch."

Sam only grunted as he gladly turned over the wheel to the older man, shrugging the stiffness from his shoulders. How could he admit that he'd completely forgotten about the other ship on the horizon?

"Nay, Cap'n, I warrant that's the last we'll see of them," continued Lawson. "No more ghosts dogging the *Truelove,* eh?"

Sam didn't agree. From where he stood, ghosts were everywhere.

"No, Jeremy, the tail on the *y* goes back this way," said Ananiah as she slowly guided the quill clutched in the boy's wind-chapped fingers. "There now, you do it for yourself."

"Aye, ma'am, if you say so." Jeremy sighed manfully, dipped the quill in the ink again and, with his tongue thrust halfway out of his mouth in concentration, formed a shaky but correct version of the proverb Ananiah had written out as a model.

"That's excellent, Jeremy, truly!" she exclaimed, clapping her hands as he smiled shyly and held up the paper to admire it himself. "Before long you'll be writing to Ben all on your own."

"What's excellent?" asked Sam as he let himself into the cabin. He tried to act as if his quarters being turned into a schoolroom happened every morning, and finding Ananiah there, her eyes merry and her fingers smudged with ink, were the most natural thing in the world. He'd do whatever it took to gain her trust. He liked seeing her there with the boy, their two blond heads bright in the slanting sunlight as they bent together over the papers, and he could so easily imagine her teaching their own son that he smiled ruefully to himself. Where she was concerned, his fancies simply had no sense of propriety.

Ananiah watched him as he smiled, holding her breath against the moment when he'd make some reference to all she'd told him. It would come, she knew it; he'd be no different from the others. Her memories of last night were muddled, too thick, the way they often were when she thought or spoke of Étienne and Martinique, as if her mind was still trying to soften the pain of the old wounds. She'd told him more than she'd ever told anyone else, and he now knew the worst.

Sam came to stand over them, his hands clasped behind his back as he admired Jeremy's penmanship. Please, please, she prayed silently, let him not denounce her before the boy.

"You've done well, Jeremy," he said, clapping the boy on the shoulder. "Better than I'd ever expect from a rascally little monkey like you. Your pa'll be mighty proud of you when you come home."

Jeremy ducked his head with pleasure, his face flushed scarlet. "It's all Mistress Snow's doing, Cap'n Colburn," he managed to mumble.

"Then it's Mistress Snow we've to thank, isn't it?"

At last Ananiah dared to meet his gaze over the boy's head, and she was struck by what she found: no scorn, no contempt, no judgment, only that familiar lopsided grin that reached clear to his eyes, eyes that were so warm she had to look away.

"I'll tell you, Jeremy, she's a sight prettier than the old rogue that learned me," he continued for Jeremy's benefit. He'd seen doubt and then bewilderment on her face before she'd looked down. Lord, what had she expected him to do to her, anyway? "Captain Jacob Jamison, out of Bridgeport, and you've never seen a meaner, uglier Connecticut captain. Took out all his hatred against the British that burned his sloop on me, a great oaf that tried so hard I'd splinter my quill and be thrashed for my trouble."

"I thought you didn't go to school," asked Ananiah, her head still bent. He would never be her lover, but surely there was no harm in learning who he was, where he'd come from.

"Not a proper school, no," he admitted. "But in the four years I was in the Old Mill, I had the forty others in my cell teaching me everything they knew from boredom alone, whether I wanted to learn or not. Oh, it wasn't a dainty kind of Cambridge education, but I learned how to read and write and cipher, navigation and physicking, and the harbors and landfalls of every place ever crossed by a Yankee sailor, a smattering of French and Spanish, plus a bit of Turk and Dutch tossed in for seasoning. I also learned what great idiots your Englishmen are, and how to live on old gristle and a splash of brack, but none of that's worth talking about now."

There, he'd gone rattling off again like some old man thrilled to find an audience. He'd bore her to death if he wasn't careful. But the expression shining in her eyes was that of a woman who was entranced, not bored, and he had to remind himself that, given her genteel upbringing, an ancient stone castle full of prisoners of war might indeed be interesting. She couldn't possibly be fascinated by *him*. His life hadn't been any different from those of a score of other mariners he could name from Salem alone.

"Ben says you was a hero in the war, Cap'n," said Jeremy with unabashed adoration.

"Nothing brave about me, lad. 'Twas only luck that carried me through alive and in one piece." Sam shrugged, and invented a reason to go to the chest beside his bunk before his hands, on their own, reached out and touched the soft, rounded flesh of her upper arm, bare beneath the puffed sleeve. He'd surely give the French credit for the new fashions they'd invented for women, and the lovely, teasing way they suited Ananiah to perfection. "On a privateer, you're fighting for gold, not glory and General Washington."

"Oh." Jeremy's face fell with the single syllable.

Sam reached out to ruffle his hair. "But your father, now, he's the hero."

"*My* pa? Ben never told me anything about *that*, Cap'n."

"Maybe because he didn't know," Sam answered easily, remembering the boy's father before he was crippled. It was a memory Jeremy would never have. He hadn't been any more a hero—whatever that was—than Sam himself, but he was a good man who'd fallen on bad times, and a little adoration from his own son couldn't hurt. "'Course, your father won't tell you that himself, and you'll have to forget who told you so, but he always fought the British with his heart on victory alone, right there up front. He was always ready to give everything he had for New England, no mistake."

And he almost did, Sam added mentally as Jeremy shook his head in delighted wonder. "Pa a hero!" he marveled proudly as he moved his pen to a fresh corner of the paper. "I'll have to write that to Ben. He thinks he knows everything, Cap'n, but he don't know this!"

Once again Sam's gaze met Ananiah's across the boy's head. Clearly she wasn't as gullible as Jeremy, but the sudden smile she flashed him said she'd keep her doubts to herself.

"You've a way with him, Sam," she said, the smile lingering. "Have you any children of your own?"

"Me?" Sam grunted incredulously. "Nay, it's a bit soon for that, don't you think?"

Ananiah blushed with embarrassment, remembering too late that he'd only been married a brief time. "I didn't mean to be so—so inquisitive."

"'Twas unexpected, that's all." He loved her discomfiture, and because of her question, his grin came dangerously close to becoming a leer. "Of course, in time I want a son or two, and a daughter to please her mother. A man needs a family to give him something worth working for. You haven't any of your own, have you?"

The guarded sadness came back into her face, and he cursed his own insensitivity. If any child had come from her wretched union with Étienne de Gramont, surely she would have told him last night. She didn't need any more heavy-handed reminders from *him*.

"Cap'n Colburn," said Jeremy sternly, "you can't go asking a lady like Mistress Snow if she's any babies when she don't have a husband. It ain't polite, Cap'n, and my ma'd light into you for asking such."

"Your ma's right, Jeremy, and I deserve her thrashing." Sam bowed slightly towards Ananiah, grateful that Jeremy had given him a way to cover his blunder. "Forgive me, ma'am."

She nodded, but her smile now was small and tight, and the moment of empathy between them was gone. It shouldn't matter if he wanted children by the score, she told herself fiercely. He wouldn't have a one by her. She pulled her shawl from the back of the chair and rose to leave.

"Nay, lass, don't go on my account," Sam said, impulsively taking her by the arm. She tensed, but didn't pull away. He saw the pulse quicken in her throat, and knew that no matter what her past had been, she couldn't deny the spark that was there between them, any more than he could, or wanted to. "You said yourself the boy needs schooling, and with these winds we'll likely make England within a fortnight."

"So soon?" she asked without thinking, without realizing how wistful her voice sounded. He'd made it clear that when they reached England she'd be on her own to find her father, and once he saw her ashore she'd likely never see Sam Colburn again. His fingers on her arm burned like fire, the warmth spreading into her blood.

*He knew the truth about her, and yet he didn't care. He still wanted her—and worse, she still wanted him.*

She swallowed convulsively, fighting against herself. Nothing had changed. He still wanted her, but he was still wed to another woman.

"The *Truelove*'s fast as the wind, Ananiah. As I recall it, that's the reason you came to me in the first place." Sam purposefully kept his tone light, remembering Jeremy, and released her arm. It took so little with her—the fragrance of lilies, one touch of her skin—and he was half out of his head with desire. "Consider this cabin yours if you wish to keep teaching Jeremy. Come back tonight after supper. I'd be powerfully pleased if he writes that letter to Ben before we see land."

"Mornings should be sufficient," she said quickly, remembering what had happened on that other night in this same cabin.

Sam remembered, too. How could he forget? He'd never drink canary wine again without tasting her lips with it. "I won't be here, if that's what's bothering you," he said gruffly. "I generally take that watch at the wheel myself."

She nodded, avoiding his gaze as she busied herself stopping the ink and wiping the quill clean. "Tonight then, Jeremy. I've one or two books among my things, and we'll try a bit of reading."

She smoothed the boy's hair fondly, and Sam felt an awful, mean pinch of jealousy. He wished she were stroking his hair instead, and he wished she hadn't agreed quite so quickly once she'd learned he'd be elsewhere. Aye, he'd stand his watch, but he'd be sure to come below before she was done playing schoolmistress. A fortnight was precious little time, and he didn't intend to waste any of it.

By nightfall the wind had come around from the west to the northeast, a mean, unseasonable wind that claimed back all the progress the *Truelove* had made in the past three days. The seas ran high and sluggish, making the tedious back-and-forth of tacking even slower. The best Sam could say for the change was that the sky had remained clear, and with a bright half-moon he was able to keep fighting the wind and the seas and make some sort of progress during the night. He worked side by side with his men, not being the kind of captain who played high-and-mighty God on the quarterdeck, and by midnight he was as weary and disgusted as the rest of them. There was no question now of pleasantly ambushing Ananiah in his cabin. He remembered how earlier in the day he'd predicted to Ananiah that they'd reach English waters within two weeks. Two weeks, hell. At this snail's pace he'd consider himself fortunate to sight land in two months.

"The…cat…ru-ru-ru—*ran!*…to…the…to the…"

"Sound it out, Jeremy," said Ananiah again. "It begins like *ran*, doesn't it? Just sound it out."

Jeremy sighed heavily, scowling down at the elusive words Ananiah had written neatly for him to read. The only book she'd been able to find among her own tightly packed belongings was a copy of Samuel Richardson's *Clarissa*, suitable in neither subject nor moral tone for a ten-year-old boy, and instead she'd written a brief story about a cat and a rat that might prove more manageable.

But as the evening dragged on and Jeremy's yawns came closer and closer together, Ananiah felt quite sure the wily rodent wouldn't meet his end in this lesson. Her own attention was wandering, and she didn't doubt Jeremy's was, too, though he continued to struggle onwards to please her.

When Sam had told her he wouldn't bother her tonight, she had, curiously, been both relieved and disappointed. She hadn't believed him, either, and as Jeremy had toiled over the rat and cat, she had listened expectantly for the sound of Sam's step in the companionway or his voice outside the door.

Her gaze wandered around the cabin, searching for any clues to the man who inhabited it. The paneling of the bulkheads was plain and unbeveled, the pine thinly whitewashed, the stern windows were bare of any curtains, and the deck was without a rug. Although everything was almost painfully tidy, there were none of the little luxuries with which most shipmasters indulged themselves, no shelf of well-read books, no extra cushions on the bunk or chairs. In fact, there was only the one chair itself, and that worn and battered beyond fashion. The only decoration was a faded, water-stained print of ships gathered at Gravesend, and a tiny round shaving mirror in a brass frame. She thought of her father's quarters on board the *Commerce*, better furnished than most drawing rooms ashore.

Ananiah wondered if the cabin's Spartan air was due to Sam's own tastes or to the emptiness of his pockets, and then she remembered the carefully patched canvas in the *Truelove*'s sails. *She* would never have let any husband of hers sail away with so few comforts. *She* would have found a score of small ways to remind him that she loved him, whether sending a supply of his favorite tobacco or embroidering his initials on his linens or at the very least making certain he had her likeness with him, whether a miniature or a cut-paper silhouette. That his new wife hadn't bothered with any of these struck Ananiah as unforgivable, and she felt scornful of the unknown Sophie and sorry for Sam. He deserved better. When he came down from the deck, she might even tell him so.

"The cap'n won't be coming below, ma'am," said Jeremy, yawning yet again as he rested his head heavily on his arm, "if that's what you're hoping for. Not that he might'nt want to, sure, but he won't on 'count of the weather."

"Has the weather changed, then?" asked Anani-ah, too quickly, embarrassed that her thoughts were transparent even to Jeremy.

"Oh, aye, ma'am, with a nor'easter that's precious cruel." He grinned sleepily and tossed his hair back from his eyes. "If'n you didn't feel the change in how the brig be riding, well then, you got far more of a sailor's stomach than the other lady."

But Ananiah *had* noticed the change; it would, she thought, be difficult not to. Now the *Truelove* seemed to spiral slowly through the waves with an uneasy, ir-regular motion that had forced her to slide her hands along the companionway for steadiness when she walked between decks. Even the lantern overhead was swinging in wide circles instead of back and forth, making her shadow and Jeremy's on the bulkheads loom huge one moment, then shrink away to tiny blots the next.

"If it's as bad as you say, then we'd best stop for tonight," she said as she pushed back her chair from the table. "You should rest while you can, Jeremy. If we're all in for a foul night, then you never know when Captain Colburn might need another pair of hands. We'll meet tomorrow, if you can be spared."

"Aye, ma'am. And thank you, ma'am." Jeremy tumbled across the deck like an overeager puppy to reach the door before her and hold it open. "Sleep pleasant, now, ma'am, and a good night to you."

The boy might need her help in reading, she thought with amusement, but in gallantry he was already learning fast, and in a few years he'd likely have half the girls in Salem sighing over their fans at him. She smiled warmly as Jeremy tugged on the knitted brim of his cap, and then he vanished down towards the crew's quarters.

Left alone, she was surprised to find the passageway dark. The small lantern that hung near the steps must have guttered out, and briefly she considered returning to Sam's cabin to borrow his. But then she thought of what he'd say if he found her with it, how he'd tease her about being frightened of the dark, and decided that if she took her time she'd find her own way well enough.

Faint moonlight filtered down through the hatch, and she leaned against the bulkheads, waiting for her eyes to adjust to the darkness. Overhead she could hear men's voices, Sam's loudest as he called out another order, and then someone swearing. This new wind sounded different, too, whipping through the standing rigging with a high-pitched banshee's wail. Ananiah pulled her shawl over her shoulders uneasily. She was too much a mariner's daughter not to know that at sea all fortune, good and bad, came with the wind, and this one had no good in it. She looked up towards the wooden planks overhead as if she could see through them, and murmured a little prayer beneath her breath to help keep Sam safe.

She sidled along the companionway in the dark, trying to remember how far her cabin was, and where the steps from the deck above were exactly, and, most importantly, where the steps to the hold might begin and yawn away into emptiness beneath her feet. The steep swaying cant of the deck only added to her disorientation, like walking along a shifting, polished mountainside blindfolded.

Her doorway could not be far, she reasoned against the pounding of her heart. The *Truelove* wasn't that large a ship. She'd walked this trip in day or lantern light before and thought nothing of it. The wind

wailed higher, and she tried to remember what Sam
had told her about being brave.

She wasn't feeling brave at all. She wished she'd
called for Jeremy to carry the cabin lantern for her.
She wished she didn't care so much what Sam thought
of her. She wished—

The man's hand clamped down hard over her mouth
before she could scream. As she reached up to claw her
way free, his other arm circled around her body and
pinned her arms against her chest. She struggled and
plunged against him in panic, but he was larger, and
far stronger, and his grip only tightened, his forearm
crushing painfully into her breasts. Her shoes scrab-
bled over the deck as he dragged her backwards
through the darkness. He turned and hauled her
clumsily with him. As suddenly as he'd grabbed her,
he set her free, and with a frightened sob she stumbled forward, turning as she moved away from him.
In a tiny square of gray moonlight, she saw stars, and
then she was falling, falling with the wail of the wind
in her ears, falling into the blackest night she'd ever
known.

## Chapter Nine

"Blast that boy for letting the light go out," muttered Sam as he reached into his pocket for the flint he carried for his pipe. He himself knew every inch of the *Truelove,* and he could find his way without hesitation from the very end of the foremast to the deepest part of the hold. Although Sam suspected Jeremy could do the same, that was no reason for him to leave everyone else on board in the dark. There'd be no more coddling the boy, he decided grimly. Tomorrow he'd get the thrashing he deserved.

The spark caught on the wick and flared briefly, and Sam closed the top. In its gimbals the lantern swung back and forth with the ship's motion, and the swinging arc of light found a patch of pale gold and scarlet on the deck. Frowning, Sam bent to pick up the cashmere shawl that Ananiah nearly always carried. It wasn't like her to leave it behind. After the crossjack had fallen, her first concern had been to untangle the shawl from the wreckage, not to consider how close she'd come to being crushed. He impulsively gathered the soft fabric in his hands and brought it to his face. There were the lilies again, mingled with the fragrance he now realized was hers alone.

The lantern's light swung back again, fading to a faint glimmer as it swept down the narrow ladder to the hold. With the shawl still in his hands, Sam barely glanced at the shadowy forms of barrels and crates below. But the shifting light found something else, as well, a drift of white muslin and pale golden hair and paler skin, and all of her lying as still as death itself.

Unwilling to trust her with anyone else, Sam carried Ananiah to his cabin and laid her as gently as he could on his bunk. Like most merchant ships, the *Truelove* did not sail with a surgeon on board, and Sam alone was accustomed to dealing with the usual strained muscles and smashed fingers. But already he could see that her injuries were beyond his experience: her skin was chalky pale and clammy to the touch, her breathing shallow, and her pulse was so faint he could scarcely find it. Yet somehow she lived, and Sam clung desperately to the fragile hope that her battered body might still recover, and he refused to consider the alternatives.

As carefully as he could, he unfastened the hooks and ties of her gown and eased it from her limp body, grimly amused by how complicated such a simple garment could be. He'd often imagined undressing her, but never under such circumstances.

Through the thin linen of her shift, he felt along the length of her arms and legs, and her rib cage, too, searching for broken bones. Miraculously he found none, but the ugly pattern of purple bruises already marking her body could be all that showed of injuries within. Worst of all was the swollen bruise on the left side of her head, where she must have struck one of the stairs as she fell. He'd seen bruises like that before, on men who'd misstepped while hauling in a sail and fallen twenty feet to the deck. Few ever regained consciousness; most died.

He pulled off her little kidskin shoes and drew the homespun coverlet over her. The bunk had been built oversized to fit him, and in it she looked like a lost, broken doll. She could almost be sleeping, her golden brown lashes feathered down across her cheeks, her full lips barely parted. He wondered if she felt any pain. He prayed she didn't.

Gently his fingers smoothed her tangled hair back from her forehead. He should never have let her wander about the brig alone. He knew the dangers to be found at sea, even if she didn't. Hadn't he learned anything when she'd nearly been killed by the falling crossjack? After all she'd suffered in her life, the one sure thing he'd thought he had to offer her was the promise to keep her safe. And just as she'd come to trust him, he'd failed.

He knelt beside the bunk and buried his face in the coverlet, his fingers curling tightly into the coarse wool. Overhead the wind still shrieked from the northeast, and he felt its wail in the darkest corners of his soul.

For the next three days, Sam abandoned the quarterdeck to Howard and Lawson, seldom leaving Ananiah's side. She grew no better, remaining still and pale, but she didn't worsen, either, and Sam was encouraged that no fever had come with the blow. He watched her, and kept her covered and warm, and wished there was something else he could do.

Word of the accident had spread quickly through the brig. One by one the crewmen came to knock softly on their master's cabin door, each with whispered messages of concern or tales of friends who'd

survived just such a fall as Mistress Snow's. Jeremy
was one of the first, sobbing so beneath the weight of
his guilt and sorrow that Sam put aside his intention
to punish him. The two Portuguese hands came together to offer a small scrimshaw crucifix that they
swore had been blessed by the pope himself, and haltingly they promised it was sure to save the young lady's life. Sam thanked them solemnly and hung the
little cross over the bunk. He'd welcome a miracle,
wherever it came from.

It was Amos Howard who brought Ananiah's maid,
and Sam was grateful for the mate's thoughtfulness.
In the accident's aftermath, he'd completely forgotten Letty's existence.

At first Letty hung back behind Amos, almost,
thought Sam, as if she were afraid of what she'd find.
Then she saw Ananiah, and with a muffled shriek of
distress she ran to her mistress's side.

"Oh, dear Lord, don't let her be dead!" she cried.
She turned back wildly towards the men, and to Sam's
surprise, she looked not to him for reassurance, but to
Amos. "Oh, Lord, what will I tell her father if she's
gone?"

"She's not dead, Letty, just unconscious," said Sam
quickly, and again he was surprised to see Amos nodding in agreement. "I don't know how long it will be
before she wakes again. We just have to wait, and pray
for the best."

Letty shook her head fiercely, her hands clenched in
fists at her side. "Miss Ananiah needs a doctor. Captain Snow wants only the best for her!"

"We're in the middle of the sea, lass," said Amos
gently. "There's no doctor to be had, else we've have
him here already. Likely a doctor couldn't do no more
for her anyways."

"But you don't know Captain Snow." Her round face crumpled as she looked from Ananiah to the two men and then back to Ananiah, and her voice rose hysterically. "He'll go mad if anything more happens to her. He'll say I shouldn't have let her leave Providence at all, and he'll be right. Look at what's come of it! My poor little lady, my poor Mistress Ananiah!"

"It's not your fault, Letty," said Amos firmly. "It was an accident. She fell and cracked her head, and there's none to blame for that."

Sam took her gently by the shoulders. "I'll make it right for you with Captain Snow, Letty, if it comes to that. You won't be faulted. What I need now from you are the things your mistress might want to make her more comfortable."

But Letty pulled free and rushed back to Ananiah, lifting the coverlet far enough to look beneath. Then she wheeled around furiously to turn on Sam.

"You've no right, taking her clothes off like that, like she was *common,* just because she's out of her wits! Oh, you think you can because you're captain, but you're bad as that wicked old Frenchman, gawking and pawing at her—"

"*Letty.*" Amos's voice silenced her at once. She stared at him, her mouth working wordlessly, and then her tears spilled over, and she ran to bury her grief against the mate's broad, gingham-covered chest.

"She didn't mean it, Cap'n, I'd swear to that," said Amos earnestly to Sam over Letty's shuddering shoulders. "'Twas the shock and all. She'll come right, and do what you asked."

Sam listened, his discomfort growing. He had little doubt now that Amos had disobeyed him in regard to seeing Letty. The obvious intimacy between them couldn't have grown any other way. Every rule of discipline and keeping an orderly ship demanded that Amos be punished, but Letty was Ananiah's responsibility, and he couldn't very well deal with only half the couple. Considering his own thoughts towards Ananiah, any kind of punishment would feel hypocritical at best.

Wearily Sam shook his head at his own weakness and stared out the stern windows to the sea. "Take her back to her quarters, Howard," he said at last. "I'll speak with her again in the morning."

"You've seen for yourself how it is between them, Letty," said Amos urgently. "He didn't think nothing of keeping her there on his own pillows, they're that familiar to her. 'Course he took her gown off her. It's likely he knows her clothes well as his own by now, though who can blame him for taking what was offered?"

"I know what I've seen, Amos, and I can't deny what you're saying." Letty snuffled back the last of her tears, wiping her eyes with the corner of her shawl. "It's just that I've been with Miss Ananiah for years and years, since we was both girls, and to see her lying there all broken and battered, well, it went straight to my heart."

"You're tenderhearted, lamb, and you know I love you for it. But your precious Miss Ananiah don't deserve your loyalty. She only brung you along to make her look respectable. She'd toss you over in a flash if she didn't need you anymore."

Troubled, Letty shook her head. "I don't know, Amos. She's always been good to me."

"Because then she as good as owns you, lass!" Amos seized her hands and drew her face so near to his their foreheads almost touched. "Can't you see? She's just like Cap'n Gill told me. She and that wicked father of hers will do most anything to get what they want. Her marrying that Frenchman was just another of their schemes, and for her to sell herself to him that way, she's just as wicked as her father. You have to believe it, Letty!"

He searched her face, desperate for her trust. She had to believe it, because he had to, too, or he'd never be able to do what George Gill had asked. An accident, he'd said, a guarantee that the Snow woman never reached London or her father. In return, Amos would be his own master at last. Anything would be worth that, especially when the woman was an idle, spoiled strumpet that the world wouldn't miss.

Easy enough, simple enough. A ship was a dangerous place for a woman. The first time he'd misjudged the distance and failed. The second he'd been more careful and should have succeeded. But he hadn't reckoned on what the terror in her eyes would do to his conscience, how he couldn't forget the sight of her falling, reaching out to him as she dropped back through the empty air, or the sickening sound of her body striking the deck far below him, the broken gasp that should have been her last. For she still lived, lived to torment him with his promise to Gill and the possibility that she could tell Colburn who had pushed her.

"You will believe me, lamb?" he asked again, and unintentionally the strain and longing showed in his voice. "You'll trust me to do what's best for us both?"

Letty's arms went around his waist as she pressed her cheek into the familiar warmth of his chest. How could anything the Snows ever offered to her compare to being wanted like this?

"I trust you, Amos," she said simply. "I'll trust you in everything."

*Ananiah was back again in the white stone house at Beau Coteau, back in the tall bed with the little steps on her side. She had told herself she would never return. Maybe instead she had never left. She tried to rise from the pillow, but her head was too heavy, thick again with the burgundy from dinner. Maybe Hélène and leaving and all the rest was only the wine too. She closed her eyes, but still the first hot tear of misery and disappointment slid down her cheek to puddle in her hair. She had wanted so much for the dream to be real.*

*The shuttered doors to the balcony were open to catch the breeze that rose at night from the water. Ananiah turned her face towards the breeze and smelled the saltiness of the sea. It reminded her of someone, a man who had once shown her kindness and love, and she opened her eyes, eager to remember more, even if it was only the fragments of a dream. The night sky was dark blue above the black, jagged outlines of the palm trees, and filled with stars like scattered diamonds.*

*Five stars, she thought in confusion, five stars in a ring....*

*The door to her room slammed shut, and she pushed herself up on her elbows, her heart pounding. Through the gap in the netting that draped the bed, she could see Étienne, the gold striped silk of his dressing gown billowing around him as he walked past the open window, his steps silent on the deep plush carpet.*

*"You retired early,* ma chérie," *he said, his voice velvet-soft with the sarcasm of false concern. He sipped from the glass in his hands, his elegant fingers*

*caressing the angled facets of the crystal. "I'm sorry that my guests did not please you."*

*Defensively she curled herself into a tight little ball, the fragile lace of her gown slipping from her shoulders. "I was ill, Étienne."*

*"You were rude," he said sharply as he threw the glass over the balcony. The crystal shattered seconds later on the walkway below. "But if my friends bored you this evening,* ma petite bonne femme, *I promise you I shall not."*

*From experience she knew better than to argue with him, or to plead that he leave her alone. She watched as he threw open the drawer to her dressing table and rummaged through the contents until he found the wide satin sashes she wore with her robes. Muttering to himself, he slowly drew out two of the heavy bright sashes, wrapping them taut between his fists, and turned towards her. She didn't know if he meant to gag her or tie her to the posts, or perhaps something worse, something he'd never done to her before. She shrank back to her side of the bed, to the very edge, until her bare shoulder brushed against the netting.*

*"Ananiah?" called a man's voice behind her. "Ananiah, lass, can you hear me?"*

*It was the man from her dream, she was sure of it, and she turned around swiftly, towards the sound of his voice. Through the gauze she could make out his shadowy figure as he stood beside the bed. He was there for her, he was real, if she could only find a way to reach him. She felt the ropes beneath the mattress creak under Étienne's weight, felt the feather bed shift her towards him, and she tore at the pale cloud of the netting, struggling to find her way to the other man, the one who wouldn't hurt her. The sheer fabric swirled around her, swallowing her like a winding sheet, and as her panic grew she feared she'd never be free of it or Étienne, never free to love the other man....*

"Ananiah, lass, listen to me!" he was saying as he held her arms still against the pillow. "I swear to God I won't let him hurt you!"

Instantly she stilled, listening, afraid to open her eyes. Instead of the cries of parrots and other wild birds in the trees outside her window, she heard the creaking of the *Truelove*'s timbers, and the rushing of the waves around her sides. The sheets she lay upon were coarse homespun, slightly damp from the ocean air, not the cutwork cambric on her bed at Beau Coteau, and the mattress seemed stuffed with lumpy wool, not feathers. And she told herself it was Sam's callused hands so gentle on her wrists, Sam's voice that wanted to calm her. Sam, not Étienne. She slowly opened her eyes, and saw she'd been right.

"You're back then, are you?" he asked levelly, as if all she'd done was step out to a shop for a skein of embroidery silk. His face said otherwise, lined and shadowed with worry and lack of sleep, his cheeks bristling with unshaven whiskers. She had brought him trouble, and she was sorry for it.

"I was with Étienne again," she said, her voice squeaking from disuse. "I didn't—"

"Hush now," he said as he touched his fingers gently across her lips to quiet her. "Four days ago you fell and struck your head, but you've been here with me the whole time since."

"I don't remember falling," she said, frowning as she tried to concentrate. She was tired, so tired, and her head throbbed from the effort of talking. "No, wait—there were stars. Five stars in a ring."

"Oh, aye, I'll warrant you saw plenty of stars, considering the blow you took." He tried to smile, but the doubt in his smoky blue eyes was apparent even to her muddled mind. "You do remember who I am, don't you, angel?"

"Oh, aye, I'll warrant I do, Samuel Colburn," she said, smiling sleepily. "You I'd never forget."

By the next morning she felt well enough to sit upright, and in the evening when Sam brought her supper, they ate together, he sitting in the chair with his long legs propped up on the edge of the bunk and she with the coverlet tucked primly up under her arms, balancing her plate in her lap. The silences between them stretched awkwardly long, and hungry as she was, Ananiah scarcely picked at the fresh cod and stale biscuit. By now she'd come to realize just how intimate his care of her must have been, and that, coupled with what had passed between them the last time she was in his cabin, made her almost too embarrassed to meet his eyes.

"You've been most kind to me here while I've been ill," she said at last, her cheeks pinking. "But it's time I returned to my own cabin."

Sam laid his fork neatly across his empty plate and settled it on the deck beside his chair. "You're not putting me out any, being here. A few more nights in the hammock over there won't bother me."

Her blush deepened. She doubted that his wife would be as sympathetic. "No, Sam, I mean it's not proper for me to be here, in your—your bed this way. What would Sophie say if she learned of it?"

"Hang Sophie!" he thundered. He dropped his legs to the deck with a thump and leaned towards her, his expression black. "Twice now on my vessel you've nearly been killed. Once I'd believe it an accident, but not twice. You're staying either locked in here or in my sight for the rest of the crossing."

"Oh, for God's sake, Sam!" said Ananiah irritably, dropping back against the pillows with her arms across her chest. She couldn't believe he'd be so cavalier about his wife, or that he'd sink to scaring her to make her stay with him. "I went wandering in the dark and I *fell* down the wretched hatch!"

"Do you remember doing that?" he demanded.

"I do remember walking down the companionway after Jeremy left," she said, hedging against her own ignorance, "and you told me the rest."

He shook his head. "That's not good enough for me, Ananiah."

"Honestly, Sam, next you'll be seeing goblins and ghosts! Why would anyone want to hurt me?"

"You tell me why, lass," he said grimly. "Maybe someone had reason to push you. The way I figure it, the only person on board who knew you before, in Providence, is your maid."

*"Letty?"* Ananiah's voice rose with her disbelief. "Letty's been with me for years. She can be cross, I'll grant you that, but she'd never wish me any real harm."

"She hasn't wished you much good, either," said Sam bluntly. "For all her shrieking and wailing like you were already dead, she only came to see you here the once while you were unconscious."

"Only once?" she asked, more hurt by Letty's lack of concern than she wanted to admit.

Sam shook his head. "But I'll call her now, if you'd rather hear it from her."

"No, I—no, that won't be necessary." There had been a time when nothing could have taken Letty from her side, a time when she'd given her not just obedience, but affection, too, and it saddened her to think that time was gone.

"And I'd swear she's dallying with one of my men," continued Sam. "Tempted him enough that he'd go against my orders to meet her again."

"Not my Letty!" she said indignantly. "I'd look to your own man first before you go accusing her of dalliances!"

Yet even as she defended her maid, Ananiah remembered how Letty had flirted with the ginger-haired mate at Newport, and she remembered, too, how sullen Letty had turned when she'd been scolded for it. She sighed deeply, wishing the answers were easier.

"Letty's been against this voyage from the beginning," she said at last. "She's always thought I should stay in Providence and wait for Captain Gill to find my father. She likes fussing over me, telling me what to do, and she wasn't happy this time, because I didn't listen. Perhaps that's the reason she's sought this man's company. I don't know. But I can't believe she's come to dislike me so much she'd wish me dead."

Her voice trailed off forlornly, and Sam remembered how no one had come to see her sail. It shouldn't surprise him that Letty's goodwill meant so much to her. Strange to think how once he'd assumed that having money meant having friends.

"I hope she hasn't, angel," he said gently. "I've got doubts enough about Amos Howard without taking on Letty as well. But for now you keep close to me, mind?"

Although Ananiah still didn't believe there was any real threat to her life, she found Sam's order an easy one to obey. Not that he sought to entertain her or favor her in any special way. More often than not, the endlessly changing demands of sailing the ship required most of his attention, and often she was sure that an hour would pass when he'd be too preoccupied to say two words to her, even though she was sitting an arm's length away.

But then, he didn't ask her more about Étienne, either, or treat her differently, the way other men had once they learned about her life on Martinique. He didn't mention Letty again, and he didn't try to frighten her with more foolishness about being in danger. Instead, he spoke to her of mundane things like the wind and the weather and how he didn't trust the new French government to be fair with American mariners any more than he did the old English one.

Yet it was what he didn't—or couldn't—put into words that made her treasure the time in his company. She knew he watched her protectively when he thought she didn't notice, and if she caught his eye he flashed her sudden, unexpected smiles meant for her alone, smiles that made her melt inside with the intimacy they implied. None of it was right, and none of it eased her conscience, but she wouldn't have traded a minute of it for a year's worth of respectability.

She was with him on the main deck when the lookout sighted another ship riding low on the horizon, her topsails just visible in the slanting afternoon sun.

"I'll have to go up and look for myself," said Sam as he squinted into the direction the lookout was pointing. "Can't make out a blasted thing from the deck."

"Wouldn't it be better just to sail away?" suggested Ananiah uneasily, knowing even as she asked that he wouldn't.

Sam shrugged. "Oh, aye, I warrant we could. We've got the weather gage on 'em. But I'd rather know who it is before we scurry off."

He grinned wickedly as he headed for the mainmast. "But don't worry, angel," he called back over his shoulder. "I won't make you follow me to the top. Lawson here will keep you out of mischief."

Lawson, at the wheel, only grunted, as embarrassed to be left with Ananiah as she was with him, and he stared steadfastly out to sea and away from her. What kind of mischief did Sam expect from her? she thought crossly as she watched him scramble up the shrouds to join the lookout. Skirts or not, she was half inclined to climb up there after him, just to see the look on his face.

She was still considering it when he returned, racing hand over hand back down to the deck with a boyish agility. "We'll make straight for her, Lawson," he declared. "I'd know the rake of those sticks in a moment, but if I'd any doubt, her house flag's bright as day, a white diamond on a green field."

Lawson's face lit with surprise. "Meaning it's the *Calliope,* Cap'n? Meaning it's Cap'n Greene?"

"Aye, unless Greene's dead and buried. He'd sooner give his wife to another man than his precious *Calliope.*" Sam rubbed his hands together with obvious delight. "It must three years since we've been in Salem at the same time, and now here the rogue turns up like he's been waiting for us. The *Calliope,* for all love!"

"Is Captain Greene a particular friend of yours?" asked Ananiah.

"Elihu Greene's been my friend since before you were born, Ananiah," Sam explained, and her heart sank. An old friend might urge Sam to keep more suitable company, and not waste his time with a woman like herself.

But Sam was too happy to notice her uneasiness. "We were born on the same street, you see, and served on the same ships as boys. He made master before I did, the black rascal, and had the good fortune to find backers for the *Calliope* before he was out of his teens. Of course you'll fancy him. Every woman does."

Yet later that evening, as Ananiah waited at the rail with Sam, watching the *Calliope*'s boat make its way across the swells to the *Truelove*, she still found herself dreading the dinner ahead. She wore her best white silk and her mother's sapphire locket, and under Sam's watchful eye a silent, sullen Letty had dressed her hair, but none of it eased her sense of foreboding. As Sam's oldest friend, this Captain Greene would be sure to know Sam's wife, and if he knew Sam's wife, he'd have no wish to know *her*.

As the boat bumped alongside, she stepped back, away from Sam, rubbing her bare arms uneasily. Even though it was July, the wind off the water was chilly for evening dress, and her head was beginning to ache again. Sam was already calling to Greene as he climbed up the side, and other men from the *Truelove*'s crew were crowding beside him, shouting down to Salem friends in the boat. She swallowed hard and drew her shoulders back, ready for her first glimpse of Elihu Greene.

She'd somehow been expecting another version of Sam, not the small, stout man who tumbled over the side as ungracefully as she had herself in Newport. Beneath a black coat sprinkled with sea spray he wore a pale blue silk waistcoat straining across his round little belly, the cut steel buttons winking in the fading sun, and more cut steel on the buckles at his knees and on his shoes. As soon as he'd found his feet, Sam clapped him so hard on the back that he almost toppled over again before he could slap Sam's shoulders in return, the pair of them grinning and roaring well-meant insults back and forth.

Suddenly Greene's gaze found her, and his round-cheeked face glowed with the kind of frank male admiration that once would have pleased Ananiah, but now only increased her uneasiness. Immediately he drew off his beaver hat and tucked it beneath his arm, and with surprising grace bowed from the waist. From long habit, Ananiah automatically returned his courtesy, and then he came bustling across the deck to seize her hand in his.

"So this is your wife, eh, Sam?" he exclaimed as he beamed at Ananiah. "I'd heard you'd done well for yourself, but I'd no idea a creaking old bachelor like you could win such a lovely lady as this one! Come here, love, and let Elihu Greene kiss the bride!"

# Chapter Ten

"My *wife?*" Sam thundered incredulously. "You want to kiss my *wife?*"

Elihu Greene's smile stretched wider, until his eyes were nearly swallowed by his cheeks. "Sam, Sam, my boy, don't tell me you're jealous of an old friend like me? I'll grant you she's a prize to be guarded, a rare gemstone, but fair's fair. Why, I can't count the times I've seen you buss my Sally!"

Sam could scarcely speak for the laughter welling up inside him. News often traveled in odd ways at sea, but where the devil had Elihu heard he'd married, anyway? Here Elihu thought he'd be able to twit him for being an overcautious husband, while in truth *he'd* be the one to laugh loudest. "You're more'n welcome to kiss my wife, Elihu," he managed to get out, "that is, if you can find the blessed creature!"

Elihu harrumphed, not believing Sam at all. He held up Ananiah's hand as if it were a prize. "Then who is this, Sam?" he demanded. "If this isn't Elias Crowninshield's youngest daughter, then I don't know who is. She's got her mother's hair, that's for certain, though she's grown a great deal handsomer since I last saw her as a girl."

"I must assure you of your mistake, sir," said Ananiah, her voice brittle as ice. "My name is Ananiah Snow, and I'm sailing with Captain Colburn as a passenger on the *Truelove*. I'm from Providence, not Salem. My father is not Elias Crowninshield, and I'm not married to Captain Colburn."

Her fingers were still in Elihu's eager grasp, but her profile seemed carved, marble cold in the setting sun, and to Sam's dismay he realized she'd retreated again behind the well-bred formality he hadn't seen since they'd left Rhode Island. He couldn't say why or how, but he knew the misunderstanding he'd found so amusing had wounded her.

Elihu's sandy eyebrows rose, but he was quick to cover his confusion. He gallantly lifted Ananiah's gloved hand and kissed the air over her knuckles, bowing low. "Forgive me, ma'am. I spoke in hasty error, not malice. Excepting, however, that you are far lovelier than any of the Crowninshield women that I can recall."

"The truth is, Elihu, you can just forget the lot of 'em," said Sam hurriedly, still watching Ananiah's immobile face. "Likely you heard I'd asked for Elias's girl Sophie, but she tossed me over for Rob Pickering long before the banns were read, and her father nearly broke me in the process. I'm still the hoary old bachelor that sends your Sally into fits of matchmaking."

Ananiah stared at Sam, too stunned at first to speak. "You're not married?" she asked at last. "Sophie's not your wife?"

Bewildered, he stared back at her. "By now she's Sophie Pickering, and may the Lord grant poor Rob the patience he'll need to live out his days with her."

"You're not married," said Ananiah again, this time as a wondering statement instead of a question, a statement that changed everything she felt about him.

Sam raked his fingers back through his hair. "Aye, I'm not, and powerfully thankful I can say so. But how the devil you came to think I was—"

He stopped abruptly, remembering Justin Forbes congratulating him in Newport. He hadn't had a chance to deny it to Justin, and she must have pieced together the rest after that. All the little references to Sophie that Ananiah had made that had struck him as strange at the time made sense now, as did the way she'd tried to warn him away from her. It all fit together painfully well. After she'd unwittingly come between Étienne and his first wife, she'd never trust herself with a wedded man again. But how would she feel towards him now that she knew he was unmarried?

His answer came swiftly enough. She tipped back her head and her shoulders relaxed, and the smile that slowly spread across her face almost blinded him with its radiance.

"You're not married," she said softly, and then began to laugh. She pressed her palm across her mouth, trying to suppress the odd mixture of joy and relief that seemed determined to spill over. What would come next between them, she couldn't tell. But the past was done and clear, and she felt almost giddy with the freedom of it.

"Seems true enough, Miss Snow," said Elihu. He released Ananiah's hand with a little pat and settled his hat back on his head. "I swear, I've heard more revelations than Saint John himself. But Sam, I do recall an offer of supper was made. Or did I misunderstand that as well?"

"Damn your supper, Elihu," growled Sam, unable to pull his gaze away from Ananiah. Standing there in the twilight in the white silk, the wind playing through her pale hair, she seemed almost to glow with a happiness that he'd never seen in her before. As old a friend as Elihu Greene was to him, he'd have given a fortune to have the evening alone with Ananiah instead. "God help me if I dare deny your stomach its supper!"

"Come now, Sam, you can act the host better than that," scolded Ananiah playfully. She found she was grateful for Elihu's visit after all, for his presence spared her having to consider how she'd treat Sam when, inevitably, they were left alone again. She tucked her hand back into Elihu's arm and tossed the long cascade of her arranged curls back over her shoulder. "I'll see to your guest, even if you won't."

Elihu leaned into Ananiah's arm, grinning triumphantly at Sam. "So it's 'Sam,' is it, Miss Snow? You'll honor this sorry rogue with his given name on your sweet lips after he's led you to believe he was married?"

Sam glowered at him, certain that Elihu's highly embellished version of this misunderstanding would be told in every tavern in Salem within a week of the *Calliope*'s arrival. He would have done the same to Elihu, of course, given the chance, but that was little comfort to his pride now. "'Sorry rogue,' is it? I'll show you a sorry rogue, Greene, if you don't hurry your overfed, meddling self below before my boot helps you along your way."

But by the time the three of them sat down at the table, Sam's humor had grudgingly improved, and as

Jeremy carefully brought in the the first dish of French beans harrico, he finally managed a tight-lipped smile at Ananiah, who flushed with relief. Eager to make the best impression on Elihu for Sam, she had worked hard with Miguel, the *Truelove*'s Gibraltar-born cook, to make the meal special, contributing from her own private stock of dried pippins for the apple pudding and sacrificing the last of the Rhode Island hens to the fowl pie, seasoned with salt pork. Three more precious bottles of her father's canary wine joined Sam's more humble sherry and rum on the table, and she'd even had Jeremy scour the ship until he found two other chairs, sparing Elihu the ignominy of perching on a sea chest while he dined.

And Sam had been right—she *did* like Elihu Greene. He made her laugh until she wept with tales of him and Sam as boys, of the tricks they'd tried to play on their sisters that somehow always went hilariously awry, or how they'd fallen asleep in the back of a farmer's wagon one market day and awakened to find themselves in Haverhill instead of Salem. There were other stories, too, of women they'd known in foreign ports, stories that Elihu's inspired telling barely rescued from bawdry. Yet even as she laughed at Elihu's tales, she was always conscious of Sam watching her, and the warmth she felt whenever their eyes happened to meet.

But her spirits foundered late in the evening when Elihu asked how she'd come to be sailing to England. As briefly as she could she explained about her father, thinking sadly as she did how much he would have enjoyed the company of the two other shipmasters tonight.

Shaking his head, Elihu leaned back in his chair, his pudgy fingers spread across his waistcoat. ''I don't like

to be the one to crush your hopes, Miss Snow," he said
with obvious reluctance, "but since you've come this
far you deserve to hear the truth. There's precious few
Yankees for guests in the Crown's prisons, and I doubt
your father's among them. Oh, their navy's still stopping our merchantmen to plunder our cargos, bold as
any pirates, and stealing our men away whenever they
please to press them into service against the French.
But it's the able-bodied seamen they're taking, not
stiff old masters like us. We're no use to 'em. Six
weeks I've just spent in Bristol, and I never heard a
word of any Yankee ships taken whole."

"But Bristol's not London," said Ananiah firmly.
"I'm certain that's where my father's being held."

She caught the look the two men exchanged, its
meaning as clear as if they'd spoken aloud. She didn't
want their pity, and she didn't share their skepticism.
She lifted her chin stubbornly. "I *will* find him, Captain Greene, and I mean to bring him home with me.
He's my father, and I won't abandon him."

"I'm not saying you will, sweetheart," said Elihu
gently. "It's just that there are many ways a man can
run afoul of his luck at sea, and English popinjays are
only one of them."

"I appreciate your concern, Captain Greene, even
if it is misplaced," she said, forcing herself to smile.
She reached out for the bottle before her and refilled
their glasses. "This wine is my father's favorite canary, and I'll ask you to drink his health against the
day he can drink yours in return."

Solemnly they raised their glasses to her father. Although Ananiah drank hers in one long swallow, the
same as the men did, the giddiness she might have
welcomed this time didn't come. Through her lashes
she glanced across at Sam, wondering if he recalled as

well as she did the last time they'd shared this same
wine, but he was staring down at the empty glass in his
fingers, his expression troubled. She swallowed hard.
So Sam had no more faith in her father's rescue than
did Elihu Greene.

Overhead, the second mate struck the bell to mark
the end of the watch. Elihu stood and yawned, again
patting his tightly stretched waistcoat. "High time I
headed back to my own berth," he said, bowing to
Ananiah. "Miss Snow, meeting you has been as great
a pleasure as any meted out to us poor deep-water
sailor-men. If your travels ever bring you to Salem,
you'll have a welcome from my Sally. I'll take it amiss
if you don't let her repay this splendid meal. And I
look forward, too, to meeting Captain Snow in happier days."

She nodded farewell, not trusting her voice. She had
sat down at the table happier than she'd been in years,
and now that she was ready to leave it, she was peril-
ously close to tears. Maybe it was the blow to her head
that made her swing so wildly from gaiety to despair.
She could think of no other reason.

"I'll come up with you, Elihu," said Sam. As he
passed Ananiah's chair, he rested his broad hand on
her shoulder in a small gesture of comfort, and she
gratefully rested her own hand on his. Strange how
well he seemed to read her moods, considering the
brief time they'd known one another.

And, she thought sadly, the brief time they had left
before they reached England.

"If you're looking to wed, Sam," asked Elihu as
soon as the two captains stood together on the *Truelove*'s deck, "what's wrong with that lass in your
cabin?"

Sam swore halfheartedly beneath his breath as he felt in his pocket for his pipe, looking across at the dark outline of the *Calliope*. The night was bright with stars and the sliver of a new moon, and he wished his own thoughts were as clear as the sky overhead. "You haven't changed your ways a bit, Elihu. Still eager enough to steer my course for me, eh?"

"Aye, when I can see plain what you're too stubborn to admit," answered Elihu evenly. He lit his own pipe before handing his flint to Sam, and waited while the sparks caught and the light flared briefly over the taller man's face. "You and your Ananiah made me feel like the old maiden aunt set down in the chimney corner to check the passions of the young persons. Lord help me, Sam, but the pair of you could scarcely keep your eyes to yourselves, let alone the rest of you!"

"You just hush up, Elihu," said Sam warmly. "There's nothing untoward between Ananiah and me."

Elihu shrugged. "Then I'll wager you wish there was. You'd be an idiot not to. The girl's beautiful and clever, and from the sapphires around her throat, I'd guess she comes with a fortune as pretty as her face. Can't think of a sweeter reason to give up all those doxies you've dawdled with in the taverns. And you know as well as I do that the chances of this girl's father turning up to make trouble for you like old Elias Crowninshield did aren't exactly overwhelming."

Sam sighed, his shoulders working restlessly beneath his coat as he considered sharing his suspicions about Ananiah's accident. But before he thought better of it. After he'd watched Letty with Ananiah earlier, he'd found it difficult to picture the little maid as the villainess he wanted her to be. Letty was dour and unpleasant, but that alone wouldn't make her a murderer. And these last days Amos Howard had been a model first mate as well, as cheerful and efficient as he'd been when he first signed on in Providence. Maybe Ananiah was right, and he'd imagined it all so as to have a reason for keeping her close. Lord knows she herself should have been reason enough.

"I hope Sally was as practical as you are about courting," he said wryly instead. "I'd always thought there should be a bit of pretty, foolish talk and kisses in the moonlight. You make marrying sound about as exciting as going to market."

Elihu chuckled, rocking back a bit on his heels. "It can be exciting enough, if both parties are as eager as you two seem to be."

"Eager's got nothing to do with it." Sam's voice grew serious. "On first sight, she's everything you say. But she was wed before to some French planter on Martinique who hurt her, hurt her bad, and now she's got scars on her soul as deep as this whole ocean."

Elihu's cheerfulness vanished, and he whistled low under his breath. "She told you this?"

"Some of it, and I can guess at the rest. Shame made her stay with him so she wouldn't disappoint her blessed father. If I thought the old man was still alive somewhere, I'd have words aplenty for him, selling off his own daughter to some French bastard like that."

"Poor little lass!" murmured Elihu. "I never would have known. I hope at least she's a widow, and the blackguard's dead."

"Life's not that just, Elihu. Seems he had another wife already, and he'd never legally been married to Ananiah at all. The worst of it is, she believes it's her fault." He kicked aimlessly at a coiled line on the deck, his fists jammed deep in his coat pockets.

"Sometimes she just disappears into herself and there's nothing I can do to reach her."

Tonight, Sam feared, would be one of those times. He'd seen the despair in her face before he'd left her, and despite the closeness they'd shared these last days, he was certain she'd be gone from his cabin when he returned.

Elihu reached out to rest his hand on Sam's arm. "Then I agree with you. As handsome as she is, a woman with that many problems would make a difficult wife at best."

Sam wheeled around to face him, appalled by his friend's callousness. "Nay, it's not like that at all! To abandon her now, when she'll still have to come to accept her father's loss— Jesus, Elihu, what kind of man do you think I am?"

"I think you're still the same softhearted lad that half drowned himself fishing kittens out of the Essex River," said Elihu with satisfaction, and, chagrined, Sam realized Elihu had bested him again. "You bring the lass back to Salem as your wife, and I promise you my Sally will welcome her with a party that they'll talk about clear to Boston. Now put your thoughts of Miss Snow aside and tell me what was selling well in Salem when you sailed."

Much later, Sam hesitated outside his cabin door. By now Jeremy would have come and cleared away the last remnants of the dinner, and Ananiah would be asleep. He could picture her at rest, curled on her side with her knees drawn up and one hand open, palm up, on the pillow beside her flushed face. The coverlet would follow the soft rise of her hip and dip over her waist, and her hair would be bound in a touchingly inept braid falling over her shoulder. He'd watched her sleep often enough these last nights, standing protectively over her in the dark as she lay in his sheets.

His fingers curled around the polished brass latch, but didn't turn it. A faint glimmer of lantern light outlined the door. If Ananiah were asleep within, she would have snuffed the lantern's wick. More likely she'd decided to return to her own cabin, rather than face him tonight. Though he knew her reasons, the fear that she'd fled from him again ate at him with a lonely hollowness.

He shook his head ruefully. Since when had he been afraid to enter his own quarters? Swiftly he turned the latch and swung the door open, ducking to clear the low beam of the door frame.

With a startled gasp, Ananiah rose from the armchair. Clearly she had fallen asleep waiting for him; her eyes were heavy-lidded and slow to focus, and one cheek was rosy where she'd rested her head on her arm. She had taken off her earbobs and necklace and held them still in her fingers, the sapphire pendant swinging gently on its chain.

"Be proud of me, Sam," she said, her voice husky with sleep. "I didn't run away."

"You shouldn't have waited for me," he said gruffly. She hadn't changed from her gown, and the white silk fell in soft, crumpled folds around her body. He liked her better this way, without artifice or ornament, and she was so lovely it almost hurt him to look at her. "You should be asleep by now."

"I wanted to talk to you first." With a soft clink, she dropped her jewelry into the seat of the chair and circled around it, her fingers trailing along the worn turnings. "I'm sorry I made such a fool of myself before Captain Greene. You've never given me any real reason to think you were married."

"How can Elihu think you're foolish, when he made the same mistake?" He pulled his arms from his coat and tossed it across the chest, trying to be careless, trying to break the spell he knew was tightening around him and Ananiah. The elaborate curls that Letty had crimped into her hair had fallen into loose waves of pale gold that he found far more beguiling, and he longed to touch them and learn if they were as soft as they looked. "Though for the life of me I can't figure out why the world's been so blessed eager to see me wed to Sophie. A sight more eager than she was, anyway."

"She didn't love you?" asked Ananiah with genuine surprise. She tried to look at him with fresh eyes, to imagine seeing his face for the first time as he stood before her—the dark hair tousled by the wind, the heavy brows now raised with bemusement and the mouth curved in a wry grin, the nicked front tooth and crescent-shaped scar on one high cheekbone. How could any woman not love a man that looked like Sam Colburn?

"Don't seem likely that Sophie did, considering how fast she found herself another man." Ill at ease, he impatiently shoved his shirtsleeves higher up over his arms and then smoothed his hair back from his forehead. "Not sure she ever did love me, when I think on it now."

Talking about who loved him and who didn't made him feel like a self-centered idiot, completely at sea for what to do with his hands or what to say next. All he wanted was to take her in his arms and kiss her and forget this genteel conversation, and with any other woman he would have already done it. But too well he remembered the wild, lost look on Ananiah's face after he'd kissed her before, and if he touched her again, now, he had no idea how she'd respond.

In confusion Ananiah turned away from him, walking to stand near the sweep of stern windows. Even with her back to him, she could feel the intensity of his gaze upon her, and she thought wistfully back to the comfortable familiarity they had shared earlier.

"This was easier when I believed you belonged to someone else," she said with a shaky little laugh. "I didn't have to consider how to behave with you."

"You don't have to consider it now," he said, his voice almost strangled with frustrated desire. He watched her unconsciously compensate for the ship's motion, her legs apart and her body swaying rhythmically from side to side, the white silk clinging to the lush curve of her hips and buttocks. He wondered if she knew how seductive the graceful movement was to him, wondered if she knew he'd never wanted a woman, any woman, as much as he wanted her right now.

"Oh, but I do, Sam," she answered, her back to him and her head bowed as she struggled to force a levity she didn't feel into her words. "I deceived myself about you, wishing you were something you weren't, just the way I deceived myself about Étienne. It's not the best of habits to have."

"For God's sake, Ananiah, it was only a misunderstanding!"

"Tonight I deceived Captain Greene, too, didn't I?" she continued as if she hadn't heard him, and Sam wasn't convinced that she had. "He believes me to be a good, decent woman that his wife would welcome into his home. What would he have said if he knew what I'd done with Étienne?"

She caught up the skirt of her gown with one hand, then let the silk slide from her fingers. "Could it be because I wore white that your friend was deluded? White for purity, white for virtue. My gown was white the night I met you, and you called me an angel. Dear God, an *angel!*" Her voice broke, and she clutched her hand across her mouth to stifle a sob. "Better I should wear black, to match the color of my soul!"

"Damn it, Ananiah, it wasn't your fault!" In three steps he had crossed the distance between them and taken her by the shoulders to steady her. He felt her whole body stiffen beneath his palms, and reflexively his fingers tightened into the soft roundness of her shoulder beneath the silk. There was no way he'd let her run from him again tonight.

"Étienne can't hurt you anymore," he whispered fiercely. "It's over, mind? It's done."

"No, it isn't Sam, not so long as I live," she whispered hoarsely. She was trembling, her back rigid and her fists clenched into tight knots at her sides. "No matter how much you wish it, what Étienne did to me can never be undone."

"The hell it can't!" His hands slid possessively down her arms and around her waist, pulling her against him. The full soft length of her body pressed into the hard muscles of his own with a fire he hadn't expected, and his grip tightened as he fought the urge to move against her. He didn't want to frighten her, but dear God, they fit together so well, the way he'd somehow always known they would.

Ananiah twisted against him as she tried to break free of the steel band of his arm. "You don't know, Sam. How could you?" she asked, her voice rising with despair and her words spilling out too fast. "You're a good man, too good for me. Listen to me!

Go back to Salem and find the kind of pretty innocent you deserve and let her make you happy and fill your house with your children and leave me alone!''

"I don't want another woman, Ananiah. I want you." With one arm still locked around her waist, he reached up and swept her hair back to the far side of her shoulder. Bared to him was the slender curve of her throat and shoulder, the rapid beat of her pulse visible in the hollow beneath her jaw. When he kissed her there, he could feel her heartbeat quicken beneath his lips.

"No, Sam, I swear to you, this isn't right." Yet even to her own ears her plea had a seductive falseness to it, her voice as eager to betray her as her body. As the roughness of his cheeks brushed over her throat, she shivered with pleasure, and she let her eyes close and her head lean back into his shoulder. Effortlessly, his lips had found the sensitive place below her ear, and she felt herself melting against him as the warmth grew in her blood. Slowly his arm loosened around her waist. His hand slipped lower, kneading the curves of her hips and belly as he drew her closer against the hard heat of his arousal.

She heard the harshness and the tiny catches of her own breathing as his lips and hands teased her further, and when his hand swept slowly upward to find and cup her breast, she gasped raggedly, and her fingers clutched at his arms for support. If he released her now, she wasn't sure her legs would hold her upright.

She'd thought she knew what passed between men and women. Étienne had taught her to please him in lovemaking that held no love, only skillful, selfish diversion. But this was different. *She* was different. With each new ripple of sensation, she realized Sam was carrying her someplace she'd never been, someplace beyond the heavy guilt Étienne had branded into her. Maybe Sam was right. If she could let herself trust him completely, if she could surrender, then maybe he could finally set her free of the past.

*Surrender,* she repeated to herself. *Surrender and be free.*

She turned in his arms to lift her face toward him, and at once his mouth found hers. With a moan that was lost between them, she tasted his desire and his urgency, an urgency she knew she shared. As he worked to unhook the fastenings on her gown, she tugged his shirt free of his breeches and slid her hands up the warm, hard muscles of his chest.

He groaned and pushed her away long enough to pull the shirt over his head. Her fingers trembling, she untied the last cord of her gown. When she shrugged her shoulders the silk slid from her body with a whispered *shush.* The shift she wore beneath was linen, sheer enough to show the dark tips of her breasts and the shadowy place at the top of her thighs, and she glanced up at him shyly through her lashes.

She saw a body made lean and muscled by a hard life, shoulders broad and hips narrow, and another scar, a faint pale ridge across the flat plane of his stomach. More differences, she marveled, more differences—where Étienne had chosen power, Sam had been given strength. Slowly she raised her gaze to meet his. There was no laughter in his eyes now, no teasing grin, and to her amazement she realized as he stood so still before her that he was waiting for her to decide. The tension in his face betrayed the effort such restraint cost him. She swallowed hard and, in a gesture that was oddly formal, held her hand out to him. He caught her by the waist and carried her to the bunk.

Mindlessly she gave herself up to the wondrous sensations he brought to her body. His mouth was hot and demanding, and his touch was more than she thought she could bear. She scarcely noticed when he tore away her shift and left her naked but for her stockings and garters, nor could she have said when he freed himself of his breeches and boots. They lay side by side on the rough coverlet, their arms and legs tangling restlessly together as they explored each other's bodies, his touch like fire to the tinder in her blood. She heard soft cries, wordless animal cries of pleasure, cries she realized belatedly were her own.

When he slipped his hand between her thighs, she didn't pull away but moved wantonly against his fingers. Another time she would have been shamed by how her hips arched against him, and by the way she grew so slick and ready beneath his touch, but now she couldn't feel shame, she couldn't think at all, her whole existence narrowed to Sam, and to the wild, strange tension coiling in her body. She sensed she was close, so close, to understanding it all.

*Surrender, and be free....*

Swiftly Sam eased her onto her back and moved between her legs, lifting her hips towards his on the narrow bunk. Her eyes flew open when he filled her and she felt her body welcoming him, tightening further to meet his thrusts. She clung to him feverishly, her arms and legs wrapping around him as she sought the completion only he could grant. With a low groan, he moved deeper into her, over her, his fingers digging into her soft flesh, and uncontrollably she felt herself begin to spin away, farther and farther out of her own being.

*Surrender...*

*But she lay trapped beneath Étienne. Powder from his wig stung her eyes and nose, and his weight pressed her heavily against the cool marble of the drawing room floor. He hadn't bothered to undress, and the heavy gold buckles at the knees of his breeches cut into her inner thighs as he used her. At her sides, her fingers fanned convulsively across the polished marble, and she prayed she could hold back the tears of shame and humiliation until he was done and had left her.*

*"You're a coldhearted bitch, aren't you, ma chère," gasped Étienne as he raised himself up to look at her. "Always keeping yourself aloof, as if the price I paid to your father for you was too slight. But I know how to reach you, my common, mercenary little whore. You can't hide forever."*

*He hooked his fingers into her pearl necklace and jerked them tight across her throat. Desperately she began to fight against him, clawing at his arms as she struggled to breathe.*

*And at last he smiled, finally pleased, and collapsed on top of her.*

# Chapter Eleven

"Ananiah?"

The gurgling gasp she made deep in her throat had nothing to do with passion, and Sam swiftly rolled onto his back, bringing her with him. The last thing he wanted to do was hurt her, but he knew he was a large man, and perhaps, inadvertently, he'd frightened her.

Still struggling to breathe, she braced her arms on his chest and shook her hair away from her face. Her eyes were huge, and the panic was only now beginning to fade from her face. Without a word from her, Sam realized furiously that Étienne had once again stolen her from him.

"Ananiah, look at me," he ordered, anger and frustration making his voice harsh. "Damn it, mark who I am!"

"You're Sam, of course," she said raggedly, her confusion clear on her face. She shifted forward on him, and flushed when she realized they were still joined. "But Étienne—"

"The devil take Étienne! It's me you're with, Ananiah, pure and simple." Lust and anger combined were making him throb within her, anger at battling a rival he'd never meet, and when she moved again he seized her arms to still her until he'd said what he had to say. "I'll not say he hasn't left his scars on you, but if he's still hurting you, it's because you're letting him. Forget him, Ananiah. Hell, I'll *make* you forget him!"

He pulled her face down and kissed her hard, his tongue echoing the intimacy that their bodies already shared. Her pale gold hair fell around them like rippled silk, and the fringed ribbons of her garters feathered across his arms. His hands slid down to her hips, rocking her until she found the rhythm with him. She drew her knees up higher and shuddered, an exquisite vibration that nearly finished him, and he knew he couldn't hold back much longer.

He slid his hand between their bodies and touched her where she was most open to him. She arched back her head and stiffened, and with a sharp, startled cry of female pleasure, she collapsed onto his chest. He met her then, his self-control gone, and again and again he plunged deep into her, until he felt himself explode with an intensity he'd never known with any other woman. But then, she wasn't any other woman—she was Ananiah, his Ananiah, and after tonight it would never be otherwise.

Afterwards, he held her close and tried, though not very hard, to remember when he'd felt so contented. The *Truelove* held easily to her course, and the sounds overhead of the few hands in this early-morning watch might have been a thousand miles away. So this, he marveled, was how it felt to be in love. Strange how he'd always thought of protecting Ananiah, of keeping her from harm, and now, instead, she seemed to be the haven he'd sought his whole life. Elihu was right, he should marry her, if marriage meant having her with him like this for the rest of his life.

Lazily he traced sweeping circles over her back and buttocks, enjoying the different textures of her hair

and skin now that he had the time to appreciate them.
She still lay sprawled over him, her breathing regular,
so relaxed that he wondered if she'd fallen asleep.
From happiness alone, he chuckled to himself and
kissed her shoulder.

With a little sniff, Ananiah roused herself and raised
her face from his chest. Her beautiful mouth was
swollen from his kisses, her eyes heavy-lidded beneath the damp tangle of her hair, and he felt himself
beginning to grow hard all over again. He touched his
thumb to the full flesh of her lower lip, and she pressed
back against it, a mere tremor of a kiss. He smiled,
and then saw a single tear spill over from the corner of
her eye and slide unevenly down her cheek.

"Why the tears, angel?" he asked tenderly.

"I'm sorry I hurt you, Sam," she whispered
hoarsely. Self-consciously she smudged the tear away
with her fingers. She ached to tell him she loved him,
that she'd always loved him, from that first moment
in the Browns' garden.

"Me?" he asked, mystified. "How could you hurt
me?"

She stared down at his chest, unable to meet his
eyes. "To speak of Étienne as I did, when I did—how
could that not wound you? I saw it in your face, clear
as if you'd spoken. No man wants to be reminded that
another has been there before him." She smiled wistfully, another tear sliding to her jaw as her fingers
curled into the coarse hair of his chest. "I wish I'd met
you long ago, Sam. I wish you had been the first, so I
could have given that much to you."

"Oh, angel." His arms tightened protectively
around her waist. He'd never been with a virgin, and
from what he'd heard from other men, they didn't
seem worth the trouble. "I wish I'd known you then

too, to save you the sorrow of marrying Gramont. But the rest of being first don't signify, at least not to me. I have you now, not him, and I mean to keep you with me a good long while."

She held the silence a hair's breath more than she should have. Sam was different from Étienne, but she'd be a fool twice over to believe that what he felt for her would last beyond this voyage. "Then the wind to England will decide how long that shall be."

"Aye, for a fair beginning." He considered telling her how he loved her then, but something in her tight-lipped smile warned him not to. She was skittish about love, and with good reason, after Gramont. He'd do better to go slowly, and although he meant to give her all the time she needed to grow accustomed to the idea, he didn't believe her when she said she wouldn't marry again. Especially not after tonight.

His hands caressed the narrow curve of her waist, and he pictured instead her belly rounded with his babe. The image pleased him, and in a way he hoped that as she lay with him now, with his seed still warm within her, he'd already gotten her with child.

"We're good together, you and me," he said instead, wishing he was better at explaining how he felt. "That kind of fire in the blood's a rare thing."

She nodded, swallowing back the sharp stab of disappointment. So it was lust that made him hold her so tenderly, desire that made him want to protect her. No wonder he hadn't cared that she wasn't a virgin. But at least he wanted her in some way, and with it he'd given her a kind of joy she hadn't dreamed of.

"Before tonight," she said softly as she pillowed her head again on his chest, "I believed that only men found pleasure in—in lying together."

Sam grunted with disgust. "If a man wants to take his pleasure alone, then there's a better way to do it than boring some poor lady silly in the process." He remembered the startled, unpracticed way she'd followed his lead, and hated Étienne the more for not having bothered to make love to her even once. "You deserve better than that."

She smiled to herself, listening to Sam's heartbeat. He might not love her, but he did care for her, and that was more than she'd ever gotten from Étienne.

*Étienne.* She held her breath, braced for the harrowing memories of him that so often struck her like waking nightmares. She dared herself further, purposefully recalling how quickly his smile could turn into a sneer, the elegant courtier's manners that he saved for guests, the scent that he wore and the snuff he favored.

But nothing happened. None of Étienne's old cruelties came back to her against her will. There was nothing beyond the muted sound of Sam's heartbeat, steady and sure, beneath her ear. Gradually she let the images of Étienne go completely, and let her mind fill instead with the man beneath her and inside her, and the unfamiliar peace that followed. Though she didn't believe that Étienne had been banished forever, for tonight at least, because of Sam, she finally seemed able to put her husband aside.

"What I don't deserve," she whispered happily as she curled closer into his body, "is you, Sam. You're far too good for me."

"You're the first to tell me that, angel." He felt his lower body tighten beneath her languorous movements, and as he hardened again he began to thrust slowly into her. "I'll warrant I have a good deal more experience at being bad."

She raised herself over him to better match his rhythm, her lips parted in a wanton half smile. "Aye, Cap'n," she said with a low, husky laugh. "I'll just warrant you do."

"You saw her alone, Letty?" demanded Amos, stunned. "When?"

"This evening," answered Letty promptly, smoothing her apron neatly over her knees. Since Ananiah had abandoned her cabin for Captain Colburn's grander quarters, she and Amos had fallen into eating together, with him bringing food and drink from the galley and her adding special treats she'd squirreled from Ananiah's private stores. But oranges and sugar candies weren't all Letty "borrowed" to please Amos. The lace cap and coral earbobs she wore tonight were her mistress's, too, and only the difference in their weight and height kept her from taking her gowns as well.

"Miss Ananiah wanted her hair dressed special for the dinner for the other captain. Her hair's like milkweed floss, all silky down that won't hold a curl, and of course she's helpless with it herself." She drew her fingers through her own dark, glossy hair, but the compliment she'd expected didn't come.

Amos scowled down at the salt pork on his plate, stirring the peas around it with his knife. "I didn't think the cap'n ever left her alone anymore."

"Not for long, he don't," said Letty tartly. "Came in and sat as if he'd every right to watch her dress."

"Likely he does." His appetite gone, Amos set the plate on the deck and shoved it away with his shoe. As they neared England, he felt his chances with Gill slipping out of his reach, and there didn't seem to be a damned thing he could do about it. The Snow

woman was never alone. Captain Colburn could keep
her on a lead and she wouldn't be any farther from his
reach.

"Miss Ananiah don't think he has it, that's clear as
day. Didn't dare raise her eyes to him the whole time,
the unhappy little creature. But then there's plenty I'd
lay at that captain's door already. I've never seen Miss
Ananiah look so poorly before, and he's the reason."

"She's a wanton little baggage, and she looks well
enough to me." Amos took Letty's hand and tugged
her across the bunk towards him. "The next time you
find your unhappy Miss Ananiah alone, you come
find me, Letty, and you find me fast."

"I can't see what sort of private business you'd want
with her." Letty pouted and made a show of holding
back the way ladies did, but in truth she liked the way
Amos gave orders to her. She'd no use for a husband
she could push to do her will.

"I told you before, lamb," he grumbled, "it's
Cap'n Gill's business, not mine."

"Well then, for Cap'n Gill's business, I suppose I
could go to her tomorrow, after breakfast, when that
great rude cap'n of yours is up on deck, bellowing like
a bull." She shuddered delicately, leaning into Amos's
shoulder. "He wakes me every morning, he does. But
that means he's not with her, and I'm certain she'll
unlatch the door to me. You meet me then, at the
door, and then you can speak your business."

He nodded, considering. He'd have to lock Letty
out of the cabin, of course, for he didn't want her to
share any of his guilt. His best chance then would be
to smother the woman, drown her screams with the
bolster. That would leave no mark. Letty had said she
hadn't looked well. Her death could be blamed on
apoplexy or some such.

He nervously wiped his palms dry on the thighs of his breeches, already hating the way he knew she'd struggle. He prayed it wouldn't take long. Shoving her down into the hold had been hard enough.

Letty looked at him uneasily, finding that his round, merry face had somehow changed. "You don't mean to harm her, do you, Amos? It's only Mr. Gill's business you want with her, isn't it?"

Amos forced himself to smile as he settled his arms comfortably around her shoulders. "'Course it is, lamb," he said heartily. "You been listening to too much scuttlebutt about how Cap'n Colburn's protecting her from mischief, when the only mischief's come from herself. And why would Cap'n Gill want to bring Miss Snow to harm, anyways? Him an' her father's been partners and friends since the war. You heard him say so yourself at Newport."

"Ah, you're right again, Amos." Letty sighed and leaned comfortably back against Amos's chest. "Miss Ananiah's been making a pretty fool of herself over Cap'n Colburn, and he's been making moon-eyes over her, but none of it's reason for her to come to more sorrow than she's already had in her life. 'Course you're right. Why under heaven would a gentleman like Cap'n Gill want to harm her?"

Amos said nothing. Troubled, he rested his cheek against the top of Letty's head and closed his eyes. He didn't know the answer himself. He wished with all his heart he did.

"Wake up, angel."

Her eyes still shut, Ananiah smiled blissfully at the sound of Sam's voice. She turned towards the side of the bunk where he should have been, pulled the coverlet higher over her bare shoulder, and promptly sank back into sleep.

Sam shook her gently. "I know it's early, sweetheart, but you don't have a choice. We have visitors."

"Visitors?" Ananiah rolled over and squinted up at him. Through the cabin windows, the sky was just beginning to pale with daybreak, an hour that Ananiah decided was inhumanly early for visitors of any kind, especially when they'd slept so little. But Sam was dressed and shaved already, with his hair tied neatly back, and for one awful moment Ananiah feared that she'd dreamed every lovely memory from the night before. God knows it wouldn't have been the first time she'd deceived herself.

But then Sam bent over and kissed her, his open mouth moving so swiftly, so surely, over hers that her doubts fled. With a contented purring deep in her throat, she reached up to slip her arms around his neck and draw him back into bed with her, where he belonged.

But instead Sam reluctantly freed himself from her embrace and stood, shaking his head at the choice he'd had to make. "You tempt me, lass, tempt me sore, but I don't fancy a pack of French sailors for an audience."

"You're not making one whit of sense." She sat up against the pillows, modestly pulling the coverlet higher over her nakedness. No, she realized as she peeked underneath, not quite naked, for he'd left her her stockings and garters, and she felt her face grow warm as she remembered how readily she'd parted with the rest. "There's not a single Frenchman on the *Truelove*'s books."

"I told you, we have guests." He heaved the strongbox that held the ship's papers and hard money onto the table, and began sorting rapidly through the contents. "A French frigate popped out of the mists on our weatherboard so fast we couldn't turn tail without seeming unmannerly. I wouldn't have wakened you, but they seem eager to come a-calling."

He jerked the kerchief from around his neck, scooped all the coins into it along with several of the papers, and tied the kerchief into a lumpy bundle. He slammed the strongbox's lid shut and slid it back under the cupboard. Then he reached up the largest carling overhead, felt for the hollowed-out opening he knew was there, and hid the kerchief and the gold inside.

"At this hour?" Ananiah was awake now, wide-awake.

Sam swept up Ananiah's white silk gown from where it lay on the deck and handed it to her. "They've lowered a boat and they're sending a lieutenant and a pack of other rascals to come aboard. I don't want them ogling you."

"Coming aboard or boarding us?" she asked as she slid from the bunk and hurriedly began to dress. "I am my father's daughter, Sam. I know the difference."

His eyes met hers, searching, and she knew the moment he decided to trust her with the truth. "I'll tell you as soon as I know myself," he said grimly. "I'd feel a sight better if they hadn't run out their guns. Last I heard, the Directory favored us Yankees, but ask poor old Louis what *their* word's worth. The devil take their jackals' brand of brotherhood! I'll see 'em in hell before they'll claim my *Truelove* as their prize."

As Ananiah struggled with the ties on her gown, she watched him load and prime a pair of battered old pistols and tuck them in his belt, where they were hidden by the skirts of his coat. The sight chilled Ananiah. She'd seen what trouble Sam's temper could cause with his fists alone, but pistols and gunpowder were different. All of Sam's size and strength would be meaningless against anyone with a pistol. And guns—open gun ports meant the French had trained their great guns on them, and she'd heard enough tales from the last war to know what that meant. One broadside from a frigate bent on taming the temper of an irate merchant captain could sweep the *Truelove*'s deck clean in minutes, killing Jeremy and Lawson and Martin and Howard and all the rest who'd be caught gaping at the rail.

And Sam. No ship in the world was worth his life. Dear Lord, she couldn't bear the possibility of losing him now, after last night.

"Swear to me you won't do anything foolish," she asked urgently. She held her arms folded tightly across her chest, not letting herself touch him. She knew her own weakness, how tempting it would be to cling to him and collapse into tears. "Can't you promise me that much, Sam?"

They both heard the hail in garbled English from the French boat alongside. He reached out and cupped her cheek in his palm, turning her face towards his.

"Take care, angel," he said quickly. "Stay here, where I'll know you'll be safe, and keep yourself from their eyes."

Ananiah clutched his wrist. "Sam, I beg you, for your own sake—"

"I'll do whatever I must, sweetheart," he said gruffly. "I can't promise you more than that." Gently he uncurled her fingers from around his wrist and lifted her hand to his lips. His eyes held hers as he kissed her palm, reminding her in a single gesture of all that had passed between them, and then he was gone.

She pressed the hand he'd kissed over her mouth, both to savor for a moment longer the memory of his lips and to hold back the fear she felt rising within her. Overhead, the deck seemed curiously silent as the *Truelove*'s crew waited and watched as the French boat came closer. No running footsteps, no swearing, no singing to match the rhythm of hauling; only the sound of the wind against the canvas and, through the standing rigging, the creaks of the *Truelove*'s timbers and the rush of the waves along her sides, and Sam's lone voice, so quiet that this once she couldn't make out his words.

*Oh, Sam* . . .

For her love, he would do whatever he believed he must. For his, how could she do less? There had to be other ways to win against Frenchmen besides pistols. She ran to her own small sea chest, which Sam had had brought to his cabin with her. She frantically dug through its contents until she found the leather portfolio that Mr. Morrow had given her before they sailed. False papers, he'd explained proudly, for travelers never knew what might happen at sea: one set for the French, and another for the Dutch. Though her father never sailed without such forgeries, other shipmasters judged them a low, dishonest trick, and Mr. Morrow had hesitantly advised her not to share their existence with Captain Colburn unless circumstances demanded it.

Ananiah decided the present circumstances could not be more demanding, and she scanned the false papers quickly. Her apprehension grew as she realized the difficult part Morrow's ingenuity would require her to play; what he expected her to do, what she *must* do to make this work. She closed her eyes and swallowed hard. Only her love for Sam could make her do this. Before she lost her nerve she added the forged French papers to the *Truelove*'s genuine ones tucked in the back of Sam's log, and prayed to God he'd understand why.

As she heard the Frenchmen scrambling up the side, she rose on her toes to look at herself in the tiny mirror Sam used for shaving. To her dismay, with her hair loose and tangled over her shoulders and her gown a crumpled mess, she looked more like some sailor's doxy than the imperious lady she'd have to be. Swiftly she retrieved her sapphire earrings and necklace from the chair and clasped them on, hoping that the sapphires at least might impress the French lieutenant. She flung her yellow shawl around her shoulders to hide as much of her gown as she could, and threw open the cabin door.

"Miss Ananiah!" Scandalized, Letty stood in the doorway, blocking Ananiah's path to the companionway as she indignantly raked her mistress from head to foot. "Look at you, miss! Lord, I'd never credit it if I'd heard the tale from another, but I can't deny what my own eyes are seeing! Colored jewels and silk satin before breakfast, and you creeping out of that man's bed, bold as sin itself! What your poor father'd say, miss! Oh, what he'd say!"

Ananiah knew quite well what he'd say, and she didn't care. She had to reach Sam before his temper got the better of him. "Please, Letty, let me pass!" she begged. "I must get to the deck at once!"

"Back to that great roan bull of yours, I'll wager." She sniffed and looked over her shoulder, wondering what was keeping Amos. "You'll be with him soon enough, but there's another with business with you first." Again she looked back, and while she was off balance, Ananiah tried to push her aside.

Letty stumbled back and gasped. "You've never laid a hand on me before, miss, not once in all the years I've served you!" She wasn't being self-righteous now; instead, she was bewildered and disbelieving, and the wounded look on her face cut straight to Ananiah's conscience.

"Letty, please, forgive me," she began, reaching out her hand to the smaller woman. "We've much to talk over, but not—"

"There's nothing left to say, miss." Letty's expression hardened. "Once I thought you was the finest lady in Providence, and I was honored to belong to your household. But Amos is right. You're no better than they say, Miss Ananiah Snow. When we're safe home again, I mean to make a life of my own, and that don't include serving one such as you."

"Letty!" cried Ananiah, shocked, but the maidservant had already turned and run. Letty had been with her since before her mother's death, since before she met and married Étienne, and there were no secrets from that past that Letty didn't know. Her betrayal left Ananiah shaken and vulnerable.

When Ananiah heard the man's harsh voice speaking in French, she squeezed her eyes shut and tried to calm her racing heart. She had thought Sam could make the past leave her alone, but she knew she'd be helpless to stop the memories once they'd begun.

*"No more, Étienne!" she heard herself crying. "You can't hurt me, because I'm not going back to you ever again!"*

And then there was Sam, speaking in awful, angry French until the harsh-voiced Frenchman interrupted him. Ananiah's eyes flew open as she remembered the

French frigate. This wasn't one of her waking nightmares. This was real, and Sam needed her. She raced up the narrow steps to the deck.

But at the top of the steps, she froze. She felt like an actress dropped into the middle of a play with no notion of what lines to speak next. Every man was turned towards her, waiting and watching. The faces of the *Truelove*'s crew were surprised, but not hostile, and they quickly blended into a familiar blur. But beside the rail stood the cluster of French sailors and marines, brilliant in their blue uniforms, with the rising sun glinting off the polished barrels of their muskets. While she saw surprise on their faces, too, there was also so much hatred and contempt and open lust that she wanted to shrink away in fear and shame. And in the middle of them stood Sam. His shock at seeing her changed so swiftly to cold fury that she almost staggered beneath its impact.

"This woman is what?" demanded the young French lieutenant in awkward English. With dismay, Ananiah realized he was the exact kind of officious popinjay that would anger Sam the fastest. Above the fine lace of his shirtfront, the man's face was marked by arrogance and smallpox scars, and the smile he granted Ananiah was a cross between a leer and a smirk. "She is the most beautiful . . . sister to *le capitaine?*"

The significant pause was as much an insult as the implied relationship, and Ananiah caught her breath as she saw Sam's fingers flex and draw into fists at his sides.

"She's an American lady, you lace-trimmed bastard," growled Sam, "and you're not fit to even ask her name."

"Since your country allied itself with my enemy Great Britain, *capitaine,* I have every right." The Frenchman's smirk widened. "The treaty of your citizen John Jay with King George, *oui?* Now you are enemy also."

"Since when?" thundered Sam, and now it was the French marines whose fingers tightened on their weapons. Soon, thought Ananiah desperately, she must speak soon and end this. She had not spoken French, Étienne's language, since she had sailed from Martinique, and she still balked at speaking it now. Yet for Sam's sake she must. She *must.*

"By the orders of Captain Landriot, date 22 Thermidor," the lieutenant was saying, "we seize and search and take vessels of America as please us."

"The hell you will!" roared Sam as he lunged at the lieutenant. With one hand he seized the lace-trimmed shirt, while the other, clenched tight in a fist, struck the lieutenant's jaw, snapping his head back. As Sam drew back to strike him again, four French sailors grabbed him and jerked their officer free. When the struggling men finally parted, Sam's face was as bloody as the Frenchman's. His arms were pinned back by the others, while one of the marines swung his musket stock into Sam's belly for good measure.

"You will free the American at once, Lieutenant!" cried Ananiah, her voice ringing out across the crowded deck. Effortlessly, the words came back to her in the distinctive island French she'd learned on Martinique, and with them flowed the careful lies constructed by Morrow. "You will touch nothing on this brig, and you will harm none of her crew. I am Ananiah de Gramont, wife of Étienne Jean-Baptiste de Gramont, citizen of the Republic, and this vessel and her contents belong to me."

# Chapter Twelve

The lieutenant swung around to stare at her, half his face covered by a bloody handkerchief. "What did you say, my girl?" he asked in French.

"I am not 'your girl,' Lieutenant," Ananiah said acidly, "and you'd do well to remember it before I must speak to your captain." As long as she didn't look back towards Sam, she'd be fine. All she had to do was mimic the wealthy French wives she'd known on Martinique.

The lieutenant hesitated, dabbing at his nose. "Madame must forgive me if I question her," he finally said, slipping unconsciously into the outlawed formality of the old bourgeois address. "Madame understands that these are difficult times for military men. I don't wish to give offense, but my duty demands I be thorough. If madame could but explain how she comes to be here?"

The lieutenant was growing more uncomfortable by the minute, but with her head high, Ananiah forced him to wait for his answer as she gazed out over the railing and adjusted the drape of her shawl. She hoped he would wonder if she'd deign to answer him; in reality she was groping for a plausible reply. For the first time she noticed the frigate across the water, how much larger it was than their own little brig, two neat rows of black guns in square ports punctuating its yellow side. It was up to her to keep those guns silent.

"As you say, Lieutenant, these are difficult times." Strange how her father now came to mind, and how he'd have laughed and approved of what she was doing. It was the same kind of ruse he'd used a score of times himself. "When I wished to travel to Boulogne-sur-Mer to visit my sister, my husband believed it safest to employ a neutral American to carry me and his cargo. Of course, had he known of this new decision to seize American vessels, he might have chosen differently."

"Of course," murmured the lieutenant, and Ananiah hated his solicitude, knowing it to be as false as Morrow's bills of lading.

"The world does not stand still." She shrugged carelessly, and prayed that Sam, with his scattershot French, wasn't following what she said. "You'll find the documents as I say in the captain's logbook, though I doubt he has the wit to recognize them for what they are. The others that state our home port as Providence, in Rhode Island, are merely to delude any British inquisitors that we fall in with."

With a brusque wave, the lieutenant sent a midshipman and a marine below to seek the papers she described. Behind her, Ananiah heard Sam swear and struggle against the men who held him.

"Ananiah, what the hell is happening? Ananiah, lass, what are you saying to this bastard?" he demanded, and it took all her will not to turn and run to him. "Damnation, Ananiah, look at me!"

To hear him beg like this tore at her heart. But if she faltered now, if she betrayed any tenderness for him, the lieutenant would pounce on the truth, and they'd all end their days in a French prison.

The French officer's knowing smile spread slowly across his battered face. The more Sam raged, the more the lieutenant believed Ananiah's story. "This Yankee is fond of you, Madame de Gramont. Who can blame him, with such a lovely passenger to share his company?"

Ananiah longed to strike the smirk from the man's face, remembering too well how the other ladies in Fort-de-France had twitted her for never taking a lover. Even if Étienne had been more permissive, her New England upbringing would never have allowed her to break her marriage vows so casually. But worse still was what she must now say to the lieutenant, how with every word she'd cheapen herself and tarnish the new treasure Sam had given her.

"For all love, Ananiah, what the hell is that bastard telling you?"

*For all love, Sam, I'm doing it all for love of you....*

"A crossing at this season can be long and tedious," the lieutenant was saying, raising one brow as he pointedly surveyed her disheveled appearance. "I trust you've found diversions to pass the time."

This awful, smirking Frenchman left her no choice. Her dishabille needed an explanation, and there could be only one that he would accept.

"My husband is an older gentleman, and understanding of such matters," she said lightly, keeping her smile arch to hide the disgust she tasted so bitterly. A corner of her shawl fluttered up into her face. The wind was freshening, and the eastern sky was dark with mounting clouds. "This Yankee is hot-tempered, true, but he has proved his worth, and I ask you to be gentle with him."

"You might have asked the same of him, madame," grumbled the lieutenant as he dabbed at his nose again with his handkerchief, his gaze, too, shifting towards the horizon.

Ananiah saw his uneasiness, and for the first time she let her hopes begin to rise. She was nearly certain he'd accepted her story. All he would need now was enough proof to convince his captain. With the weather turning, he would want to hurry back to his own ship, and perhaps he'd give the lading bills only a cursory scan. Beneath her shawl, Ananiah's thumb worked her ring around and around her finger as she willed the Frenchman to leave.

The midshipman came trotting up the steps, his hand full of papers. "It's all just as that lady says, sir," he said excitedly as he gave the papers to the lieutenant. "And, sir, we found another woman as well!"

Ananiah's head whipped around in time to see the two French sailors haul Letty stumbling to the deck. She was pale with fear and seasickness from the rising waves, and her knees buckled beneath her as the sailors dragged her back to her feet. Ananiah felt her own mouth grow dry. How could she have forgotten Letty? Letty would know nothing of her story, and could unwittingly tear it full of holes with a handful of the wrong words.

"Letty , you ignorant girl!" she said crossly, hoping that Letty would remember enough French to be able to answer. "Can't you see that these men are French, not English, and will not hurt you?"

But Letty stayed silent, her eyes round with fear, and Ananiah felt her own confidence begin to crumble.

"I should have left you at Beau Coteau with Monsieur de Gramont, Letty," she said, trying desperately to make Letty understand as she prayed the lieutenant hadn't heard the tremor in her voice. "What use will you be to me in Boulogne if you're like this now?"

Still Letty didn't answer, and to Ananiah it seemed the silence around her grew more ominous by the moment. Lord, what kind of fool had she been to believe she could save them all herself! Her panic rose, and at last she let herself look to Sam for reassurance.

One look, and her heart plummeted. His face was stern and immobile, the lines around his mouth were carved deep, and the blue eyes she loved so well were as cold as the sea. His French might be clumsy, but he'd understood enough to damn her.

Refolding the *Truelove*'s papers, the lieutenant reached out and chucked Letty beneath her chin with a familiarity he'd never have dared with Ananiah. "Listen to your mistress, you sullen little baggage." He laughed when Letty jerked her face away from his hand. "Your lady is too tenderhearted. If you were mine, I'd thrash that plump bottom of yours until you learned to obey. Eh, madame?" He winked broadly at Ananiah.

As the sailors around him guffawed, he nodded at the men who held Sam and handed the papers out to the other captain. "You are free to go, *Capitaine* Colburn, yes?" he said in English with a wary, unconscious duck of his head. "If before you said you sail for a citizen of France, you would have had no troubles from me."

Encouraged that Sam didn't try to strike him again, he motioned for his men to return to the boat. "Farewell, *capitaine*. You have a pretty brig, and a prettier lady." He turned and bowed neatly to Ananiah. *"Au revoir, madame, et bonne chance!"*

Without answering, Sam turned his back on both Ananiah and the departing Frenchmen. He stuffed the papers into his pocket unread as he went striding to the helm.

"Away aloft there!" he roared, and all around him men raced up through the rigging. "Ready about! I don't want us caught with our breeches down when this blow hits!"

Miserable, Ananiah hung back, the one person on the deck with no purpose. She looked for Letty, hoping at least she could explain to her, but the maid had found comfort of her own, and stood sobbing against Amos Howard's chest. The mate's broad hands moved gently up and down Letty's back, and the tenderness of the gesture made Ananiah painfully aware of what she herself had lost. Over Letty's dark hair, his gaze met Ananiah's, his round face so openly distorted by hatred that Ananiah gasped. So he blamed her, too, for what she'd had to do to Letty. Lord, did they all hate her this much?

Her eyes stinging with unshed tears, she turned away from them, towards the helm. Sam had taken the wheel himself and was bawling out more orders, his eyes intent on the mass of dark clouds swirling overhead. He couldn't have made his disinterest in her any more clear. The deck angled sharply beneath Ananiah's feet as the waves grew higher, and as she grabbed at the larboard shrouds to keep her footing, she barely caught at her shawl before the wind whipped it from her shoulders. Awkwardly she wrapped it more tightly around her body and knotted the ends at her waist.

"Best t' go below, miss," Lawson shouted through cupped hands at her across the deck. "The cap'n wouldn't want you comin' to no harm."

Ananiah shook her head and pretended she couldn't hear him as she carefully began to make her way aft. She didn't agree with Lawson. Right now she doubted very much that the captain would care if the wind picked her up and tossed her clear to France, but not even a nor'wester could make her go without at least trying to talk to Sam.

"What the hell are you doing here?" he shouted at her as she stopped near the mainmast, clinging with both hands to the pin rack around its base. Against the dark gray clouds, his untied hair glowed like dark fire as it blew back in the wind, wild flames to match his anger. "Take yourself below, Ananiah, else I'll have one of the men haul you off. Or would you heed me any better if I gave you orders in French, Madame de Gramont?"

"That's not fair, Sam, as well you'd know if you listened to your brains instead of your pride!" Because of the weather they were shouting at each other to be heard, but Ananiah knew that anger swelled their voices as much as the wind. "I hate Étienne de Gramont! I've never used his name since I left him, nor spoken his language until this morning! What I did—what I said—I never would have done it had there been any other way!"

"You expect me to believe that, when you've come all tricked out with a set of papers that say otherwise? Or didn't you believe I had the 'wit' to read 'em for myself?"

She winced to hear her own words tossed back at her. "Mr. Morrow told me not to show them to you because you wouldn't approve, and he was right!"

"Damnation, it's not Morrow's trickery I care about, Ananiah, it's yours! Playing at being some fine French bitch proud to give her poor husband another set of horns, and making me look no better than the bull you've bought for stud! Oh, aye, and you enjoyed it, too, didn't you, being the great lady again that always gets what she wants?"

She stared at him in disbelief, stunned that he had so misunderstood her actions.

He looked past her, to the brig's bow and the sea beyond, and the muscles in his chest and arms strained beneath his coat as he struggled to hold the wheel steady. "You couldn't even trust me to take care of you when I'd sworn I would, could you?" he shouted, biting off each word. "Nay, you had to do it your own way, and make a fool out of me. Not an hour out of my bed and you've set yourself up like a Dock Street whore, dancing your wares under that Frenchman's nose!"

"It wasn't like that, Sam!" she cried in anguish. "It wasn't like that at all!"

His gaze swung back from the sea to her. The fury in his eyes was almost more than she could bear. "Then why the devil did you do it, Ananiah?"

A cold wall of spray flew over them as the *Truelove*'s bowsprit crashed through the crest of a wave higher than her freeboard. Ananiah gasped as the salt water struck her, soaking her to the skin. She released one hand from her grip on the rack long enough to pull the weight of her sodden hair from her face, and immediately felt the drag of the wind yank her body towards starboard. Sam made no move to help her, and as she steadied herself with both hands she realized bitterly that she'd been right to guess that he no longer cared.

"I did it for you, Sam Colburn!" she shouted into the storm. Drenched by the spray that swept again across the deck, she was glad he couldn't see the tears on her cheeks. Perhaps it wouldn't matter to him anymore, but to her it did. "I did it to keep your precious *Truelove* from the French, and I did it to keep you from getting yourself killed in a fight you couldn't win! God help me, Sam, I did it because I love you!"

She searched his face for his answer, any answer, watching and waiting and waiting as the wind and spray lashed around them both. But it seemed his expression grew harder, if that was possible, the set of his mouth more unforgiving, and she knew he did not believe her. She had given Sam the greatest secret her heart held, and not even that was enough to wipe the fury from his face.

She felt a hand grip her firmly by the upper arm. "Come wit' me now, miss," said Lawson into her ear as he gently pried her cold-stiffened fingers free of the rack. "This storm's no place for any lady."

She saw how Sam nodded curtly to Lawson, not to her, and she let the older man lead her away.

The cabin was dark except for one guttering candle swinging in its gimbals, the deadlights in place over the stern windows keeping out even the storm's green-gray light. Slowly, Ananiah pulled off her sodden clothes and let them drop to the deck. She pinched the candle out, and though it still wanted hours until noon, she crawled back into the bunk. Curled on her side in the dark, she listened numbly to the *Truelove*'s timbers creak and protest against the waves' beating. If she turned her face into the pillow, she could smell Sam's scent on the worn linen, close her eyes and almost believe he was with her still.

Almost, but not enough.

* * *

In the twenty-four years since Sam had first gone to sea as a boy, he'd weathered hurricanes and blizzards, and lightning that had shattered a barquentine's mainmast, but in all that time he'd never seen a storm to match this one for sheer cussed meanness. Sheets of rain and spray meshed with the clouds to form a seamless curtain that masked the sun and stars, and only the bells at the end of each watch could separate day from night. And always there was the wind, driving the swells into waves, and the waves into heaving, shining mountains frosted with spume that tossed the brig as carelessly as if it were a child's toy boat.

At the end of the second day, the patched old mainsail split, and on the third morning it was the foresail that shredded and tore away from its yard. Left without a choice, Sam ordered the exhausted crewmen to snug down the sheets that were left and ride out the storm as best they could under bare poles. Still the *Truelove* hurtled onward before the wind, Sam struggling to control the helm. Together with another man on the opposite side of the wheel, most often Lawson, Sam held tight to the spokes, his torn, callused palms cushioned with rag bindings, until his hands shook as he fought to steer the brig up and over the waves and away from the dangerous valleys in the swells.

Because the sun and stars were hidden, the only guide for navigation was the mariner's compass in the binnacle, and south by southeast became the one constant in a gray, distorted world. If they'd been able to remain on course, they would have reached an English landfall days earlier. Now they were sure to be past it, though not even Sam could guess how far, or what lay ahead.

By the fifth day, the men were beyond exhaustion, bound by the growing, unspoken fear that this storm had no end. With no fire in the galley, there was no hot food or drink and no dry clothing. Enough seawater had forced its way through the hatches and down the companionways to make the crew's quarters nearly as wet as the deck above. Though there were smashed fingers, bruises, and a broken arm, incredibly, no one had been lost to the waves. Saved to drown together, the pessismists muttered, and now when the Portuguese topmen told their beads, the other men fell quiet and listened for the first time on the voyage.

Sam understood their fear and the superstition that went with it, and spared the crew as much as he dared. He couldn't deny the weight of the responsibility that lay on him, the faith they put in him to miraculously bring them through safe. He drove himself relentlessly. Not a watch passed that he wasn't on deck with the others. He slept no more than an hour at a time, and gulped the cold food when he remembered to eat.

And if it seemed a kind of punishment, then so it was. The endless hours at the wheel gave him all the time he needed to realize what he'd done to Ananiah. He could tell himself forever that his quarrel had been with the Frenchmen, not her, that the sight of their uniforms on his quarterdeck reminded him too strongly of what he'd seen of war as a boy. He could argue that his temper had gotten the better of him, and spilled over unintentionally onto her. He could say that she hadn't been in any real danger when she'd slipped on the deck, that for him to hold the wheel steady had been more important to the safety of everyone on board. He could tell himself all this, and he did.

But the truth didn't change. Ananiah had been clever and resourceful, and she'd risked everything she could because she loved him. Damnation, she *loved* him, and in return he'd called her a whore. The woman he loved, dearer to him than anything else in life, the woman he wanted for his wife. Five minutes of his blind anger had destroyed the fragile trust they'd built between them, and there was no way to go back and rebuild it.

His last glimpse of her face haunted him. The pain he'd seen in her eyes was nothing compared to the resignation there with it. He had told her to trust him, swearing that he was different from Étienne, and the night when she'd shared his bed she'd believed him, he knew it. But she didn't now. He doubted she ever would again. Words like that could not be unsaid, no matter how sweet the apologies.

There wasn't a man on board that couldn't guess why Sam chose to sling a hammock among them instead of retreating to his own quarters. None of them was foolhardy enough to mention it in the captain's hearing until, on the storm's sixth day, Lawson dropped heavily onto the bench across from his captain at the mess table. Sam smiled wearily as he leaned forward with his elbows on the rough planks, a cup of cold black coffee in the mug before him.

"Evans says the *Truelove*'s weeping so bad now there's more'n a foot of water in the well." Sam rubbed his fingers into his bloodshot eyes, willing them to stay open just a little while longer. "Through the hatches or through the sides, 'tis all the same. Pumps don't amount to much in seas like these. Next watch we'll try lightening her, and jettison some of the heavier stuffs in the forehold.''

With his palms flat on the table, Lawson shook his head. They'd sailed together long enough to know what didn't need to be said. The odds against finding a safe harbor were insurmountable, and unless the storm's fury abated soon, the *Truelove* would become too waterlogged to float. "So when, Cap'n," he asked softly, "will you take yourself off to speak to the lady?''

"What, on account of them being her goods going over the side?''

"Nay, she wouldn't care a fig for the lot o' it," said Lawson doggedly. "Don't go playing the fool with me, Cap'n. You know very well what needs to be said to Miss Snow.''

Sam pulled himself upright, his chin up and his eyes narrowed. "Miss Snow's none of your affair, Lawson.''

Again Lawson shook his head. "Any other time an' you'd be right, but you know same as me that if you don't take the chance t' see her now, you might not get another.''

"Damn it, we're not fin up yet!''

"Then go tell the lass so. She's a gallant little creature, but she must be scared witless, all lonesome in that cabin." Lawson drummed his fingers on the table, staring down at them self-consciously, as if they didn't belong to him. "After what she done for us, she deserves better, and you know that, too, Sam Colburn.''

"What she don't deserve is me." Sam's shoulders felt too heavy to shrug. "After what I've done to her, I wouldn't expect her to take me back even if I crawled on my belly and begged.''

"I reckon that's for the lady to decide.''

"It's done with her, Bob," said Sam bleakly. "Done, mind?"

Lawson rose stiffly to his feet, retying the scarf over his tarred hat as he waited for Sam to join him to return to the deck. "I've never been one for churchgoing, and I can't say for certain what follows after living this life," he said carefully. "But whatever comes, I wouldn't want to be you a-facing it down if'n you don't go make things right with Miss Snow first. Then, if you've a mind, you can say it's done between the two o' you, an' not before."

But Sam only shook his head.

When the knock came at the cabin door, Ananiah and Jeremy were sitting side by side on the bunk, their backs braced against the bulkhead to keep them from tumbling forward with the rocking of the waves. After six days, they scarcely noticed the motion. Their legs were curled beneath them Indian-style to keep their feet clear of the seawater that flooded the cabin's deck, the little waves that slapped against the legs of the table and chair mimicking the ones that hammered against the deadlights. Spread across Ananiah's lap was the Old Testament she and Jeremy had begun reading when, on account of his age, he, too, had been banished from the deck. By now Jeremy could make out most words, excepting the longest Hebrew names. With cheerful pride, he predicted how surprised Ben would be that he could read. Silently Ananiah prayed the boy would live to have that opportunity. He'd been her only company, and as together they'd pretended not to be afraid, each for the sake of the other, Ananiah had been forced to think of something other than Sam.

The knocking on the door startled them both. "Who d'you think that be?" asked Jeremy, staring at the door as if he could see through the oak. The rest of the crew had been so occupied with the storm that these last days he and Ananiah might have been the only two people on board.

"You wait here," said Ananiah as she slid off the bunk. "No use in both of us with wet feet." As if anything, she thought wryly, could possibly get any wetter. She'd long ago abandoned shoes and stockings, and with her skirt held immodestly high above her knees she waded towards the door. The water was cold and dirty, and she didn't like to think too closely about what might be swimming between her toes. With her shoulder she shoved the door open, and another stream of water rushed in, past the boots of a young sailor named Stimson.

"Mister Howard said to fetch you, miss," he said, purposefully slicking back his wet hair with both hands, still somehow aware of her as a lady. "Said the cap'n was asking for you t' come t' him topsides."

Her heart racing, Ananiah hurried clumsily back through the water to get her bedraggled shawl.

"You'll come back, won't you, Ananiah?" asked Jeremy, his voice quavering as he clutched the Bible to his chest.

"Of course I will," Ananiah declared with a certainty she didn't feel. She didn't need to be told how grim their situation was, and though she suspected Jeremy didn't either, for his sake she could pretend a little longer. She held her arms out to the boy, and he flew into them, hugging her fiercely before he remembered he was too old for such coddling. Manfully he pulled free with a loud sniff, but Ananiah kissed him on the forehead anyway.

"Try not to worry, Jeremy," she said gently. "You know Captain Colburn's doing everything he can for us. I'll back as soon as I've seen him."

Stimson had gone on without her, and on her own she fought her way up the steps to the deck. The wind struck her with a ferocity she hadn't expected, and she struggled to keep hold of the lifelines that had been strung between the masts. She was shocked by how much of the standing rigging had been carried away, and by the long gap, like a toothless smile, where the larboard rail had been. Overhead, the tatters of the mainsail cracked in the wind, and there was another sound, too, in the distance, a repetitive crash and boom that she couldn't place.

The brig was riding far too low, and waves swept easily across the deck. Men were struggling to haul barrels and crates up through the main hatch and then shove them over the side. Too little, too late—even Ananiah could recognize that the *Truelove* was a dying ship. Through the spray she could barely make out Sam's tall, broad-shouldered figure at the wheel, and her heart lurched. Too often these last days and nights she had wondered if she'd see him again in his life.

"Miss Snow?" someone shouted to her above the wind, and she twisted back to look over her shoulder. The blow that came next caught her off balance, striking her hard on her back. She felt her feet sliding out from under her on the slanting, slippery deck. Her hands reached out reflexively to break her fall, and she let go of the lifeline she'd been clutching. Though she clawed desperately at the deck, she was falling fast, too fast, with nothing to stop her as she plunged through the gap where the larboard rail had been.

For one moment she felt weightless, hanging in the air as the ship pitched away from her. Then the cold black grip of the water swept over her, clutching at her flailing arms and legs, drawing her deeper into a wave that had no bottom and no end, and she knew then that she was lost.

# Chapter Thirteen

Sam refused to believe his eyes. To see Ananiah there in the mist before him was only another part of this nightmare that had no end. She should be below in his cabin with the boy, as safe as anyone could be on a sinking ship. He swore bitterly, cursing himself for having failed her so completely, and wishing for her sake she'd never met him. For his own sake, though, that was different. She was the best thing that had ever happened to him.

He squinted harder, but her graceful figure didn't disappear, her knotted yellow shawl bright above the dark deck. Before this was done, he would tell her he loved her, and kiss her farewell. One last time, that was all, once more for them both.

As he watched, one of the men came up behind her, and she turned expectantly. Too late, Sam recognized Howard's barrel chest, and too late he saw the other man's broad arm swing back and purposefully slam into Ananiah. Too late, he watched her crumple, spin, and slide across the deck and over the side.

And then, too soon, she was gone.

"Ananiah, no!" Without a thought, he abandoned the wheel to Lawson alone, and lunged frantically towards the taffrail. Already the *Truelove* was racing past the place where she'd disappeared. He shouted her name again into the wind, vainly scanning the black water for a sign of her.

Too late.

The *Truelove* heeled abruptly as Lawson lost control of the wheel, the brig's wake curving like a plume in response. Bobbing in the white foam that streamed behind the rudder was the yellow of Ananiah's shawl, and in the same instant that he saw it Sam dived over the rail.

He was a strong swimmer, but he hadn't reckoned on the pull of the stormy water. Twice the waves washed over him, sweeping him along in their path, and then, suddenly, the patch of bright yellow was bobbing before him. He lunged for it and caught one end, wrapping it tightly around his fist as he tugged it towards him, tumbling Ananiah's body through the water to him. Swiftly he linked his arm around her chest to lift her shoulders clear of the water, but her head lolled forward, and her arms drifted limply on the current.

"Damn it, angel, I won't let you go like this," gasped Sam as he squeezed her hard, trying to force air into her lungs. He didn't know how much water she'd swallowed, or how long she'd been trapped beneath the waves, but he refused to consider that she might already have drowned and be no more than a corpse in his arms. "Come on, lass, breathe for me!"

Another wave rose and lifted them forward, and he held her tight. There'd be no help from the *Truelove,* now vanished into the night, and he quickly shoved away the thought of her crew's distress. There was nothing he could do for them now. This was hard enough work, keeping himself and Ananiah afloat in a heavy sea, and awkwardly he worked his waterlogged boots off. That was better, but he knew he was tiring.

Not far to their left bobbed a large, flat crate, and Sam dragged Ananiah towards it. He grabbed the crate and pulled himself over it, and Ananiah with him. Supported by the floating wood, breathing hard, he realized how exhausted he'd become. What did he expect, when he'd hardly slept or eaten in a week? He looked down at Ananiah, limp and white against his arm, and gently pushed her hair back from her face.

"Forgive me, Ananiah," he said hoarsely as he ran his fingers along her throat, feeling for a pulse. The beat was faint, if it was there at all. "None of this has turned out the way I wanted, but God help me, I love you still."

He lowered his mouth to hers, rhythmically trying to breathe his life back into her. Over and over he forced air into her lungs, long past the time when anyone else would have given her up as lost. Still she did not move, and her lips remained cold and lifeless beneath his own.

*Come on, lass,* he prayed, *you're all I have left now.*

Suddenly her eyelids fluttered open and she began gasping convulsively, and Sam flipped her over on her side, holding her tight around the waist as she coughed up half a wave's worth of seawater. At last she gulped for air alone, in great wracking gasps that were almost sobs.

"You're all right, angel," he said into her ear. "You'll be all right now."

She twisted about in his arms, disoriented by the way her lower body floated weightlessly. With stiff, clumsy movements, she tried to kick her legs out of the water.

"I'm cold, Sam," she rasped, clutching at Sam's shirt. Their makeshift float bobbed precariously, and he struggled to keep it steady and their heads and shoulders above the water.

"I am, too, love, but there's not a precious thing I can do about it." He shifted her body so that it rested more closely against his, hoping at least to share what little warmth his blood still had with her. She hadn't drowned, but the danger from shock was still very real. And how long would either of them survive drifting aimlessly in the open sea like this?

Another wave caught them and lifted them forward, and with an odd jolt of recognition Sam saw that a rum cask that had gone over the side soon after Ananiah was still with them, floating not twenty paces to their left. How had he become so thick-witted that he hadn't noticed? They weren't drifting at all. They were moving forward.

Now he remembered the distant roar of the breakers he'd been hearing from the *Truelove*'s deck through the fog. Breakers meant land, waves striking a shoreline. Spain, if they were lucky, maybe Finisterre, or they could have been blown as far south as São Vincent in Portugal. He'd never had much trade with either country, but they both had the reputation of being kind to castaways, and he and Ananiah could be back on their way to London within a few days. If the current held, if the crate they clung to held together long enough, if no rocks and no undertow stood between them and the land, then they might have a chance.

"Not much longer, Ananiah," he promised, as much for his own sake as for hers. "We're almost there, I swear it."

Her mind was too numb to ask where there might be, any more than she wondered why Sam was making her cling to an worn old crate covered with wet splinters. Sam must have a reason. He always did. She burrowed closer into his chest, her bare legs tangling between his underwater in a way that made her smile.

"I still love you, too, Sam," she mumbled thickly into his chest, but the words were lost in the sound of the waves.

When Ananiah woke, the sun was already hot on her back, though the hard-packed sand she lay upon still held the chill of the night before. She shrugged off the shawl that had been her coverlet, and with every muscle aching in protest, she pushed herself up onto her knees and brushed the damp sand away from her face.

"Sam?" The impression in the sand beside her showed where he'd lain, followed by the long trail of his footprints down the beach. On the tall rocks that had shaded her he'd spread his coat to dry, the water still dripping from it in little rivulets. "Sam, where are you?"

She didn't like being alone, not here, and she rose stiffly to her feet to follow Sam's footprints. Although the rising sun was bright in a cloudless sky, the sea beneath it was still restless from the storm, its surface rough with whitecaps, and the wide, flat beach was littered with flotsam washed ashore, branches and bottles, shattered crates and barrels, broken spars and torn planking.

And Sam and herself, too, she thought, remembering how they'd been carried by the storm's last great waves, how in the dark they'd barely dragged themselves clear of the high-water mark before collapsing on the sand. Slowly she picked her way through the wreckage, her legs unsteady beneath her. Though she'd slept, she still felt exhausted.

"Sam?" Her call rose forlornly over the deserted beach. The sand ended in a sheer cliff of rock, and beyond that she could see nothing, no trees or grass or paths to mark a way to the top. The land didn't look like any description of England she'd ever heard, but then, perhaps they'd been carried to France instead. She cupped her hands around her mouth and shouted louder. "Sam Colburn!"

She spotted him then, beside a little outcropping of dark rocks, and though she called again, he didn't turn. He sat with his legs bent before him, his arms resting on his knees, staring out at the ocean.

Breathless, she sank down on the sand beside him, her hand outstretched to take his arm. But one look at his face and she withdrew, overwhelmed by the depth of the loss she saw etched deep in his every feature.

"They're all dead, Ananiah." His eyes didn't move from the empty horizon. "Bob Lawson, Israel Martin, Daniel Evans, and the others, even Jeremy and that plump little maid of yours."

"You don't know that for sure, Sam. We're alive, aren't we?"

"Did you know I shipped alongside Bob Lawson for sixteen years? He could've been his own master, but he followed me instead. Sixteen *years,* for all love! That's longer than I knew my own father."

"The *Truelove* rode out that storm for nearly a week, and you've no proof she didn't last the night, with the worst of the winds past."

"Proof! For God's sake, Ananiah, the proof's scattered all over this beach!" He snatched up a long, broken pole with a green-striped end that lay at his feet. "This is—nay, *was*—the forward oar on the starboard side of the longboat. This little notch, here, that's where the oarlock had shaken loose and worn the wood away. I had Evans set it to rights before we left Salem in June. Jesus, Evans has three little daughters, all fair like their mother, and now those pretty little girls will never know how much he loved them!" His voice broke, and he hurled the shattered oar into the water.

His grief and sorrow were too much for him to weather alone, and she felt her eyes well up with tears as she hugged her knees to her chest. "Perhaps they're in the boats now," she said, rushing her words in desperation. "Perhaps they'll find us soon, and then we can all leave this place together."

"Those boats were stove in on the first night. The *Truelove*'s gone, Ananiah, and her people with her, and if none of their bodies have washed up here with us, it's only because the fish found them first. They're all dead from trusting me, *me,* their captain!"

The tears streamed down her cheeks unchecked, the horror he described too great for her to accept. Not Letty, not Jeremy, not torn apart by sharks; no, somehow they must still live.

"I trusted you, too, Sam," she said haltingly, "and you saved me."

"Oh, aye, and I warrant you'll thank me till the end of your days, as well." At last he looked at her, his eyes red-rimmed and fierce. He hurt inside, the hollow pain so great he didn't know how he survived it. He'd lost his friends and his crew. He'd lost his brig—not merely his livelihood, but his one great possession, the one thing that defined him, as a mariner and a man. There was nothing of worth left in him at all, yet Ananiah still looked at him with a kind of devotion he knew he didn't deserve.

"Look where I've brought you!" he said, his anguish raw. "Do you have any notion at all of where we are, Ananiah?"

She hesitated from uncertainty. "France?"

"Aye, and there's Mary Antoinette's Versailles, directly over those rocks," he said bitterly. Blast her infernal, unrealistic optimism that refused to accept the *Truelove*'s loss, just as she'd denied her father's. "We're in Africa, ma'am, on the same sorry shore that's brought a thousand others to grief. Morocco, the Barbary Coast. Sand and rocks and no water, and not a charitable Christian in the whole damned country. No other decent vessels will dare venture close enough to this coast to spot us, for fear of having the same thing happen to them. You'll never find your father now, and no one will ever find you, either. I'd have been kinder far to let you drown than to save you for this."

She shoved her hair, stiff from the salt, back from her face and held it there with her hand. "What would you have me say, Sam? That I'm sorry you saved me? That I'd rather I'd drowned without your help, so you could have stayed to die with the others? You made that choice, not me."

He didn't answer and he didn't look at her, turning away from her instead to stare once again at the water. She was right, he'd made the choice to save her, and no matter how much unhappiness his decision would bring her, he knew selfishly that he'd make it again. One more reason for her to blame him, one less reason for her to offer her love.

But to Ananiah his silence could only mean that he would rather have died with the others than live with her. How more blatant could his rejection be? She'd sworn after Étienne that she'd never give another man the power to hurt her that came with love. She loved Sam, and she'd trusted him with the gifts of her heart and her body. But he was no different from Étienne, and neither was the pain she'd gotten in return.

Her throat closed with misery, and she bowed her head beneath the helplessness that weighed down upon her. He was right. There was nothing left for her in this life, not on this deserted beach.

"Damn you, Sam!" she cried through her tears, swaying as she scrambled clumsily to her feet. She couldn't stay here beside him, not like this. "Damn you and your choices and your trust! Why did you bother to save my life if you hated me this much?"

She turned and ran stumbling across the beach near the water, her feet leaving only faint prints in the hard-packed sand that the reach of the surf soon swept away. There was nothing left at all.

"Ananiah!" He seized her by the arm, dragging her to a stop as he pulled her around to face him. "Ananiah, please."

She halted, her heart pounding. He was the captain, and captains didn't say "please" to anyone. She wondered why she'd never noticed how long his lashes were, or the faint trail of freckles along the bridge of his nose, almost buried beneath his tan. His hold loosened on her arm, and she knew that if she wanted him to he would let her go.

"Please, Ananiah, I—" He stopped, searching her face for an answer to a question he dared not ask. He knew now there were other ways of losing her than to the sea.

She waited, wondering at the fear she saw so plainly in his eyes. She was the one with reason to be afraid, not him. *He* would never be afraid of anything.

His fingers spread and slid along her arm, tracing the blue veins that carried the blood to her heart. Because he loved her, she was alive. Her eyes were heavy-lidded from weeping and shadowed from exhaustion, her hair was tangled and stiff from the salt water, her green silk gown tattered and stained and split at the shoulders, and yet she'd never been more beautiful in his eyes than she was at this moment, because he loved her, and she was alive.

"Don't ever say those things again, Ananiah," he said, his voice harsh from emotions he couldn't have defined. "I love you, mind? I love you!"

Before she could answer, his mouth had found hers, and the fire between them was instantaneous. Her hands threaded around his waist and beneath his torn shirt, holding him tight as he lifted her feet from the sand. There was a desperate urgency to their desire this time, and their movements were frantic as they kissed and touched and clung to each other. Love seemed the one true way to reaffirm the life they miraculously still shared, and this passion they shared would bind them together forever, no matter how brief forever might be.

Mindlessly they toppled over onto the sand, pulling at the little clothing the storm had left them. Wavelets rippled around their bodies and tugged the sand from beneath them as the water retreated back to the ocean. The fever in their blood left them no patience for tenderness or teasing caresses, and when he entered her she cried out her welcome, drawing him deeper, her legs crossed possessively across his back. Overwhelmed by her need, she arched against him as his thrusts grew more savage, more demanding, until at last they could climb no higher, and the delirious power of the release that came left them gasping and spent.

Afterwards they lay together in silence, neither one willing to break with words the peace their union had brought. With her eyes closed against the sun, Ananiah traced her fingertips across the broad muscles of Sam's back. Beneath this bright sky, she felt closer to him than she ever had to any other person, her love binding her to him in a way that went far beyond the intertwining of their bodies.

She followed the line of his jaw, softened by a week's worth of new whiskers, and smoothed his hair away from his forehead. "What happens next, Sam?"

"I wish the hell I knew." With a groan, he rolled away from her and pushed himself up on his elbows. Lost in the pleasure they'd made for each other, he'd been able to forget how serious their situation was. "I'd feel a good deal better if we had water."

Just the mention of water made her realize how thirsty she was, how her tongue seemed to stick to the roof of her mouth. She sighed and sat upright, pulling what was left of her gown over her legs. The silk had shrunk so that it barely reached her knees, every seam straining, and soon she knew she'd be reduced to her shift and nothing else.

She shaded her eyes with her hand and looked back at the cliffs. "Perhaps we might find a spring, there, in the rocks."

"Nay, lass, I've already searched. This is the most barren, godforsaken place I've ever seen." He raked his fingers through his hair and braided it to keep it from falling in his face. "Haven't you noticed that there aren't any gulls or other birds? No grass or trees or weeds? Even the tide pools are empty. There's nothing but us and the rocks, and whatever waveson I can salvage from the wreck."

He smiled crookedly, unable to bite back his bitterness. "Maybe I'll find a cask of your father's fine canary so we can drink again to our good fortune."

She touched his arm, understanding what it must cost him to refer to the *Truelove* as a wreck. "I'm sorry, Sam," she said softly. "Sorry for everything."

He covered her hand with his own, not trusting himself to try thanking her. No matter how grim his loss, it would have been a thousand times worse without her. This, then, must be what Elihu had meant when he spoke about how much he loved his Sally. He leaned across and kissed Ananiah, his lips meeting hers with a sweetness that rapidly grew more heated before he broke away.

"Jesus, but this sun is hot, and it's not even noon." He scowled up at the sky and wiped his shirtsleeve over his forehead. The waves that had lapped around them earlier had retreated with the tide, and the wet sand around them was steaming in the heat.

Ananiah busied herself trying to comb her fingers through the snarls in her hair, looking down at the sand. Warm though it was, what he felt had little to do with the weather. She knew because she felt it, too, and if he kissed her again she might burst into flame.

"Here, lass, let me do it." He crouched down behind her, taking the tangled mass of pale gold from her hands. As he began to work deftly through the knots, she let her eyes close and her head arch back, and a little purr of pleasure sounded deep in her throat. He shook his head wryly as he looked down at the arcs of her lashes and at her parted lips. Making a simple sailor's pigtail had never before had quite this effect on him. His fingers brushed against her bare shoulder and the gold chain that had been hidden by her hair.

"I can't believe you didn't lose this," he said as he lifted the chain free of her gown. Hanging from it was the heart-shaped pendant he remembered from the first night he'd met her.

"I can't, either." She carefully brushed the sand and white salt away from the sapphires, marveling that the necklace had stayed around her neck. "It was my mother's. I remember her wearing it with blue satin when I was a little girl. Perhaps, somehow, she was watching over me last night."

"Then I hope she's not done yet." He separated a thin ribbon of her hair to loop and tie around the end of the pigtail and drew it tight. "We'll need everything we can in that line."

Sam was already thinking of how he could construct some sort of shelter for them tonight from driftwood, and how best to rig her yellow shawl as a flag to catch the eye of the lookout on any vessel that might pass them. But first would have to come something to drink. Before she'd awakened he'd pulled and rolled four different kegs and casks from the surf, two of which had sloshed in a promising way. From the brands, the contents were more likely wine or brandy than the water he'd prefer, but as long as it was wet and not gone off with seawater, he'd be thankful.

He bent over and kissed the bridge of Ananiah's nose. Already her fair skin was bright pink; if she didn't get out of the sun soon she'd be burned to blisters by nightfall. "Now you take yourself back into the shade by the rocks, while I see what the tide's brought us."

"No, Sam, I won't!" She rose swiftly, the new braid swinging between her shoulder blades. "I can search the beach every bit as well as you."

"Nay, lass, I can't allow it." From where he sat, she was worse than naked, the tattered silk provocatively revealing more of her long legs than it hid, and he climbed quickly to his feet before he could be distracted. "You've suffered enough. You should rest. You're not accustomed to this kind of sun. This isn't Rhode Island, you know."

"It was just as hot on Martinique," she declared stubbornly. "Sam, I'm not some dainty bit of porcelain to be locked away in a cabinet. If my great-great-grandmother could fight off a war party of Iroquois braves all by herself, then I can certainly sort through broken crates."

He frowned and shook his head. With a faint sheen of perspiration on her cheekbones and forehead and wisps of pale hair curling from the braid, he thought she looked exactly like a fragile porcelain figure. The last thing he wanted was her taken ill with sunstroke.

Ananiah lifted her chin higher. "You can't stop me, you know. Unless you mean to tie me to those rocks yourself, then I'm going to help."

"Like you helped me with that French frigate?"

"Oh, Sam," she said wistfully. "That all seems a long time ago, doesn't it? If the French had taken the *Truelove,* we might all have been better off."

"More likely they went down with all hands in the same blow. I never did see a Frenchman who could hold his wits together in a stiff wind." His expression softened and he smiled crookedly. "It's done now, lass, and we can't change anything that's gone before us. But next time, mind you tell me first before you set yourself to help me. And another thing..."

He reached down and ripped off the trailing torn panel of her gown, and she yelped in surprise. "I know it was hardly decent, Sam," she began indignantly, "but since I have no other—"

"Oh, hush now." He tied knots in the corners of the silk piece and twisted the edges to make an impromptu hat. He plunked the hat on her head, eyeing her critically as he tugged it forward to shade her face. "If you're so bound to play the wrecker with me, then at least I want you outfitted for it. And fetch your shawl, too. You'll be hot as blazes, I know, but I don't want you getting sunburned."

She tried to look up to see the hat, and couldn't resist adjusting the angle. "Shall I set a new fashion, Sam?" she asked ingenuously. *"Capote à le naufrage, Monsieur le Capitaine?"*

He grimaced. "No more French prattle, Ananiah. You're trial enough in American."

Finally the bung on the hogshead gave way beneath Sam's determined hammering, the oak piece cracking in two and falling back into the barrel. Carefully Sam tipped the hogshead forward far enough to pour some of the contents into his hand, and Ananiah leaned eagerly across his arm. But as the purplish red liquid spilled into his hand, she jerked back, gagging from the sour smell that came from the barrel.

Sam swore with disgust and shook his hand clean. "That's the last of them, lass, and not any fit to drink." Ringed around them on the beach were the other casks he'd found: one had held ship's biscuit, still edible once they found something to drink with it, but the other two had leaked so badly that their contents were mostly seawater. "Yet foul as this is, we may be desperate enough to try it for lack of anything better.''

Ananiah shook her head. Her mouth felt as dry as the sand around her, but the stench of the sour wine was still too strong to consider stomaching. ''I don't think I could, Sam.''

''Let's hope we don't have to.'' He'd heard stories from other sailors of castaways so parched they'd drink their own urine or, worse yet, cannabalize the bodies of dead companions, and he prayed she wouldn't learn how bad things could become. ''We might still find something before the tide turns.''

Ananiah nodded, too weary to speak, and headed back out to the flats left by the receding tide. Along with Sam, she had already pulled enough driftwood clear of the waterline to fashion a crude roof among the rocks for them to sleep beneath, and he was carefully collecting old spars, timbers, and bits of cordage in hopes of building some sort of boat or raft. But none of it would matter unless they found water.

The sand was damp and hot beneath her bare feet, and beneath the late-afternoon sun the horizon splintered into bright, shimmering mirages. She was lightheaded from thirst and exhaustion, and she didn't see the oak rim buried in the sand until she tripped over it. Sprawled facedown, she borrowed one of Sam's oaths as she sat up and glared back at whatever had caught her foot. Then, slowly, she realized what it was.

''Sam!'' she shouted as she began to scoop away the sand with both hands. She uncovered the brand of the His Majesty's Navy, and dug faster. ''I found another barrel!''

Not just any barrel, as Sam was quick to point out, but a pipe, and inside it was one hundred and forty-six gallons of English ale, as pure as if it had just come from the brewery. More than enough to keep them from perishing, enough to keep them alive for weeks. Though Sam was careful to measure out a frugal allowance, they gulped their first swallows in honor of His Majesty King George the III, and his naval victualing yard at Portsmouth.

Later that night, they lay together on the beach, Ananiah's head pillowed on Sam's shoulder. The sky was full of stars, stars in the same constellations Ananiah had studied with her father on their roof as a child long ago in Providence. She sighed and burrowed closer beneath Sam's arm. Providence and Rhode Island might have belonged to another world compared to the one she found herself in now.

"Is drowning considered a bad way to die?" she asked softly.

Sam snorted. "You tell me, angel. You came precious close to doing just that last night." His arm tightened protectively around her, and his voice softened. "Are you thinking of Jeremy and Letty and the rest?"

"How could I not?" she said sadly. "It doesn't seem fair."

"Nay, but then little in this life is. If the world were fair, you and I would be lying cozy in a feather bed in the best room in the best inn on the road from Bristol to London." He sighed heavily. "I can't help thinking on them in the *Truelove,* too. I only hope they went quick, and that they're in a better place now. Excepting Howard, of course, may the devil take him straight away for what he did to you."

"To me?" Ananiah propped herself up on one arm. "I know you think he was bent on harming me, but I don't—"

"He pushed you overboard, Ananiah," he said bluntly. "I saw him from the helm. Knocked you over knowing you'd never have a chance, and I'll warrant he's the one that tossed you down into the hold as well."

"But why, Sam?" she asked plaintively. "I scarcely knew the man."

"I don't know, love, and now we likely never will." He reached up gently to stroke her cheek, and tried to smile. He loved her so much, and yet again and again he'd come so close to losing her.

"Sam?"

His answer came as a wordless rumble deep in his chest that she felt beneath her palm.

"Sam," she said again, her voice scarcely more than a whisper. "You don't believe my father's still alive, either, do you?"

"Oh, Ananiah," he said sorrowfully, and she laid her fingers across his lips before he could say more.

"You believe I'm on a fool's errand after a dead man, but you've never told me so. You've never tried to stop me, and I think for that I love you most of all."

The poignancy in her voice tore at his heart. Dead or alive, that wicked old man didn't deserve a daughter like this one, any more than he himself deserved her for a lover.

"Look at you, Miss Snow," he said, striving to lighten her mood. "What would your father say of you now, eh? Tippling ale in your shift with a raggedy castaway sailor-man. Did you ever believe you'd fall so low?"

Ananiah smiled. "Oh, no, Sam," she said softly as she lowered her lips to his. "I never dreamed I'd rise so high."

# Chapter Fourteen

"From these cliffs, I warrant that we're south of Tangier, closer to Mogador," said Sam the next morning as he scratched a crude map of the coast into the sand. They sat side by side in the shade of their makeshift hut, the hot sun filtering through the driftwood. "How much closer I can't say. I cleared Cape Verde once, when I was scarce more than a boy, but the captain was right cautious, and we never did hail this shore. But then, old Captain Norwich was a wiser man than another Salem shipmaster I could name, eh?"

He hurried on before she could say something meant to ease his guilt. Longing for the comfort he didn't deserve, he'd intentionally said that bit about the wiser man knowing she'd defend him, then perversely punished himself by not letting her speak.

Ananiah bit her lip, frowning at the curving coastline in the sand as she pretended not to know what he was doing. There had been an oddly euphoric quality to yesterday, a shared joy in simply being alive, but this morning Sam was all grim seriousness, and she knew nothing she might say would help his temper.

"Couldn't we make some sort of boat or raft and travel by the water?" she suggested warily. "I can't quite imagine a sailor like yourself walking when he might float.''

"You're forgetting that I'm a sailor without a damned cockleshell left to my name, Ananiah," he said sharply. If she'd meant it as a jest, then she'd sorely misjudged his humor, and his pride with it.

"What I haven't forgotten is that none of our misfortune is your fault," she snapped with an edginess that matched his own, "something that you'd do well to remember, too. I'm sorry if my question strikes you as foolish, but I would appreciate a civil answer from you in response."

He scowled at her, surprised she'd spoken up. Stranded on a desert shore, most ladies would have wept and bemoaned their fate. But the worse Ananiah's lot seemed to be, the stronger she became. Maybe there was some of that staunch old Indian-fighter blood in her after all.

Seeing her with her pale eyes bright with challenge and her sunburned cheeks flushed deeper, he hoped there was. He had always liked her fragility, how she needed his protection, but to his own surprise, he liked her this way, too, liked the spirit that would fight him back. Not many others had ever dared.

His scowl softened as he studied her. She looked at once very determined and very young with her peeling pink nose. Maybe she'd been this feisty before she married Étienne de Gramont and had the spirit beaten from her young body. As far as he knew, the nightmare of her husband's memory hadn't plagued her once since the wreck—the one good thing might have come from losing the *Truelove*. Nay, he amended, not one, but two. He'd told Ananiah he loved her, and, miraculously, she'd said she loved him back.

He brushed his fingertips along her cheek. "Ah, you're right, love," he admitted grudgingly. "You do merit an answer."

Her eyebrows rose questioningly. This was more of an apology than she'd ever heard from him before or ever expected, but she was wise enough to let it pass without comment.

"There's a wicked undertow beyond those rocks that would grab any raft or boat we could build and suck us below in an instant," he continued gruffly. "I've been shipwrecked once, and I've no mind to repeat the process. It's a blessed miracle we came ashore safe as we did."

She nodded, and with her finger she traced along the map marked in the sand. "Is Mogador such a grand city?"

"It don't matter if it is or not. It's got a harbor, meaning vessels to take us out of this godforsaken land, and an American consul—a Baltimore man, I recall—to book us passage."

Ananiah nodded. She knew from her father that consuls were fine, useful men to come across in foreign lands. "How far is it?"

"Could be ten miles, could be a hundred. But I warrant somewhere up top those cliffs there's bound to be a village or town before that, someplace with water and horses. All we'll have to do is find a passage up the side."

Ananiah gazed thoughtfully up at the cliffs behind them. The cliffs were sheer gray stone, splintered and crumbling like shale in places where the ocean had worn at it, and at their highest point they rose perhaps two hundred feet from the beach. No garden wall, this. To climb so high, with such precarious footing—even imagining it made her heart pound. But

for him she would try. If he believed she could do it,
then she would.

"Let's be off then, Sam." She briskly dusted the
sand from her knees as she rose, wanting to be on her
way before her resolve faded. "We can leave this
hour."

"Hold now, lass, it's not that simple." He caught
her arm and gently pulled her back down beside him.
"I've no idea how many days' journey this will take.
We'll only be able to take as much of the ale and bread
as we can carry, and pray it will be enough, or that
we'll find a spring or well along the way."

He looked down at her bare feet, slim and smooth
from wearing kidskin slippers, and he shook his head.
"I wish to God you had a decent pair of shoes."

"I don't see you sprouting little goats' hooves
yourself, Sam Colburn," she said, self-consciously
tucking her own feet beneath her tattered shift. It
suddenly mattered intensely to her that she prove herself to him. "But I swear I won't complain, and I
won't hold you back. You'll see."

"We'll stay here another two days," he said firmly.
He didn't understand why she was so eager to leave
now, and he almost considered explaining more about
what they might have to endure. Not that they had
much choice: if they stayed where they were, they'd
likely die of starvation or dehydration when their
meager scavenged rations were gone. "I want you to
rest and drink your fill while you can, mind?"

She looked up at him through her lashes, her eyes
narrowed suspiciously. "And what about you? What
will you be doing?"

"Oh, hell, Ananiah, have it your way!" He groaned
with exasperation, and with one arm around her waist,
he neatly flipped her onto her back. "We'll stay here

another two days so *I* can rest. And that's an end to it."

They set out early in the gray morning, before the sun had risen and while the air was still almost chilly on Ananiah's bare arms and legs. She had filled their small collection of scavenged bottles with the ale, stopping the tops with more scraps torn from her gown, and Sam had knotted little slings from bits of line and cordage to hold each bottle. He had planned to tie them all from a rope over his shoulder, but Ananiah had argued that the more liquid they could carry the better, and insisted on bearing her share as well, four bottles dangling from a rough cord. Though the weight of the filled glass swung heavily against her back and hip as she walked, she was proud to be useful.

But by late afternoon the rough hemp had worn her shoulder raw, and no matter how many times she refolded her ragged shawl to serve as a pad, she still felt the rope cutting into her flesh. It seemed they'd been trudging the same glittering sand for years, not hours, as they followed the jagged coastline. Each time they rounded another long rocky point, they'd look expectantly upwards, to the cliffs ahead, but they had yet to find any sort of passage or break in the forbidding walls of stone.

She was swaying from fatigue by the time Sam decided they'd halt for the night, and she sank down onto the sand where they'd stopped, too exhausted to travel a step farther than she must. With a whimper of pain that she tried to swallow, she eased the rope with the bottles from her shoulder. When Sam pulled her back against his chest, she was too weary to move.

Carefully Sam drew away the shawl, noting how she stiffened as the soft, worn fabric slipped across her shoulder. Then he saw the angry raw blisters beside the gold chain of her necklace, and he swore under his breath.

"For God's sake, Ananiah, why didn't you tell me?" he demanded, his brows drawn together with concern.

"I swore to you that I wouldn't complain, and I didn't." She shifted away from his displeasure, trying to shield her shoulder with her hand. "It's not that bad, Sam. I'll be fine in the morning. Truly, it doesn't hurt."

"I don't believe you," he said flatly. "In heat like this I've seen a scratch go putrid in three hours."

Without hesitating, he unplugged one of the bottles that she had carried and splashed the precious ale onto her shoulder. She gasped and squeezed her eyes shut as the alcohol spilled into the open blisters, but she didn't cry out, and his estimation of her rose another notch. When he was done, he kissed her gently by way of apology, and she opened her eyes and smiled weakly.

He noted how she lightly touched the locket around her neck for comfort, the sapphires winking in the setting sun. Sam wondered cynically where her dead mother's protection was now. Though, come to think on it, he wasn't doing much of a job of it, either.

On the third afternoon, they found the break in the cliff that they'd been searching for. Instead of a single sheer face, the rock zigzagged in a pattern of ledges and crevices.

"Are you still game, lass?" Sam asked as they stood at the base of the rocks. Slung across his broad back were the last two bottles of warm, flat ale, and wrapped in his coat were the final bits of dry biscuit.

Ananiah craned her head back to look upwards. From the waterline, the cliffs had seemed surmountable, the ledges almost like carved stairs. But this close, she could see how far apart the ledges really were, and her confidence faltered again.

She lowered her chin, and her gaze met Sam's, his eyes intensely blue above the dark beard. But the beard couldn't hide how hollowed his cheeks had become, and at night, when they lay together, she now could feel his ribs beneath the flat planes of muscle. There had been no more barrels of food or drink to be found in the surf, and the beaches they'd crossed had been as barren as the one they'd first been cast upon. She'd become so accustomed to hunger and thirst and exhaustion that it frightened her. She tried to smile at Sam as her throat tightened. They were very close to the end of everything, and she didn't want to lose him like this.

Wordlessly she threaded her fingers into his, and together they began the long climb to the top.

"Don't look down!" Sam ordered quickly as he grabbed Ananiah back from the edge. They had stopped to rest here, where the ledge of rock was wide enough to sit, and for the first time she had realized how high they'd climbed, over a hundred feet from the beach. Heights didn't bother Sam, not after twenty years of climbing through rigging, but he'd seen how her eyes had widened and her face had paled beneath her sunburn as she leaned unsteadily forward. Swiftly he shoved her back against the warm wall of stone, holding his arm protectively over her chest, and felt her shudder.

"I didn't know we were so high," she said with a shaky, nervous laugh. He had warned her not to look, and she felt foolish for having done it anyway. "It would be so easy to fall, wouldn't it?"

"It's as easy to fall from three feet as from thirty," said Sam, "or as difficult, if you want to be cheerful about it. You're more'n steady enough. I'll make a topman from you yet."

Ananiah took the compliment along with the bottle. The air was hot and still, her shift was pasted damply to her body, and below them the ocean stretched out endlessly beneath the glittering sun. Climbing the rocks barefoot was painfully different from walking across sand, and her feet were sore and bruised from loose stones. She swallowed only enough of the warm, sour-tasting ale to moisten her mouth, returned the bottle to Sam, and tipped her head back against the rock. Her fingers brushed against something small and dry on the ledge beside her, and she started.

Frowning, again Sam steadied her. "Here now, lass, no more hopping about—"

"No, look, Sam, *look!*" Excitedly she held out to him three dried, empty locust shells, the tracery of the brittle, folded wings still impossibly delicate. "They had to come from somewhere, somewhere with trees and water and fruit and— Oh, Sam, I know we're almost there!"

She thought of the desert villages she'd read about in the Bible, built around oases. She could easily imagine wells and fountains surrounded by nodding palm trees, and there would be all the water they could wish to drink, cool, fresh water, and more water to wash away the salt and sand that caked her skin. Mysterious gentlemen and ladies in long robes would greet them in the old-fashioned English of the Old Testament, and offer them oranges and dates to eat before they gave them horses to ride to the house of the American consul. And she and Sam were almost there.

The sun was a red circle of fire low over the ocean by the time Sam boosted her up over the final edge of the cliff. She grabbed her last handhold and pulled herself up, eager for her first glimpse of the village that would welcome them.

Instead, there was nothing.

As far as she could see, in every direction, the sand was smooth and unmarked and washed bloodred from the setting sun. No village, no people, no welcome to carry them to Mogador.

No water, no food.

No hope.

As he put his arms around her, Sam swore with a bitterness Ananiah understood. She said nothing; there seemed nothing left to say. Long after dark they still sat together in each other's arms on the edge of the cliff, staring silently at the emptiness that would be their fate.

At last Ananiah must have fallen asleep, because she woke. Sam was still curled around her, his arm and one leg possessively thrown across her body, his breath warm and even on her shoulder as he slept. The sky overhead was a deep, velvety blue, pricked by a thousand stars and the silver crescent of a new moon. Disoriented by sleep, she moved closer into Sam's body and wondered for a long, drowsy moment at how distant the drumming of the surf had become. Then she remembered, and with a sigh she turned over to look again at the bleak emptiness of the desert.

Yet now the desert wasn't empty. Far, far across the hills of sand she saw a bright flicker, the unmistakable light of a fire in the darkness. She shook Sam's shoulder, and immediately he jerked awake beneath her hand, instantly alert.

But as she opened her mouth to tell him what she'd seen, the night was filled with a chorus of wild screams and shrieks. Moving from instinct, Sam had barely enough time to roll Ananiah beneath him to shield her before the pack of men raced over the nearest dune and were upon them. Their robes were ghostly in the moonlight, and their dark-skinned faces were obscured in the dark. In those seconds, all Sam saw were the scimitars, shining as bright and sure as death, that swept down towards his head, and all he thought of was Ananiah, and how now she'd never know how much he loved her.

Trapped beneath Sam, Ananiah struggled to see what was happening. She heard the footsteps around her, but saw only a crowd of dark bare feet kicking wildly in the sand as the wild shrieks and war cries rose. Then Sam was torn, twisting and fighting, away from her just as she felt herself dragged and lifted to her feet. She screamed Sam's name and tried to break free, but a dozen hands on her arms and legs held her fast.

Where was he? she thought frantically as she struggled to turn, why didn't he answer her? Please God they hadn't killed him already!

A tall man with a long, curling beard came to stand before her, and the others held her tighter and pushed her forward. The tall man took her chin in his hand and forced her head up, leaving her throat exposed. She caught the flash of the scimitar's blade as it arced through the air towards her, and with a terrified whimper she closed her eyes and waited for the blade to slice into her throat.

She felt the edge against her skin, the steel cold in the warm air, felt the tip catch her necklace and cut effortlessly through the gold chain. The locket dropped neatly into the tall man's open hand, and with a little shove of contempt he released her chin. He smiled at her, saying guttural words she didn't understand. With the sword's blade he lifted her braid from her shoulder. Deftly he severed the length of rope that held the end, and roughly raked his fingers through her hair until it floated free about her shoulders. The other men reached out to touch her hair, sliding it between their fingers as they nodded and smiled, and to Ananiah their smiles were far worse than the shrieks had been. Fear gave her strength, and when the tall man reached forward again to touch her, she broke free and stumbled backwards, calling Sam's name wildly. Dear God, where was he?

When the men caught her again, their hands were not as gentle, and they forced her to her knees before the tall man. They pulled her hands back behind her waist, binding her wrists together with rough cords as the tall man twisted his fingers in her hair and yanked her head back, compelling her to look up at him. He smiled, his teeth large and yellow against his black beard, and Ananiah's heart twisted with remembered fear.

She had never seen the Arab before this night, but the cruelty in his eyes, the pleasure he so clearly took in the pain he brought her, the way the cords on her wrists twisted into the skin of her wrists—all this she had learned too well from Étienne. The sand she knelt upon became the parquet floor at Beau Coteau, and the sharp, high cheekbones of the Arab's face blurred into her husband's familiar expression of bored disdain.

*"Je vous demande pardon, monseigneur,"* she begged, the way Étienne preferred, her voice shaking. She would suffer less if she obeyed. *"Je vous demande miséricorde, mon maître!"*

From where they held him, Sam heard the French words of her pleading and saw that her eyes were blank with terror. God in heaven, these bastards would make her mad without even knowing what they'd done. She needed him, needed him now. Heedless of the scimitars held to his chest, Sam wrenched free and pulled the gag from his mouth, and in a dozen steps he had Ananiah in his arms.

*"Esposa,"* Sam said loudly. *"Mi esposa."* In the handful of words their captors had spoken, he'd heard a similarity between their speech and Spanish. It was a gamble that they'd understand him in return, a terrible gamble. He'd find no help from Ananiah; she was trembling in his arms, her back stiff against his chest, still lost in whatever nightmare Étienne had called her into again.

The men hung back uncertainly, realizing he wouldn't let them take her from him again, and looked to the tall man for guidance.

"Wife," Sam repeated in English. To make his possession clearer still, he moved one hand beneath her breast, cradling the soft flesh, and the other low on her belly, his fingers spread with an intimacy that would cross any language. "The woman's my wife, damn your black souls, and I won't let you have her."

The tall man's expression darkened. Shouting threats at Sam, he circled his scimitar through the air overhead, and then abruptly thrust it back into his sash and turned his back. The other men quickly swarmed around Sam and Ananiah, prodding at them to hasten, and for once Sam allowed himself to be led. They were still prisoners, but he was certain now that only alive would they have any value to the Arabs.

They were herded to the camp with the fire Ananiah had seen, and given a warm mixture of camel's milk and brackish water to drink. Sam gulped it gratefully, thinking wryly how under other circumstances he wouldn't have touched the foul brew. He forced Ananiah to drink, and as she did he saw her eyes clear and then grow wary. He was glad she'd come back to him. He hadn't been sure she would, for wherever it was she retreated to within herself could be no worse than where they were now.

Because it was still night, they were ordered to lie down on the sand to rest. No one tried to separate them again, but Sam was well aware of the two guards standing watch.

"What will they do to us?" whispered Ananiah, shivering. The Arabs had taken her shawl and Sam's coat and shirt, and she clung to Sam as much for warmth in the chilly night as for comfort.

"Nothing, I hope," Sam said with forced lightness as he stroked her hair. The Arab men had never seen pale gold hair like hers, and with a heavy heart he knew it would raise her price in the slave markets. European and American women were rarities, especially ones as young and lovely as Ananiah. If she was lucky, she'd be bought by some fat merchant as a prized second wife; if she wasn't, she'd become the most expensive novelty in a Tangier brothel. Either would kill her. But he wouldn't let that happen to her, not his Ananiah. Somehow he would save her, save them both. "We're worthless to them if we die."

"We'll be ransomed, then?" she asked, with an eager hope he found unbearable. "I've heard my father speak of New England crews and captains held by the bey in Tunis because we have no treaties with the Barbary states. But once their ransoms were paid, they were free to leave. Is that the case here, as well?"

He nodded, unwilling to explain the other, more likely possibilities in her case.

"We will have to trust in Mr. Morrow to send our ransoms. But oh, Lord, Sam, we could be here for months." She sighed and curled her fingers into his. "What did you say to the others when you held me?"

"I didn't think you noticed."

"I think you saved my life again," she said softly. "How could I not notice that?"

His fingers tightened around hers. "I was a sight more charitable to you with these rogues than you were with me before the Frenchmen," he said gruffly. "I told them you were my wife."

"Oh, Sam...." How she wished it could be true!

"Listen to me, sweetheart." He rose up on one elbow so that he could see her upturned face in the moonlight, and behind them he heard the guard bark a warning. "I love you more than I could ever begin to tell you, and I can't consider living the rest of my life without you in it. I'm not easy with words, Ananiah, but I swear that's God's own truth."

"Sam—"

"Nay, hear me out. I want you to be my wife. We belong together, and I won't hear you say otherwise, because you know it same as I do. Jesus, Ananiah, think of the fine rascally children we'll have together!" He kissed her gently, touched by the tears he saw in her eyes. "Marry me, Ananiah Snow. When this is all over, love, promise me you'll be my wife."

She touched her fingers to his lips, wishing somehow she could make him take back the words he'd spoken. Those words had broken her heart, and now she'd have to do the same to him. "I love you so much, Sam," she said brokenly, "but I can't marry you."

"Why the devil not?" He stared at her, refusing to believe her. "Is it the money? That you're rich, and now, with the *Truelove* lost, I've nothing?"

"No!" she cried out, loud enough to rouse the guard again. "No, Sam, never that! Likely you won't believe it, but these last days with you on the beach have been happier than all the years in my father's great house! I love you so much—"

"Then why the hell won't you say yes?"

"Because you deserve someone better!"

"Damnation, Ananiah, don't begin that nonsense again! I love you, and I want to marry you, and nothing that Étienne de Gramont did or said will ever change that!"

She closed her eyes as the first tear slid down her cheek, and with bittersweet pleasure let herself imagine the life he wanted for them: the comfortable house in Salem, the suppers with Elihu and Sally Greene, and, most of all, the fine rascally children that would bear his name, sons that would have their father's broad shoulders and daughters blessed with his blue-gray eyes.

She wept for Sam and she wept for herself, and for the future they'd never be able to share. "I can't, Sam, I swear I can't," she whispered through her tears. "Not even you can change the past."

Sam held her until her sobs became no more than little hiccups in her sleep and the first gray of dawn showed over the sand, and not once in that time did he believe she'd really refused him.

# Chapter Fifteen

Once again Ananiah felt herself slipping forward off the padded wooden saddle, and she grabbed reflexively at the camel's hump to keep from falling. The sun was too hot, and the rhythmic, rolling gait of the camel was like a giant cradle rocking her to sleep. She yawned and stretched her shoulders, struggling to shake off the drowsiness. If she fell, the whole procession of fifteen camels and ten men would be forced to stop while she remounted and the camel's heavy packs readjusted. Hamet would not be pleased.

He was her master, and he rode ahead of her as he had these last five days, his long back curved above his camel's hump. Beside his outstretched legs she could see the butt of his musket, and outlined beneath his tunic was the curve of his scimitar's blade.

Since the first night, he had not tried to hurt her again, but he had made it clear in every other way that she was his property, and valuable property at that. She had been given a special salve for the open blisters on her shoulder and the cuts on her feet from climbing the cliffs. The ties had been removed from her wrists, and she was free to walk wherever she chose when they stopped to rest and water the camels. Her shawl had been returned to her to shield her head and shoulders from the sun, and each evening she was given all the water and camel's milk she wished, and handfuls of a dry root that tasted like ground walnuts.

When the tents were raised with nightfall, Hamet pointedly offered her a corner of his, but she had chosen instead to sleep outside beside Sam, and, surprisingly, Hamet had let her. Curled together beneath the endless sky, they had said little, but only in Sam's arms did Ananiah feel safe.

She twisted around in the saddle, craning her neck to see Sam two camels behind hers. She could just make out the top of his head; his dark hair, with its chestnut streaks, so different from that of the Arabs. With a sigh, she turned around, wishing it were night and she were with him again. Though they were permitted to sleep side by side, Hamet forbade them any contact during the day, and Sam's master had agreed.

Sam belonged to a short, wizened man named Seid; his two sons had been the first to touch Sam, and so by their laws had claimed him as their own. But Ananiah, as the prize, had gone without question to Hamet.

As if he had heard her thoughts, Hamet turned now to look at her, coldly, contemptuously, and with her head high she returned his stare. His head and shoulders were swathed in a stained cotton headdress that he wore as regally as a crown, his imperious manner worthy of any king. Inwardly she shivered beneath his gaze, shamed by how openly he regarded her bare legs, outstretched across the camel's saddle.

He twitched the single cord attached to his camel's left nostril, and with a wheezing snort of protest the animal wheeled clumsily about, then stopped. More willingly Ananiah's camel halted as well. Hamet spoke to her sharply in words she didn't understand, his voice raised as if she were deaf, and then urged his camel back down the line.

Shading her eyes, Ananiah judged the angle of the sun. It was still morning, not quite noon, and too early for the customary midday rest in their travel. Nor was there any sign of the well or other watering place that usually marked their breaks. Curious, she leaned back to look where Hamet had ridden.

He was speaking to Seid and his two sons, his hands slicing angrily through the air while the older man shook his head in vehement denial. Ananiah shifted to the left on the saddle so that she could see Sam.

Sitting high on his camel, he dwarfed the smaller men around him. His bare arms and chest were burned almost as dark as an Arab's. With good reason, Seid didn't trust him, and each morning Sam's wrists were lashed to the wooden pommel and his feet tied around the animal's chest, forcing him awkwardly forward on the uncomfortable saddle. It hurt Ananiah to see him like this, and she thought for the thousandth time of the consul in Mogador who would set them free.

Sam wearily rolled his shoulders and tossed his hair back from his eyes. Her eyes met his and for her sake he consciously shrugged off the weariness. He smiled, his grin white and boyish against the dark beard he'd grown, and she forgot Hamet and the blinding sun and the ache in her legs from the saddle, forgot everything except Sam. She would never be the wife he wanted, but still she loved him with all her heart.

Seid's voice rose shrilly as he argued with Hamet, and Ananiah looked back just as Seid's younger son slipped his hand onto the hilt of his scimitar. Hamet saw it, too, and at once his own scimitar was drawn, the sun glancing off the polished blade. No one spoke or moved. The only sound in the hot, still air was the creaking of the camel's packs and the jingling of the bells on their harness.

His gaze unwavering, his scimitar level, Hamet reached into the small woven bag he wore slung on a thong beneath his tunic. Seid held out his open palm, and into it Hamet dropped five small gold coins, counting them as they fell. Still Seid waited, and with a grunt Hamet added Ananiah's sapphire locket to the coins. Immediately Seid's gnarled fingers closed shut, and without a word he turned his camel's head to the north, away from the others. His sons followed, each leading another camel packed heavily with goods they'd scavenged from the coast. Irritably Seid grabbed the lead on Sam's camel and tugged the animal along after him as Hamet returned to the front of the column.

"No, Hamet, wait!" cried Ananiah as soon as she realized what was happening. "Where are they going? Oh, please, no, you can't let them take him away! My God, you cannot do this!"

Hamet coldly ignored her, his expression immovable. Frantically Ananiah pulled on the single rein, trying to force her camel to turn, but the animal ignored her, too, plodding steadfastly after Hamet's.

"Sam, wait for me!" She couldn't let him go without her. If he disappeared now, she knew, she *knew,* she'd never see him again. Desperate, she twisted around the side of the camel's hump, clinging to the trailing blankets that padded the saddle as she tried to lower herself the eight feet to the ground. Startled by the shifting weight, the camel bellowed and lurched to one side, and Ananiah tumbled to the sand, barely rolling free of the camel's legs. She scrambled to her feet and rushed towards Sam, shouting his name, her unbraided hair streaming out behind her.

As she ran, she saw him snap the wooden pommel of the saddle and swing his bound hands into Seid's chest, and with a startled gasp the older man toppled backwards from his camel. Sam frantically searched for Ananiah, but saw only her riderless camel.

"Sam, here!" she shouted, her breath short. Running through the sand was like running through heavy snow, her feet sinking deep with every step. His eyes lit when he found her, and despite the urgency of the moment, she knew what it was to be cherished.

"Ananiah, love, don't let them sell—"

But Sam's warning was lost when the butt of a musket slammed into the back of his head, Seid's son triumphant as Sam pitched forward, his eyes empty as he fell across the camel's neck. One more time Ananiah screamed his name, and then the hands were around her waist, catching her, holding her back, keeping her away from him, and she struggled until something hard struck her head and the same darkness that had claimed Sam swallowed her as well.

"It dinna serve you well to fight, my wee lady," said the woman sadly, the burr of Scotland thick in her speech. "Ye displeased your master most dreadful."

Slowly Ananiah opened her eyes. Above the rough mat on which she lay, the top of the tent fluttered slightly in the breezes that came with nightfall. Outside the tent she heard the rise and fall of the men's guttural voices as they talked among themselves, heard a woman's laugh and an infant's sleepy wail, and the soft jingling of silver bells as the camels foraged for dry moss and tested the lengths of their tethers. The sides of the tent were open, and the smoky scent of roasting meat hung in the air.

The woman leaned over her, her dark, kohl-rimmed eyes troubled. She gently rested a hand on Ananiah's arm to restrain her. "Ye mus' rest now," she ordered softly. "Ye must not risk Hamet's wrath agin."

"You speak English?" Confused, Ananiah stared at the woman. With her tawny skin and black hair, her long robes, there was little doubt that she was an Arab, no matter how she spoke.

"My name is Ezimah." The woman patted Ananiah's arm with satisfaction and sat back on her heels. "When I was but a lass, before Hamet bought me, I was slave to th' household of a Scottish merchant in Tangier. But though I served him true in ev'ry way and learned his speech to please him, he dinna take me back wit' him to his Edinburgh," she said sadly. "Ye have his look. Might ye know of him? Master Henry Cronan?"

"I'm from Providence, in New England, not Scotland," answered Ananiah warily. She must have been brought to some town or village, for there had been no women among the Arabs who had captured her and Sam. "Where are we now?"

Ezimah ignored her question, her gaze shifting self-consciously away from Ananiah's. "Ah, then ye be an American, like the others."

"The others? Is Captain Colburn here, too, a tall, handsome man with blue eyes?"

Ezimah's brow furrowed, and she lowered her chin and clicked her tongue. "Nay, nay, lady, that one went north to Seid's village. Hamet dinna want a lion like him in our tents." Her chin still ducked, she glanced up at Ananiah uncertainly. "Hamet says he was your husband."

"He was—is—very dear to me," said Ananiah softly, doubting she'd ever see Sam again.

"He be of no matter to ye any longer, lady," said Ezimah firmly. "Ye must abide by Hamet's wishes now, for he be your master until he sells ye to another."

"Sells me!" repeated Ananiah, stunned. "I'm a free American, and not his to sell! In my country my father is a wealthy man. If he takes me to a city, I'll arrange to have whatever ransom paid he wishes."

Ezimah shook her head. "Hamet has taken ye, and ye be his. Who ye were in your land matters not. Ye be fair an' young, an' your hair would tempt a sultan. Hamet will gain more from selling ye than any ransom."

Suddenly Ananiah recalled the last words Sam had tried to speak to her, about not letting them sell something. Even as she'd spoken happily about the ransoms, he had known the truth. As a woman, a slave, she would never leave this country again. She'd never find her father or return to her home. Worst of all, she'd never again see Sam, and he'd known it, too. No wonder he'd fought so desperately to stay by her side. Her throat tightened, and she bowed her head, overwhelmed by her sense of powerlessness and loss.

"Hamet must know, lady," Ezimah was asking. "Do ye carry within ye the sweet fruit of ye husband's seed? A man such as that one would sire fine sons, and ye price would be higher if ye were carryin' his child."

Ananiah closed her eyes, too aware of the bitter irony of Ezimah's question.

"There's no child," she said, her voice no more than a hoarse whisper.

"But so soon you canna know for certain. A man like that one—"

"No," said Ananiah. "There is no child."

*Patience.* More than anything else, that was what Sam needed if he wanted to survive, if he wanted to save Ananiah. Patience. Hell, he'd never been patient a single day in his whole life, and now his life depended on it.

The first day had been the worst, strapped to the camel like old dunnage, with his head hanging lower than his feet. No wonder he'd come to retching all over the stinking beast's flea-ridden hide. His head had throbbed and his mouth had tasted worse than the camel smelled, and the miserable bastards that thought they owned him hadn't give him one drop of water until they stopped at dusk. If he'd been able to stand when they cut him down, he would have throttled all three of them.

The next day, and the days after that, they made him walk. His wrists were tied together on a long lead, and if he failed to keep pace with the camels, Abdallah, the younger son, would curse and strike him across the back and shoulders with the same heavy stick he used on the camels. Patience, Sam told himself, patience, and he bit back the blasphemies that came to his own lips and accepted the blows and the leash and the taunts.

With patience, he memorized the course they took across the empty desert so that he could retrace their path back to Ananiah. He studied the wells where they stopped for water and the valleys where they made their camps, for these would be his only landmarks when he returned for her. He never doubted he'd come back for her; he only prayed he'd be in time. At night, when exhaustion should have claimed him, he saw her running across the sand towards him, her hair bleached to the palest gold, her arms outstretched and her face so full of love that the memory became a kind of torture to him. Damnation, how could he be patient when wicked bastards like Hamet had his Ananiah?

Because patience was all he had on his side.

Patience would make his captors careless. Already they trusted too much to their numbers, as if an old man and two young fools were enough to stop Sam. They let him see the strange plunder they'd found along the coast, washed ashore from other ships as unlucky as the *Truelove:* French wine their faith prohibited them from drinking but not from selling, a crate of lace-trimmed handkerchiefs, a rusted axe and three knives, and some poor lost captain's engraved presentation sword. And the small carved box whose saltwater-split sides bulged with Spanish-milled *dollares,* heavy silver coins with fluted edges that Seid counted out gleefully on the sand in the moonlight. Sam watched Seid pack away the box and the knives. When the time came, he would need both.

He pretended not to understand their commands, pretended the blow had dulled his wits, and soon they didn't bother to tie his ankles at night. Even Abdallah lost interest in the sport of goading him. To them he'd become as much a beast as the camels, though of less use. They now spoke freely before him, and he learned that Mogador was their destination. On the night before they reached the city, Abdallah spoke with such salacious enthusiasm of a young dancer he would meet there that Seid cuffed him in disgust and ordered both his sons to sleep.

And then, at last, Sam's patience was rewarded.

* * *

The crude spindle circled more slowly in the air as the wispy hairs tightened into a single thread. Carefully Ananiah drew her fingers along the thread to smooth it, and added more of the carded camels' hair to the end. Out of boredom she'd asked Ezimah to teach her to spin like the other women, and though Ezimah had at first refused, fearing Hamet's reaction, she had finally given Ananiah an old spindle and showed her how to turn the camels' soft belly hair into thread to be woven into tents or clothing. Only Ezimah was permitted to speak to her, but from a distance the other women in the village approved of her industry.

Ananiah knew otherwise. To concentrate on the growing length of thread, to watch the circle of the dangling spindle, this wasn't virtuous industry, it was only the one tiny way she had to keep her sanity.

It was not that she was mistreated. Under Hamet's protection, she was given no responsibilities, and instead sat idle while the others cooked or tended the camels and their children. When the tents were struck each morning, she was never asked to help or to carry anything as the whole village walked to the next night's camp, and new clothing, a long woman's robe, was provided when her old shift finally disintegrated. The choicest bits of roasted kid were offered to her at meals, with fresh camel milk and ground grain that made her feel like a goose being fattened for market. Which, she supposed grimly, was just what she was.

"If he means to sell me," Ananiah asked Ezimah as they sat together in the shade of the tent, "then why does Hamet keep me here?" Trapped in the middle of the desert, she felt as isolated as if she were still at sea. In a city, surrounded by other people, there might be a chance to escape, or a least to communicate with someone who might help her.

"Ye be here because Hamet wishes it, lady. When he believes ye be ready to travel again, he'll take ye." Ezimah's smile was meant to be kind, but Ananiah couldn't share her unquestioning acceptance of Hamet's will. "Ye canna keep thinkin' on that pretty fellow Seid took. He'll forget ye, no mistake, if Seid even let him live. A man can always find hisself another woman."

"Not Captain Colburn," said Ananiah sadly, remembering how many times Sam had risked his own life to save hers. She didn't any more believe he was dead than that he had found another woman. Lost to her, yes, but not dead. He would never be able to find her now, not after Hamet had moved his camp a dozen times in the past three weeks. The wind swept the sand clean each night, even of the tracks of fifty people and thirty camels.

Plainly skeptical of sentimental attachments, Ezimah pressed her thin lips together in disapproval. "Ye should be grateful, lady, that Hamet lets ye grow plump an' comely, so ye be worthy of a wealthy new master," she said sternly. "Hamet means to do th' best for ye he can."

Ananiah kept silent, scowling down at the twisting spindle. Closer to the truth would be that Hamet meant to do the best he could for his own pocketbook. Ezimah couldn't understand why she hated Hamet so much, but then, how could she? She'd been a slave all her life. As Hamet's concubine, all she knew of love were the cold, empty couplings that Ananiah heard each night in the tent they all shared. Ezimah would never know anything like what Ananiah had found with Sam, or what she had lost because of Hamet's greed.

Without bothering to greet either woman, Hamet stalked into the tent, kicking aside Ezimah's ball of thread with deliberate carelessness. Murmuring apologies for her clumsiness, she scurried after it across the sand, while Ananiah glared at Hamet, sprawled indolently across one of the rush mats that served as both beds and chairs.

"You should treat Ezimah better," she said warmly. "It's wrong for her to believe that was her fault, not yours."

She knew that he refused to understand a word she said in English, and so she repeated it as best she could in the Arabic she'd learned, driven to speak by a kind of courage born of fatalism. By separating her from Sam, Hamet had already done the worst he could to her. She had nothing left to lose, and each day she grew less afraid of Hamet.

"If I were Ezimah," she continued, "I'd take one of those sticks you use to poke the poor camels and beat you with it myself."

"Hold your tongue, jackal's bitch!" Abruptly Hamet sat upright, his long beard shaking as he shouted angrily at her, but Ananiah ignored him and calmly returned to her spinning. He'd ignored her often enough when it suited him—it was another way he reminded her of Étienne—but, also like Étienne, he couldn't hurt her any more unless she let him. She remembered what Sam had told her long ago in Newport, that if you could but hide your fears, the world would call you brave. He'd sworn she was no coward then. What, she wondered, would he make of her now?

The hollow calabash used for water crashed to the sand at her feet where Hamet had thrown it. Furious, Hamet yanked away the spindle and thrust the gourd into her hands. She understood his orders readily enough, even without him pointing towards the well on the far side of the clustered tents, near to where the camels were tethered. She'd never before been allowed to wander out of sight of Hamet's tent, and curiosity made it easy for her to obey. With her head held high and the calabash tucked under her arm, she hurried out into the hot sun.

Two other women were standing by the low wall of the well, one with a sleeping baby tucked in a sling across her back. Ananiah smiled, but at once the women ducked their heads and scuttled away. Sorry, yet not surprised, Ananiah sighed as she set the calabash beside the well. Even if Hamet's orders hadn't been clear enough, in the Arabs' eyes she was also an unclean heathen, a Christian, and best avoided. Slowly she lowered the bucket down into the well, smelling the dank, brackish water. As she stared down into the black water, she remembered how the waves had looked from the taffrail of the *Truelove*.

Behind her she heard the camels bellow and scuffle, their little bells jingling wildly. Several men were shouting at one another in anger, their voices growing closer as the men came running, their footsteps deadened by the sand. Ananiah turned with the full bucket in her hand, and an old man with long white hair fell gasping at her feet. His clothing was filthy and tattered—the mark of a slave less favored than she—and his long beard touched the sand as he struggled to regain his breath before his angry master reached him.

His shaking fingers twisted in the fabric of her skirt as he raised himself up. ''Annie, girl,'' he gasped. ''My little Annie!''

The full bucket of water dropped unnoticed from Ananiah's hands, and with a wordless cry of wonder she sank down to embrace her father.

# Chapter Sixteen

"Don't hurt him!" shouted Ananiah in Arabic. "If you hurt him, I'll have Hamet beat you instead!"

The angry man hesitated, his thick stick still raised in his hand. She was a mere woman, a slave, a Christian unbeliever, but Hamet had made it clear enough that she was under his protection. "The worthless creature has disobeyed me! He is mine, and he must be punished for his insolence to his master!"

"He is my father," said Ananiah, "and you won't touch him again."

Gently she helped her father back to his feet, shocked by the change in him. In the months since she had waved farewell to him in Providence, his hair had changed from blond to silver, and the stout, sturdy build that had always tested the buttons on his waistcoats had shrunken away into a bent old man's. But below his bristling white brows, his eyes were the same as she remembered, pale like her own, but with a fierce, angry defiance.

"Beating's too kind by half for that black bastard, Annie," he managed to gasp as he hung onto Ananiah's arm for support. "I'd flail the hide from his rotten carcass and—"

"Hush, father, not now." Ananiah slipped her arm around his back, every rib clearly outlined. His body might be wasted, but his spirit—and his tongue—hadn't diminished a bit. "I'll take you with me where you can rest."

"Giving orders to your own father now, too, are you, girl?" he asked, with as much irritation as he could muster. "There was a time when you hopped when I spoke."

"Times are different, Father. Now come with me." A small crowd of Arabs had gathered at a distance to watch, and the man with the stick still stood before them uncertainly. Ananiah didn't wish to give him any more time to reconsider. "Hamet's tent is on the far side of the camp."

But Hamet himself now came rushing towards them, Ezimah running to keep pace. His tunic billowed around his tall, lean body, and his right hand rested on the hilt of the scimitar at his waist. To her dismay, Ananiah felt her father pull himself upright and let go of the support of her arm. She had a swift, terrible premonition of her father's temper clashing against Hamet's, and of her father dead in an instant by the other's sword.

"Now you let me talk to this filthy rogue, Annie," he said, but with a little shake of her head she stepped in front of him. They were nearly the same height, and she had the advantage of being young and strong.

"Hamet, listen to me!" she called. "I would ask a favor of you!"

"You have no right to ask me the favor of lying at my feet to beg for your life!" Hamet answered furiously. "Infidel whore! I send you for water, and instead you interfere in matters of no concern to you! This worthless old cur is nothing to you!"

He raised his hand to strike her, and fleetingly she feared she'd gone too far. Somehow she forced herself to hold his gaze without flinching, without letting her fear show, and behind her back her father swore. She lifted her chin a fraction higher.

"This man is everything to me," she said, speaking slowly both for effect and to choose her words carefully in the unfamiliar language. "This man is my father."

Hamet scowled in disbelief, looking from Ananiah's face to her father's and back again. Ananiah knew he'd be unable to deny the resemblance. All her life she'd been told how much she favored her father.

"I left my homeland to find him," she continued, stumbling over a few words she didn't know, "and now my search has been rewarded. For the honor I bear my father, Hamet, I ask you to take him from a master who beats him."

"I beat him because he deserves it!" cried the indignant master to Hamet. "He is too old and worthless for any labor, and though he promised me five hundred dollars ransom, all I have from him is the food and water he has eaten!"

Captain Snow shoved past his daughter. "Damn your greedy heathen soul! I've written five letters to George Gill in Providence asking for your blood money, and if he hasn't sent it yet, it's because you're too stupid to make sure my letters get to a Yankee ship!"

Ananiah grabbed his arm and pulled him back. "Father, they'll kill you if you don't stop!" she said in English, and with obvious reluctance he limited himself to a loud, contemptuous growl.

Ananiah turned back to Hamet. "I grant that my father is old and troublesome and worthless for labor, as his master says. But he is valuable to you for his ransom, and I promise to keep him with me and away from mischief until the money comes."

Hamet tugged on his earlobe, considering, and Ananiah offered her final argument.

"If he stays with me, and you are my master—" it was the first time she had called him that "—then it would seem fair that you should claim your share of his ransom."

"It is done." Hamet's open hand swept through the air, quickly silencing the protests of the other man. "But if your father disturbs my peace again, I will slit his throat, and still take his ransom for my trouble."

"Bugger his trouble," muttered Captain Snow in English, and Ananiah swiftly pulled him away from the others before Hamet could make good his threat. Her promise had likely saved her father's life, but he wasn't going to make it an easy one for her to keep.

"So why the devil aren't you home, daughter, snug in Providence where I left you?" John Snow wiped his fingers around the wooden bowl to gather the last bit of the milk and grain and sucked them clean. It was after dark, the first time he'd been left alone with Ananiah, who'd warned him that Ezimah understood English.

Ananiah smiled happily. "I came looking for you, Father. Everyone said I should give you up for dead, but I didn't listen to them." She briefly considered telling him about Sam, then decided there'd be time enough later. Her father was a shrewd man; if she told him even a little about Sam, he'd soon guess the intimacy of their relationship, and he wouldn't like it. "And now I've found you, even though I had to be shipwrecked first."

"It was a damned fool thing to do, Ananiah," he said sharply.

Ananiah's smile faded, and with it her carefully tended hope of pleasing her father. "I thought the English had captured you, and I meant to have them set you free."

"And a half-witted scheme that would have been, too. The English bastards near had me, all right, but they drove us onto the rocks on this infernal coast rather than bring us in decently." In the twilight his pale eyes burned with the bitterness he'd always had towards anything English. "But at least that would have been me alone. Now look what you've done for yourself, rushing off across the ocean like you'd straw for brains. Has Hamet put his filthy hands on you?"

Ananiah shook her head, and he grunted. "Likely he's just saving you for the slave market. You'll end up in some sultan's harem, dancing naked for the heathens, and there won't be a damned thing I'll be able to do to stop it."

Ananiah lowered her chin so that he wouldn't be able to see the tears that filled her eyes. She had pictured their reunion so differently: her father grateful and proud of her initiative as he embraced her amid the elegance of some English lord's chambers, with all the bystanders duly touched by her filial devotion.

"Where is the rest of the *Commerce*'s crew?" she asked, hoping to divert his irritation from her. "Are any of them prisoners here, too?"

"Likely all drowned, the cowardly bastards," he said in disgust. "Took off in the boats against my orders. Aren't any of 'em alive that I've seen, and I wouldn't spend a shilling to ransom them if they are. I've lost enough already, what with the *Commerce* and her cargo."

Ananiah had always heard her father describe himself, and proudly, too, as a hard captain, and here was the proof. But how different this was from the way Sam had grieved for the men lost with the *Truelove!*

He leaned forward across his folded knees. "I'll wager George Gill didn't know what you were about, did he?"

"He followed me to Newport, and tried to make me come back with him," she said. "He said he was going to go to England himself to rescue you."

He grunted approvingly. "I didn't think George would cotton to any of your foolishness, though God knows why he went off to London. I've sent him letters enough telling him where I was, asking him to make the ransom these bandits expect."

"He'd rather keep the money himself," said Ananiah. "I know he's your friend, Father, but I don't like him."

"He's the best friend you have left in Providence," declared Captain Snow. "I know he was put out when you turned down that mealymouthed boy of his, but look how he came after you clear to Newport, when it would have been in his interests to let you disappear!"

Ananiah frowned. "I don't see how he'd gain from that."

"Because he'd inherit, that's why. To keep that whoreson Gramont from touching my money, I made sure it all goes to George if you and I die first. 'Course, I didn't expect we'd both end up rotting together in the desert like this, either."

"We're not dead yet, Father." Ananiah trailed her fingers through the sand at her feet, thinking of how many times since she'd left Providence that George

Gill had come close to changing from a rich man to a very rich one.

"Aye, there's something to be said for that, isn't there?" he said gruffly. To Ananiah's surprise, he reached out and took her hand. "You don't know how it grieves me to see you like this, Annie. Wearing rags, your pretty face turned brown as a savage's, bowing down to Hamet to save your old father's neck—Whatever would I say to your mother, eh?"

Her eyes met his, and found a warmth she would never have expected. Her face crumpled, and the tears she'd held back spilled over. Wordlessly, he held out his arms to her, and in the corner of Hamet's tent Ananiah found the reality of their reunion far better than anything she'd dreamed.

They packed and left for another camp in the morning, settling by nightfall in a rock-strewn valley around an ancient well. Among the rocks grew windswept thornbushes, their knobby branches immediately torn apart and eaten by the camels.

The tents had barely been raised for the night when three strange men appeared on camels over the crest of the dune. Their skin was darker than that of the Arabs, and their clothing and their camels' saddle cloths far richer. They wore slippers of yellow leather, and large white turbans, and wrapped over their shoulders against the cool of the evening were woven blankets; the tallest man had already drawn his partially over his turban like a hood.

But what had caught the attention of Hamet, and all the other Arabs, was how heavily, and elegantly, armed the three were. Each carried a new, long-barreled musket with a powder horn and a worked bag for bullets slung across his chest, a scimitar and two long knives at his waist, and a pair of heavy horse pistols in holsters across his saddle.

"Moors," said Captain Snow with relish. "Now we'll see Hamet and his lads jig to another's tune fast enough!"

Ananiah, standing beside her father at the opening of Hamet's tent, didn't share his delight at the strangers' arrival. Uneasily she rubbed her thumb against her finger where her ring had been. So many weapons could only mean violence and death, and she wanted no part of it.

"Like three fine gentlemen from Prospect Street a-calling on a ragtag flock of South County farmers, eh, Annie?" her father continued gleefully.

Hamet had welcomed the newcomers warily; desert hospitality could hardly let him turn them away from water. Their camels knelt, and the Moors dismounted, their movements stiff from a long day's journey. The first two feigned polite interest as Hamet, fearful that they'd come to rob him, complained passionately of his poverty, while the third didn't even pretend to listen, instead leading his camel to the trough near the well.

With his head cocked, Captain Snow's gaze flicked over his daughter, his eyes narrowing shrewdly. "Go ahead, Annie, show yourself to them," he urged. "We'll gain nothing from hiding, and I'll wager they'd rather look at you than my old face. Those fellows wouldn't lose a ransom note like these imbecile Arabs!"

"Oh, Father, no!" She didn't like these tall, dark-skinned men with their black beards and their long knives. "I can't just walk up to them for no reason at all!"

"Aye, you can, my girl, if you want us to ever see Providence again." He gave her a firm little pat that was nearly a shove. "Go to the well for water, or some such."

As much as she hated Hamet, at least she knew what to expect of him, and that he wouldn't hurt her. The Moors were different but perhaps her father was right about them. With a sigh, she fetched the calabash for water and headed for the well, her bare feet carefully finding a way among the rocks.

The hooded stranger was more concerned with watering his camel than with ogling her, and Ananiah hoped her father was watching so that he wouldn't blame her. Cool water sloshed across the front of her tunic as she pulled the bucket from the well. She swore in Arabic at her own clumsiness, and the Moor chuckled. It was one thing to fault herself, another to be laughed at by a stranger, and she turned swiftly to rebuke him. With a little splash, something fell into the hollowed gourd full of water, and she gasped when the water stilled and she recognized her mother's sapphire locket.

"Keep at what you're doing, angel," said Sam urgently, his voice low, for her ears alone. "Try emptying that bucket into the trough, but for God's sake, don't look at me."

Ananiah felt as wooden as the bucket in her hands as she made herself do as he said. *Sam here, here for her....* She was afraid to believe it. He was wise not to let her see his face, for it she did, there'd be no keeping her joy to herself. She wasn't enough of an actress for that. Her heart pounding, she glanced at his hand, patting the camel's neck as it drank. Beneath the dark stain, there was no mistaking his long fingers and broad, callused palms.

"How did you find me?" she asked breathlessly. "Where are Seid and the others?"

"Later, sweetheart, when we've more time." His voice hardened. "Hamet hasn't hurt you, has he?"

"Oh, no. I'm far too valuable to him for that."

"You're more valuable to me. Tonight, while they sleep, I'll come for you."

"No, don't, not to the tent," she warned. As she spoke, she took the necklace from the water and tied it securely in one corner of her tunic. She couldn't risk any of the others seeing it. "Hamet will hear you. I'll meet you beyond that dune, there."

"You're sure, Ananiah?" The concern in his voice warmed her, and she smiled.

"I'm sure." She began to lower the bucket into the well once again, hoping her movements appeared more natural than they seemed to her. "But I won't be alone. I'm bringing my father."

"Your father?" Sam repeated, mystified. "What the hell are you talking about?"

"I know it's hard to believe, but he's a prisoner here, too. Look back towards Hamet and the tent behind him. The white-haired man that's watching us. That's him."

"Sweet Jesus."

"I can't leave him, Sam," Ananiah said desperately, hearing the dismay in his voice.

"I didn't say we would, did I?" He sighed heavily. "I wouldn't leave a dog with Hamet, let alone your father. Bring him with you tonight. Behind the dune, mind?"

"Behind the dune." Finally full, the camel lifted its head, water dripping from its chin, and gave a satisfied toss to its head. Ananiah stepped back, knowing she should return to her father now. And yet still she

didn't move, hugging the full calabash to her chest
even as he clicked his tongue to lead the camel away to
rejoin the two Moors.

"I love you, Sam," she said softly, not even certain
he could hear her. With her head down to hide the
foolish smile she couldn't keep back, she walked
slowly back toward the tent. Tonight she would be free
again, she thought joyfully. Tonight she would be with
Sam.

"You could have made yourself more agreeable, my
girl," said her father bitterly. "I'd have thought after
that folderol marriage of yours you'd at least have
learned how to catch a man's fancy, even if he's a
bloody heathen Moor."

"Hush, Father, he's not a Moor," said Ananiah as
she carried the water into the tent. His jab about her
marriage stung. Because she had blamed herself for
much of what had gone so wrong with Étienne, and
because she had been so shamed by it, she had never
told her father how bad it had become, letting him
believe that the return of Étienne's first wife was her
only reason for leaving Martinique. Her father had
believed she was innocent, when she needed that kind
of faith most.

"Well, he don't look like the president of the United
States, either," he said irritably as he followed her.
"How the hell do you know he's not a Moor? You
scarce bothered to say how-d'ye-do to him."

Outside, she could see Sam and the two Moors pre-
paring to leave, with Hamet so visibly relieved that he
was nearly dancing his farewells, and she knew she
wouldn't have much more time alone with her father.
She set the water down beside Hamet's mat and nervously smoothed back her hair. The time for truth had
come sooner than she'd expected.

"Father, I know him." Her thumb worked hard in her closed palm. "His name is Samuel Colburn, Captain Colburn, and he was the master of the ship that brought me to this coast. He's a Salem man, and you're as much a Moor as he is."

He looked at her sharply. "Why's he here, rigged out that way?"

"He's come to rescue us."

"I'm no fool, daughter," he said bluntly. "I figured that much for myself. I mean, why's he come for you? What kind of money did you promise him, eh?"

"Not a cent, not that he'd ask for it." She closed her eyes for a long moment, wishing he'd said something, anything, other than this. She swallowed hard. "He loves me, Father. That was enough."

"Enough to risk his neck? Nay, Annie, no man does that, save in those silly London lady-novels you favor." With his hands at his waist, he shook his head and looked up at her from beneath the white thatch of his brows. "Do you pretend to love him too?"

She nodded miserably. "But there's no pretending about it. I love him more than my own life."

"If things don't go well with that rogue Hamet, you may get the chance to prove your words." He shook his head again and sighed. "At least this Colburn's come after you, which is more than that jackanapes Gramont would have done."

"Sam's nothing like Étienne!"

"He'd best not be, or off you go to Bedlam." To her surprise, he took her gently by the shoulders, an odd, uncharacteristic smile twisting his mouth.

"All I want for you is to be happy, Annie," he said gruffly. "I've always given you everything you could want. I never would've made up that match with Gramont if I didn't think he'd please you. If you want this man Colburn, why, then he's yours, and that's an end to it. Leastways I'll know this one's not out to rob me by chattering like a monkey in French.''

Ananiah's own smile was tight with everything she couldn't find words for. Her father made it all sound so easy. She wished to God it was.

It was nearly time.

Wide-awake, every muscle tense with anticipation, Ananiah lay on her mat, listening to the staggered pattern of Hamet's snores. Cautiously she eased herself up onto her elbows. Hamet lay flat on his back, his unsheathed knife ready beside his relaxed hand, and curled beneath one arm—for warmth, not affection—was Ezimah. Ananiah dug into the sand beneath her mat, found the heart-shaped locket where she'd buried it for safekeeping, and slipped it around her neck for luck.

''Ananiah?'' her father whispered softly outside the tent. ''Show a leg, girl!''

Ananiah's chest tightened with excitement. Only a few minutes more, and she'd be back with Sam. Earlier in the evening she had worked the pegs nearest her mat loose, and now she could easily roll up the edge of the tent. Scarcely daring to breathe, she glanced one more time at the dark, still shadows of Hamet and Ezimah, then wriggled beneath the rough fabric.

Her father was waiting, his hand grasping hers to pull her to her feet. His pale eyes were charged with a reckless confidence, his thin shoulders squared almost to the point of swaggering, and to Ananiah he seemed once again the commanding figure she remembered.

The moon was in its final quarter, a thin crescent that gave little light as father and daughter hurried between the tents, their footsteps muffled by the sand. Hamet posted no guards in his camp, trusting instead that each of his men would defend his own family and possessions, and there was always the chance that some light sleeper might hear them and call the others.

Their feet sank deep as they climbed to the top of the dune, Ananiah grasping her father's hand to keep from sliding backwards. Near the crest, he pulled her to a halt.

"You go on ahead, Annie," he said, breathing hard. "I've got to run back for a moment."

She shook her head. "No, Father, you have to come with me. Sam's waiting for us."

"I won't be long, I swear it." He squeezed her fingers affectionately. "On with you, now. You'll be safe enough with your love-struck fellow for company."

He turned and plunged down the dune, heading back to the little cluster of tents before Ananiah could stop him.

"Ananiah!" Sam's embrace lifted her off her feet as he swept her over the crest of the dune in his arms. She gasped with surprise and clung to his shoulders, and from sheer, dizzying relief she buried her face against his chest. Even in the unfamiliar clothes, he smelled like Sam, her Sam, and she hugged him closer, afraid that somehow he'd disappear if she didn't.

"You've become no more than a featherweight, angel," he said with real concern, his hands as he held her judging how close to the skin her bones had become. "I thought you said Hamet treated you well."

"I'm fine, Sam, I swear. Better than fine now." She smiled tremulously and touched his cheek, still disbelieving, and then her voice broke beneath the flood of her emotions. "Oh, Sam, I thought I'd never see you again!"

He kissed her hungrily, reminding himself how infinitely dear and precious she was to him. There had been too many nights and days for him as well, when he thought her forever beyond his reach, the sum of his heart lost in the vastness of the desert. Now that she'd come back in his arms, nothing would ever make him part with her again.

Suddenly she broke away from him, her eyes wide. "My father."

Sam loved the way she was still breathless, nearly panting, from his kisses, and he pulled her close again, not really hearing what she said.

"My father, Sam," she said again. This time he heard the anxiety in her voice, and reluctantly he set her down, his hand lingering at her waist. "He promised he'd be only a moment, that he had to go back."

"He picked a hell of a time for it." He ran his fingers though his beard, scratching his jaw. As much as he wanted to kiss her again, it was high time they were on their way. He was certain that Hamet would follow when he discovered his loss, and they needed to gain as much of a lead as they could. He glanced back at Rais bel Cossim and Bel Mooden. Waiting with the camels, their long-barreled muskets in their hands, the two Moors watched him with Ananiah with such studiedly blank expressions that Sam almost laughed.

"Who are they, Sam?" asked Ananiah uneasily. To her the Moors seemed every bit as threatening as the Arabs.

"Friends for as long as we need them. They've been paid well enough for their loyalty." Seid's cache of Spanish *dollares* had been more than sufficient to hire the two men and the camels; the remainder had been left with a merchant banker for safekeeping in Santa Cruz. "They're not such bad men, angel."

"But how do you know they won't turn around and make us slaves, too?"

Sam smiled. "Because they know they'll never see the rest of the silver I've promised them unless we all arrive safe at Mogador."

Ananiah nodded, rubbing her bare arms. If Sam believed he could trust the two men with the muskets, then she would, too. She looked longingly back towards the camp. "Perhaps I should go find Father."

"Nay, you'll do no such thing." Sam's arm circled more tightly around her waist. "I'll give him another two minutes, and then—"

With a loud grunt, Captain Snow charged over the crest of the dune to face the twin muskets of the Moors, aimed at his chest.

"That's a pretty welcome for your father," he said unsteadily as Ananiah ran to him.

With a little cry, she stopped and stared at the blood-splattered front of his tunic. "God in heaven, Father, what has happened?"

He held his hand out towards her to show her the long knife with a wickedly curved blade. It was Hamet's knife, the polished steel blotched dark in the faint moonlight.

"For your sake, Annie, I owed that to Hamet," he said grimly, and though his lips were curved in a grin of triumph, Ananiah saw how his fingers trembled. "He should've known better than to toy with my daughter."

# Chapter Seventeen

"Then you've earned my thanks as well, sir." Sam stepped forward and rested his hand on Snow's shoulder. Killing Hamet must have taken every bit of strength the older man had; to Sam he seemed small and frail, and he felt Snow begin to sway beneath his hand. As unobtrusively as he could, he slid his arm beneath the man's shoulders to support him. "Can you ride a camel?"

"I don't have any notion of being left here, if that's what you're asking. Of course I can ride." Snow glared at Sam, his temper undiminished though his weakness was clear to everyone else. "Annie, girl, go fetch one of those coverlets. Damned Arabs would let a man roast alive by the day and freeze by night."

"We'd best be off." Slowly Sam led him towards the kneeling camels, noting how Snow let the bloody knife slip to the sand, forgotten. "I don't know how much time you bought us, but the more distance we can put between us and this camp, the better. You and your daughter can ride together."

"You're Colburn," declared Captain Snow.

"Aye, I'm Samuel Colburn." Conscious of Snow's blunt appraisal, Sam wondered uncomfortably how much Ananiah had told her father. It might, he thought, be wiser to be spell it out. "I was master of the brig *Truelove* out of Salem, and I lost a cargo of yours worth seven thousand American dollars when we foundered off this coast. About all I saved was your daughter, Miss Snow being a particular friend of mine."

"She'd damned well better be more than a friend, if it's already cost me seven thousand dollars." Ananiah draped a wide Moorish *haick* over her father's shoulders as he stiffly climbed on the camel's saddle. As he complained, his words were slurring without his realizing it. "Seven thousand! You've picked a right royal rogue this time, daughter."

"Oh, hush, Father," she scolded softly. "Mr. Morrow told me you always overinsure every venture so that you profit even from a loss."

Too frightened for him to be embarrassed by what he was saying, Ananiah scrambled across the saddle in front of him, and gently pulled his hands around her waist. His skin was as cold as he complained it was, cold and clammy, though the air tonight was still warm. He was shivering as he leaned heavily against her, already either asleep or unconscious, and she realized she'd have to hold his hands herself or he'd topple over. She pulled the *haick* tight around him and knotted the ends around her own waist in a kind of sling to help hold him securely. From behind he would be bolstered by a pack of provisions lashed to the saddle.

She watched as Sam carefully wiped Hamet's knife clean in the sand. Although she knew her father was a hard man who had survived six years of war and a lifetime of questionable deeds, she couldn't reconcile herself to the image of her father murdering a sleep-

ing man—even Hamet. And what had he done to poor
Ezimah?

"Do you think my father really did as he says?" Her
father's beard prickled the back of her arm where he
lay against her. "Killed Hamet because of me?"

"Aye, from the looks of this, and of him, I'd say he
did." Sam straightened, and tucked the knife into his
belt, trying not to remember Seid and his two sons,
and their blood dark around them in the sand where
he'd slit their throats. God willing, she'd never need to
know. "I'd warrant love can make us do most anything. Look at how far you've come for him."

He quickly mounted his camel, and the four ani-
mals lurched to their feet. Sam caught the lead on her
camel and tied it to his own as they began to move.
Rais bel Cossim and Bel Mooden rode in front, with
their muskets across their saddles. From the height of
the camel's hump, Sam glanced back one more time at
the still-sleeping camp of Arabs.

Ananiah couldn't, not without imagining what had
happened in Hamet's tent. "How far until we reach a
town?"

"Eight days' travel, maybe nine." He shook his
head, his eyes hidden in the shadows beneath the turban. "Ananiah, your father may have saved our lives
tonight, and I swear we'll do everything we can to
preserve his. But mind that he is old, and that he has
been a slave for many months."

"I know. You don't have to tell me." She tried to
smile. "But after finally finding him here..."

"Let him sleep now, angel. That may be what he
needs most. By morning he'll likely be cursing every
Colburn that ever drew a breath."

"Likely he will." Her smile this time was genuine, if fleeting. "Seven thousand dollars is a great deal of money."

They traveled without stopping through the long night, the camels never breaking their pace, never seeming to tire. Although Ananiah's back grew stiff from supporting her father, she did not complain, and with each step she resolutely willed him to grow stronger, to survive. Several times he muttered words she didn't understand, and shifted his body more firmly against hers.

But her will alone wasn't enough. She wasn't sure when in the night she first felt the warmth that marked his fever, but by the time the horizon was gray with dawn and they had reached a watering hole, her own back was drenched with his sweat.

Before her camel had settled to its knees, Sam and Bel Cossim were already untying her father and lifting him, still unconscious, from the saddle. As Ananiah climbed wearily down herself, Bel Cossim spoke excitedly in Spanish, and Sam swore.

"What is it?" Ananiah asked. "What has—"

She stopped when she saw her father draped between the arms of the two other men, and her hand flew to her mouth in horror. The heavy *haick* was soaked through with her father's blood, the ends of his long white hair dyed crimson with it, and she knew there was no use in hoping any longer.

"So Hamet didn't go without a fight after all," said Sam grimly as they laid Captain Snow on the sand beside the well. "Caught him between the ribs, from the look of it. I can't believe he's hung on this long."

Ananiah dropped to her knees beside her father. She dipped the edge of her shawl in the bucket of water that Bel Mooden had drawn for her, and gently wiped her father's ashen face. If his skin hadn't been burning from the fever of infection, she would have believed him dead already.

She took his hand in hers, linking her slim fingers into his rough, gnarled ones. Once, when she was very young, her father had promised to give her the world. Over her mother's protests, he had put her on his back, with her tiny arms wrapped tight around his neck, and carried her to the very top of the mainmast of his ship to show her all of Providence and the river and docks spread out before her—her world. She had laughed and clapped her hands, knowing he'd kept his promise. In his own way, since then, for her he always had.

"Oh, Father," she said sadly as she drew the wet cloth over his forehead. "Why didn't you tell me you'd been hurt, too?"

To her surprise, his eyelids fluttered open. "Didn't want you getting taken again on account of me," he rasped, each word framed by a painful wheeze. "You wouldn't have left me, even if I'd ordered you to."

She bowed her head over his chest. "I'm sorry."

"Don't be. You're too kind, girl, same as your mother was."

Her necklace hung free from her tunic as she bent over him, and briefly his eyes focussed on the swinging gold heart, the blue stones flashing in the rising sun. "Same—same as your mother."

"Don't try to talk," she urged. "Save your strength."

"Eh, what am I saving it for?" He tried to laugh, a shaky cackle that ended in a cough. A small bubble of blood showed at the corner of his mouth, and Ananiah wiped it away. "Marry this one, Annie."

She raised her eyes to look across her father to Sam. He'd kept apart on purpose, giving her this time with her father, while being there if she needed him. He rested back on his heels with his hands on his knees, his turban gone and his long, dark hair loose around his face. She was sure he'd heard her father's words, but all she found in his eyes was the reflection of her own sorrow.

"He came after you. Marry him," her father said again, his voice so weak she had to bend close to hear him. "Give me grandchildren."

Her fingers twisted around his. "Father, don't."

"Call the first boy after me, Annie. Promise me—"

His mouth worked convulsively as he struggled to say one more word, his head arched back, and then he was gone.

Though it didn't matter any longer, she wiped away the blood that flecked his lips before she closed his eyes, eyes so much like her own. She turned his hand over in her own one last time, keeping her loss at bay by studying the thick calluses on his palms and the crisscross of old scars along his fingers, the freckles from age and sun, and the way one thumbnail was torn ragged.

She hadn't promised. Why had he asked of her the one thing she could never do?

The harsh sob choked her throat without bringing the tears that could ease her pain. She wrapped her arms tightly around her body, hugging her misery to herself.

"Ananiah, love," said Sam, holding out his arms, his comfort, to her.

Another sob shuddered through her body as she shook her head. "I can't, Sam. I can't. The one thing he asked of me, and I couldn't swear to it."

"Ananiah, listen to me—"

"No!" The single word wailed out over the empty desert. "You don't know why, Sam. How could you? He told me to marry you, Sam. He wanted me to promise that I'd have your children, his grandchildren. He wanted me to name a son for him. He wanted to know that when he died, he'd live on still, in me and my children."

At last her tears came, ripped from the long-buried anguish in her soul.

"When Hélène de Gramont returned, I was three months gone with Etienne's child. The last night, the last time, he—he used me badly, to try to make me stay. The pains began before I'd even reached the gates. But I couldn't stay with him. I couldn't. It was the English minister and his wife who found me by the road the next morning. They say I almost died. I wish I had. When the fever passed, the baby was gone, and the midwife said there'd never be another. *Never.*"

She could scarcely see him through her tears. "I love you, Sam Colburn, but I'll never be your wife, because I can't give you what will make you happy, any more than I could promise my poor father something that will never happen. Never, Sam. Never."

"I won't hear it, Ananiah," Sam said harshly as he came around her father's body and pulled her up into his arms. "I won't hear you deny what you feel for me."

"No, Sam, I won't say it!" she cried. "Neither one of us can change what's happened, and I won't let you pretend otherwise!"

She struggled against him, but he held her fast, drawing her closer against his body. She couldn't fight both him and her grief, and finally she crumpled, sobbing, against his chest.

His arms relaxed around her, stroking down the length of her back and soothing instead of restraining her, and he murmured meaningless little words of comfort while he tried to sort through his own roiling emotions. He had dreamed of making a family with her, of their children in their home, and now she said his dreams of Colburn sons to carry on his name would never become reality. He couldn't tell her it didn't matter, because, to him, it did. It had mattered to her father, too, enough for it to be his last request to her. And clearly, painfully, it mattered to her. The desolation of her grief was as much for what she'd lost for herself as for her father.

Sam thought of how she had suffered because of Étienne, likely far more than he'd ever learn, her youth and trust abused for her husband's cruel amusement. Yet she had survived. It was her vulnerability that had first attracted Sam and made him want to protect her, but it was her strength that had made him love her.

She was a part of him now, and he couldn't imagine the rest of his life without her in it. It was for her that he'd come back across the desert, not for the nebulous ghosts of unborn children, and he loved her too much ever to let her go from him again.

He sighed deeply, and she stirred and pushed away from him to search his face. Her eyes were swollen from weeping, her hair was tangled, and her father's blood stained her clothes and hands.

"Please don't hate me, Sam," she said, her voice uneven from crying. He had been silent too long, she thought in despair. But what else could she expect? "I couldn't bear that."

"How could I hate you? I loved you before, and I love you still. Nothing can change that."

She began to smile, then closed her eyes, wincing as if the effort hurt. "I love you, too."

With his fingers he gently wiped away the tears beneath her closed eyes. He wanted more from her, but for now, he knew, this was all the promise of a future she could give.

They buried Captain Snow deep in the sand, wrapped in the blanket and blessed with the prayers that Ananiah and Sam said together. She hated leaving her father like this, without burying clothes or a coffin or a Christian minister to speak the proper service, but they were at least a week away from any town, and even she knew they couldn't carry his corpse in the heat.

For Ananiah, the days that followed were strangely seamless, and with her grief still fresh, she welcomed the empty sameness of the landscape. They rode at night and into the early morning, resting in the afternoon when the sun was hottest.

Though there had never been any sign that Hamet's people had tried to follow, Rais bel Cossim insisted that they not lag. No fires, no cooked food, only dried figs and unleavened bread eaten as they traveled from one well to the next. It was true, he admitted modestly through Sam's translation, that he and Bel Mooden were warriors equal to a score of unclean Arabs, and true, too, that Captain Colburn had the courage and strength of a lion, for all that he was a Christian, but they were only three, and the open desert was a dangerous place to be attacked.

"The courage and strength of a lion." Ananiah had liked that, especially since Sam had looked so sheepish and unlionlike when he repeated it. But it suited him, the same way the Moorish clothing seemed to suit him. From beneath the drape of her shawl, she stole a glance at him, riding beside her. The long white robes emphasized how tanned he'd become, his blue-gray eyes startling in contrast to his dark skin and hair. Beneath the robes he wore a sleeveless red coat with tiny brass buttons, unbuttoned over the curling hair of his chest, and in the sash at his waist he carried a scimitar. He was so very handsome and she loved him so much that it broke her heart to know that when they reached the port at Mogador, this particular lion would most likely be gone from her life forever. She would find passage back to Rhode Island, and live out her days alone in her father's house. She had no idea what Sam planned next, and she didn't want to ask, because it wouldn't include her.

He still told her he loved her, and she believed he did. Eyes like his didn't lie. But since the day of her father's death, there had been no more mention of marriage. She told herself again that only a fool would expect any.

And where Sam Colburn was concerned, she was the greatest fool in the world.

They waited until sunset to enter the lower town of Santa Cruz, for Rais bel Cossim still wished them to be as unobtrusive as possible. But soon after they had come through the town's gates and down the single main street, they were trailed by a growing crowd of men and boys, some merely curious, but others waving sticks and shouting taunts at them. Rais and Bel

Mooden shouted back, waving their scimitars, but the mob still hung close at the heels of their camels.

Resolutely Ananiah stared straight ahead, her heart pounding. Ignore them, she told herself. *Ignore them!* On either side of the street, rough stone houses formed a wall, funneling the mob of men closer to them. A thrown stone hit her camel, and he squealed and jostled sideways.

"Cover your face," ordered Sam curtly, shielding her camel with his own as best he could. "Use your shawl, your hands, anything."

Ananiah tugged her shawl over her head and across her mouth, the way she'd seen Ezmiah do before strangers. One man, bolder and angrier than the others, darted forward, taunting her as he reached up to grab her bare foot. Reflexively Ananiah swung her foot and kicked him hard on the forehead, sending him staggering back.

Bel Mooden's scimitar slashed down through the crowd, and came back red with blood. Shrill screams of pain and fear echoed in the narrow street, and another rock struck the wall beyond Ananiah's head, but the crowd dropped back, unwilling to continue if their victims meant to fight back, and within a few blocks they were conspicuously alone.

Bel Mooden grinned at her, his even ivory teeth fierce in his black beard, and touched his palm lightly to his chest, over his heart, as he addressed Ananiah, beside him.

"He says for a woman you are very brave," Sam translated. "I could have told him that."

Ananiah laughed, excitement and relief mingling to make her giddy. "Tell him that the men in Santa Cruz need more genteel manners around ladies."

"They've no experience with ladies, let alone manners. You might have noticed that you were the only woman on the street." She hadn't laughed since her father had died, and Sam had missed it. He wished he could think of something to make her do it again, but Bel Mooden was speaking, with Rais nodding in agreement behind him.

"What's he saying, Sam?" The laughter had stayed in her eyes, making it hard for Sam to concentrate on the Moor's words.

"He says you have the courageous heart of a lioness. He thinks you're a worthy mate for me." Sam smiled, though his eyes were guarded, unsure of her reaction. "I could have told him that, too."

Ananiah's merriment faded, and she looked down at the pommel of her saddle. Lioness or not, she wasn't brave enough to face this yet, and the four of them traveled to the north end of the town in silence.

For once they didn't push onward, but stayed the night with a distant cousin of Rais bel Cossim, a smith, who pointedly told Sam and Ananiah to sleep beneath the awning over the walled yard around his shop. But as if to make up for not inviting them into his house, the cousin sent out to them a lavish dinner, a baked fish much like salmon, bread and sweet butter, dates, and a dish made from seasoned millet and roast lamb called couscous.

With a sigh of pure contentment, Ananiah set her wooden platter, still half filled with untouched food, down on the ground beside her and leaned back against the wall, savoring the sun's warmth, which still lingered in the limestone. "That was delicious, but I can't eat another bite. I've gone so long with eating next to nothing that I don't know if I'll ever be able to sit through a dinner with ten removes again."

Sam, beside her, ran his fingers along her arm, noting how the bones of her wrist seemed to jut through her skin. "You should eat more, angel. When I bring you to Mr. Peterson's house in Mogador, his wife will think I've starved you."

She didn't answer, preferring to concentrate on the little circles his fingers were tracing on the inside of her arm, rather than on the opinions of the American consul's wife. Mrs. Peterson meant Mogador, and Mogador meant parting with Sam, and that would come soon enough.

Wistfully she looked up at Sam from beneath her lashes, and he smiled lazily down at her. The small walled courtyard seemed almost cozy after the openness of the desert, and with the two Moors dining inside, she was alone with him for the first time since they'd been captured by the Arabs.

Sam poked at the fire before them with a stick, the light from the rekindled flames flaring briefly across his face. "When I first saw you, you were wearing diamonds and kidskin gloves and plumes in your hair, and I thought you were the most beautiful creature I'd ever seen."

"You wouldn't think that now," she said quickly. The compliment, the easy bantering, reminded her too much of what she would lose when he left.

"Oh, aye, I would. I do." He gently pushed her hair back from her face to see her better, and marveled again at how lovely she was. "But think of all the suffering you'd have been spared if I'd left you on that wall."

Suddenly skittish, she shifted away from his hand, retreating again behind the pale curtain of her hair. "You sound like my father. He thought I should have stayed in Providence, too."

"Did he now?" He smiled, thinking how young she looked with her white-blond hair loose and tangled and her cheeks browned by the sun, like some farmer girl. "You know, I'd made up my mind to dislike your father, but when I met him, I liked him right well. We were two of a kind, that old man and me. For one thing, we both loved you."

She wished he wouldn't speak of love, not tonight, and she hugged her knees and stared into the fire. "What he said about you marrying me, Sam—I shouldn't have told you that. I don't want you feeling obliged, or pitying me. Likely my father just meant to cheat George Gill."

He frowned, wondering why she was so eager to change the subject. The devil knew he'd given her time enough, time that for him had finally run out. "What the hell does George Gill have to do with me feeling obliged?"

Relieved to have distracted him, she spoke rapidly. "Father was so determined to keep Étienne from ever making a claim on his fortune that he made Mr. Gill his heir if I happened to die first. I'm just glad Mr. Gill won't know how close he's come to surviving me."

"Maybe he did know." The teasing left Sam's face, and his expression hardened, along with his voice. "When Gill came after you in Newport, I thought Amos Howard was dancing a little too sharp to another master's tune. Maybe he was working for Gill and not for me all along, from the time the crossjack fell to when he pushed you overboard. Maybe—"

"Sam, it's done." She rested her hand briefly on his arm to steady him. "Howard's dead, and I'm not, and there's nothing gainful in guessing the rest. I've never cared for Mr. Gill, but I don't think he'd ever be that—that *evil*. He was my father's friend."

"Queer sort of friend." But Sam knew she was right. The *Truelove* and everything on her were done, finished, but the threat to her while she was in his safekeeping was caught up in everything else he felt for her.

Her eyes were enormous in the firelight, and her lips were parted in an unconscious invitation. He reached out to her arm, and with his fingertips slid the wide sleeve of her tunic up over her shoulder. No shift, no petticoats, only warm, smooth, rosy skin. Gently his fingers kneaded the muscles of her shoulders. He heard the little catch in her breathing, saw how she swayed towards him, as if blown by the wind.

"Little lioness," he murmured as he pulled her into his lap. He ran his lips along her throat, and his beard feathered across her skin. She shivered and arched away, her expression unreadable. She rested her hands lightly on his shoulders and swung her leg across the hard muscles of his thighs. Like a drift of snow, the worn white cloth of her tunic settled across him, and he drew her closer, achingly aware of the soft warmth of her, so near to the center of his own desire. He slowly slid his hands deep into her wide sleeves. His open fingers nearly spanned her back, his thumbs tracing the quivering undercurve of her breasts. The sleeves of her tunic hid her body, making his a blind man's touch, the fabric whispering over his wrists.

She held her breath until his hands moved forward to the fullness of her breasts, and when he found and teased the darker crests, she closed her eyes from a joy so intense she gasped. She had forgotten the rainbow of sensation that came with his caresses. She'd forgotten the fire he brought to her blood, and the power he brought to his loving.

Slowly, slowly, she brought her lips to his, in a kiss so bittersweet she almost wept. No, she hadn't forgotten. As long as she lived, she never would. What she'd done instead was to try not to remember, and she hadn't fooled her beleaguered heart for a minute.

"I love you, Sam," she whispered sorrowfully.

"Then marry me, Ananiah. If you love me, marry me."

She gasped and drew back. Her eyes were wild as she searched his face. "I told you that you didn't have to do this."

"And I'm telling you I do. I've never loved any other woman the way I love you."

"And I'll never love any man more than I love you." She shook her head, still not quite able to believe what he was offering. "You would want me? Knowing everything?"

"Aye, knowing everything. I love you, and I'll marry you the day we reach Mogador, if you'll have me." Didn't she realize what her hesitation was doing to him? "Damnation, Ananiah, what do I have to do to convince you?"

His mouth crushed down on hers, marking her forever as his as she melted against him. He raised her long enough to sweep aside the cloth that lay crumpled between them, then lowered her swiftly, his fingers clutching her hips as he filled her completely. She curled her legs around his waist, drawing him deeper, and he took her soft cries of joy into his mouth, and took them, too, as her acceptance.

"The first thing I mean to do," declared Ananiah, "is to call for a bath, with hot, fresh water and French lavender soap."

"You do that," agreed Sam, "for I warrant I know what you'll be doing after that."

Ananiah grinned at him as she guided her mule along the narrow trail. After the desert, the way from Santa Cruz to Mogador had been an easy one, following close to the coast. The land they crossed was cultivated in green fields, fresh food and water were plentiful, and they had been able to trade their camels in favor of faster mules.

"I haven't slept on a proper bedstead, with sheets and pillows and a featherbed, since July." She lowered her chin demurely, but her grin widened. "That is, Captain Colburn, if a bed is what you're proposing should follow a bath."

"Add one more night to your tally, love, for I've no mind to let you *sleep* on one this evening, either."

Blushing, Ananiah glanced at Bel Mooden, on the mule before hers, thankful for the thousandth time that the Moor understood no English. "Mrs. Peterson might not let us stay together until after we're wed."

Sam snorted. "Hang Mrs. Peterson! We've come this far together, and I'm not about to abandon you for her niceties!"

Ahead of them, Bel Mooden had reached the crest of the sandy hill. He stopped and stood in his stirrups, waving excitedly for them to follow. "Mogador!" he cried. "*¡He aquí!* Mogador!"

Eagerly Ananiah urged her mule up the hill, and spread before her was the city of Swearah, with the island of Mogador guarding the harbor to the sea. From this distance the water in the bay looked glassy-smooth, and the vessels in port, from tiny fishing craft to large European and American ships, were all sitting peacefully at their moorings. The buildings and houses were whitewashed plaster over stone, their roofs all green tile, as neat and regular as a child's play village. It was, thought Ananiah, almost too neat to be real. Then, far in the distance, she saw the bright patch of an American flag dancing in the breeze from the water.

"Look, Sam, look!" she shouted joyfully. "There, by the longest wharf. Can you see the red and white stripes? It must be raised over the consul's house. Oh, Sam, we really will be able to go home again!"

But Sam wasn't looking, not at her, not at the flag. His face had gone ashen beneath his tan, and his whole body was rigid. The reins were wrapped so tightly in his hands that his mule whinnied in complaint. He stared at the ships in the harbor, afraid to blink or look away in case he'd imagined what he now saw before him.

For riding neatly at her anchor, every spar and sail in place, was the *Truelove*.

# Chapter Eighteen

"I knew they could have survived the storm!" Ananiah cried joyfully when he pointed the brig out to her. "Oh, Sam, I can't believe it—Jeremy and Letty and Mr. Lawson and everyone else, they didn't drown after all, any more than we did!"

"And my *Truelove* still swims." He was still too stunned for rejoicing. It was unbelievable, a miracle. When last he'd stood on the brig's deck, he would have given her an hour afloat at best, and yet here she was, as trim as ever, and with all the storm's damage put to rights—Lawson's work, he'd warrant. So all his grief and sorrow had been for nothing. His crew, God willing, must be alive. He still had the right to call himself captain and owner, and when he married Ananiah, it wouldn't be as a pauper.

"I must go out to her at once." He dug his heels into the mule's sides, trying unsuccessfully to make the animal move faster. The brig looked well enough from this distance, but he needed to learn for himself how she fared, how many of his crew had survived, how they'd come to be in Mogador—a thousand questions. "Bel Mooden will take you to the consulate, angel. I'll join you there as soon as I can."

"No, Sam, I won't!" she declared. "After I've been cast away and nearly drowned with you, and kidnapped with you, and traipsed across the desert by camel for weeks and weeks with you, I am not going let you send me off to drink tea with a lady I don't even know while you go to see everyone on the *Truelove* and have them make a great fuss over your deliverance, and anyway, I don't want to be apart from you, ever!"

He looked over at her, startled back to the present by her indignation, and slowly a smile spread across his face. For all that he loved his precious brig, it couldn't begin to compare with what he felt for Ananiah, and he simply stared at her, unable to find the words for the incredible good fortune he'd had in finding her and the happiness she'd brought.

Ananiah shoved her hair back from her face. "Well, I won't go, Sam. It's just not fair."

"And if the world were fair, angel, I wouldn't even be able to dream of a woman like you." He didn't want to be away from her, either, not even for a few hours, and he considered bringing her with him to the brig. But there was no way with any conscience he could take her through a waterfront dressed, or undressed, as she was. It had less to do with any Muslim preferences than with his own wish to keep her charms to himself. With her tunic frayed above her bare, tanned legs, and only the last remnant of her tattered shawl over her shoulders for decency, he wouldn't have let her go to the docks in a Christian town like Providence.

"I'd take you with me, love, but you're hardly dressed for it." He leaned across to take her hand and raised it to his lips. "I'm a jealous man in love, and I don't want any other men ogling you. I know how sailors are.''

"So do I. I'm marrying one.'' She sighed, realizing there was no use arguing, and squeezed his fingers. "You will take care? I'm not sure I should trust you, sailors being what they are.''

"You'll find nothing to complain about from this sailor.''

"I shall remember that, as long as you remember how much I love you.'' She smiled wistfully, imagining what Rhode Island ladies would make of him, looking so impossibly dashing in his beard and *haick,* with a scimitar at his waist. Not that she'd give them the chance to find out. Women in love could be jealous, too. "And Sam—mind you bring back my clothes from my cabin. I don't intend to be left behind again.''

"You poor creature! Look at you!'' Mrs. Peterson swept across the tiled floor of the consulate's entry hall to seize Ananiah's shoulders with an impulsiveness that made Bel Mooden's hand fly to the hilt to his scimitar. "But, child, I don't understand. Mr. Peterson had received word, most reliable word, too, that Miss Ananiah Snow of Providence had perished at sea, drowned.''

"I was lost overboard, ma'am, but I survived, and was made a slave by Arabs, and escaped.'' Ananiah noticed how Mrs. Peterson had stopped short of embracing her, and had now retreated two steps. Lord, how much she must need that bath! "I am quite alive.''

"Indeed! We've seen our share of our poor seafaring brothers made slaves, to be sure. Arranging redemptions is one of Mr. Peterson's most troublesome responsibilities. But never before a lady!''

She shook her head, her amber earbobs swinging as she dabbed her handkerchief to her forehead. Her face was flushed and filmed with perspiration; like the other American and English ladies in the city, she continued to dress as if she were still at home, in heavy sateen, with whalebone stays and the proper number of petticoats. She made Ananiah feel hot just looking at her. "Mr. Peterson will have to sort all of this out. He is at present calling on the pasha with another gentleman, but when he returns he'll know what's to be done with you. Oh, Miss Snow, truly your deliverance is the work of divine heaven!"

"More truly, ma'am, it's the work of Captain Samuel Colburn of Salem. He's the one that rescued me." Ananiah smiled shyly. "We plan to be married as soon as we can stand before a Christian minister. Today, if it can be arranged."

"Today!" Mrs. Peterson's painted eyebrows arched skyward. "Dear child, I wish you joy on your betrothal, but a wedding simply cannot be arranged in a day. We have few enough celebrations here in our little community. First you must rest, recover, have gowns made, and then we shall have a ball in your honor, before we can have a wedding."

But Ananiah didn't want a grand wedding among well-meaning strangers. All she wanted was Sam.

"You are most kind, ma'am, but I should prefer today. It would, I think, be best. I have, you see, spent many weeks in Captain Colburn's company." She smiled sweetly. Perhaps, she thought, there was more of her father's perversity in her than she'd realized. "Many weeks, and quite alone."

Mrs. Peterson needed no further explanation, and her gaze focussed critically on Ananiah's waistline. "You are right, of course. Celebrations can come after a wedding as well as before. But, pray, where is the bridegroom?'' She glanced doubtfully at Bel Mooden, who was scowling beside Ananiah.

''Captain Colburn is at the harbor,'' Ananiah said happily. Lord, she couldn't even say his name without grinning! ''He didn't know until today that his brig had been saved from the same storm in which we were lost. He will join me here as soon as he has visited the *Truelove,* and seen that everything there is in order.''

But despite her own euphoria, Ananiah didn't miss how the consul's wife started at the *Truelove*'s name, or the way she patted her handkerchief against her cheeks to mask her discomfort.

''Indeed,'' the consul's wife said faintly, her troubled eyes avoiding Ananiah's. ''Mr. Peterson must sort this out directly. But come now, child, let's try to wash and dress you like a decent Christian woman again.''

The courage of Rais bel Cossim before an enemy had never been questioned, but because he couldn't swim, he balked at crossing the deep water of the bay, and alone Sam was rowed by a shirtless hired boatman to the *Truelove*'s mooring. He smiled at the familiar feeling of being afloat, even in this battered old boat. He had been three months on land, the longest time since he'd been a prisoner in the last war.

Eagerly he studied the *Truelove* as the boat drew closer, taking in the new mast and railings, and the new, unpatched sails. Lawson's work, without a doubt, and though the brig's restoration pleased him, he wondered how Lawson had paid for it. Perhaps Peterson had advanced the funds; thank God he'd still have silver left from Seid's hoard after he paid the two Moors.

Lawson's work, and not Howard's. Sam sighed restlessly. He'd have to keep hold of his temper around Howard, if the man still lived, or he'd kill him outright for what he'd done to Ananiah.

He could see only one man on watch, a balding, thick-shouldered man he didn't recognize from the back. A new crewman wouldn't be so uncommon, but Sam prayed he hadn't been signed on to replace an old friend lost in the storm.

He frowned to see the rope ladder left hanging over the side—careless negligence in a strange port, especially if most of the crew were ashore. Tossing the boatman two coins in payment, he caught the ladder as the boat bobbed alongside the brig's gently curving sides, and swung himself up.

"Shove off, you black devil!" bellowed an unfamiliar voice as Sam climbed onto the deck. The thick-shouldered man stalked slowly towards him, slapping a cudgel in his open hand. "We've no use for thieves like you on board this ship!"

Sam belatedly remembered his Moorish dress. He couldn't really fault the man for not recognizing him as the captain, or even as an American, but it wasn't exactly the homecoming he'd expected, and the man's belligerence still rankled. He tugged off his turban, his damp hair blowing back, and looked levelly at the sailor. "You should pull up that ladder if you don't want visitors. What's your name, man?"

He scowled, clearly surprised that Sam spoke English, and North Shore English like his own at that. "My name's no concern of yours. Off with you now, or cap'n's orders say I'll stove your head in for your trouble!"

"And my orders say you'll talk civil to me, or you'll be the one with a stoved-in head." Justified or not, he hated the idea of any man giving orders in his place on his ship, and his hands curled into fists at his side. "I'm Samuel Colburn, master and owner of this vessel, and I'm willing to account your insolence to ignorance once. Once, but not again."

"Master, you say." The man smirked and spat contemptuously over the side. "And I'm the bloody pashaw hisself. Off with you, mate."

"Cap'n Colburn!" With a yelp, Jeremy hurled himself at Sam like a frantic puppy. "Oh, sir, they said you was drowned, you an' Miss Snow both, but I knew you wasn't. I knew you'd come back!"

Sam bent down to catch the boy in his arms, his eyes still on the man with the cudgel. "Aye, lad, you know I wouldn't desert the *Truelove,* nor you, neither. And Miss Snow's well enough, too."

He rose slowly, his arm still resting protectively around Jeremy's shoulder. "But this fellow here don't seem to believe me. I expect it's because he's new, but then, he could just be thick in the head."

"That be Mr. Clagget, Cap'n," said Jeremy, unaware of the growing tension between the two men. "And *this* be Cap'n Colburn, Mr. Clagget. He be everything he says. I know 'cause he be from Salem, same as me, an' he knows my pa, an' my brother Ben, an' 'cause I sailed with him long as I can remember. Longer, maybe."

Amos Howard stalked up the companionway. "Damn you, boy, quit your yammering! I'll thrash you but good if—"

Then he saw Sam, and he froze as still as if he'd seen a ghost.

What Sam saw was the man who'd tried to kill the woman he loved, the man who had taken his place on his ship.

Clagget hawked and spat again. "This bastard claims he's the master, Cap'n Howard. I thought you was, but the boy here says otherways."

"The boy don't know what he's talking about." With obvious effort, Howard composed his face, but white-hot anger had replaced the surprise in his round blue eyes. "You've no place on board the *Truelove,* Colburn. You abandoned her—jumped ship—and you abandoned us, and then you up and vanished. I'm the one that brought her in safe, and seen her put back to rights. *I* did, y'hear, not you! Mr. Gill saw to it that the courts declared her salvage, fair as morning, and he paid their price."

"Gill!" Sam didn't want to believe it: Captain Snow's friend, the friend who'd benefit most from Ananiah's death, now claimed his brig, along with her fortune.

"Aye, George Gill, and a fine, honest gentleman he is, coming here to bring home the body of his poor dead friend John Snow," declared Howard, his confidence rising as he sensed Sam's discomfiture. "It's his money that's brought this vessel 'round from the hulk she was, and he made me captain. You're nothing now, Colburn."

"The hell I'm not, and you know it!" thundered Sam. He pushed Jeremy to one side, unwilling to have the boy in the middle of what would happen next. And it was inevitable that something would. On Howard's side were Gill and the influence his money could buy, the Moroccan courts that had condemned the *Truelove,* and most likely Peterson as well. Beside that, Sam's own balance seemed pitifully slight: only the conviction that the brig was still rightfully his, and the willingness to fight to prove it. But most of all he had Ananiah.

"Was that your price then, Howard? If you'd do murder for him, then he'd make you a captain?"

"You've got no proof." But sweat glistened on Howard's forehead in the hot sun, and the other men who had gradually come onto the deck around them could hear the edge of desperation creeping into his words. Even Clagget, his own first mate, had stepped back to the circle of the others.

"I've got the proof of my own eyes, Howard." He stood with his legs spread wide, swaying slightly in answer to the *Truelove*'s motion, and the breeze that tossed his dark hair and his white tunic only emphasized the coiled tension that radiated from his body.

"I saw you push her," continued Sam. "I didn't abandon my command—I went to try to save her. And the other accidents—the crossjack and the open hatch to the hold—I'd warrant those were your doing, too, weren't they?"

"The little whore deserved to die!" cried Howard. "Ask Mr. Gill! She shamed all of Providence, spreading her legs for that Frenchman in his wife's bed!"

Sam's jaw tightened. "She's alive, Howard," he said softly, "and she's going to be my wife."

Panicking, Howard reached beneath his coat for the broad sailor's knife he wore at his waist. But with an icy scrape of metal Sam had drawn the scimitar from its scabbard. The sunlight glinted off the watered steel as he raised it high, then lowered it slowly, one hand over the other on the hilt, until it was even with Howard's chin. Every freckle seemed to stand out in relief against Howard's pale cheeks, and his throat jerked convulsively as he let the knife drop from his fingers to the deck.

"You'll never get the *Truelove* back!" Howard's voice shook through his bluster. "Gill will see to that. And your little bitch's life won't be worth a tinker's dam when he finds out she's in Mogador!"

Howard's laugh rattled with fear. "So what will you do, Colburn? Slaughter me like the heathen you're pretending to be? Here, on *my* deck, before a score of witnesses?"

"Three times you tried to kill my Ananiah." Sam stared at Howard; the freckled face seemed oddly distant and distorted, as if Sam were studying him from the wrong end of a spyglass. On Howard's bare forearm was a tattoo with five stars in a ring, the stars Ananiah had seen before he shoved her into the hold.

He felt the easy balance of the scimitar in his clasped hands. The weight was designed to make the cutting edge sing through the air as it sliced into skin and flesh and bone. He hated this man for all he'd done. He could kill him. Aye, he could do it now.

Instead, he thrust the scimitar back into the scabbard. Too easy, he thought, a coward's justice. He'd killed for patriotism, he'd killed to survive, but to kill for love, her love—she wouldn't want that.

*You will take care? she'd said. Remember how much I love you.*

He tore the scimitar and scabbard from his chest and threw them both away. The red cord on the scabbard was like a curling trail of blood as it slid across the holystoned deck. The men backed away superstitiously, unwilling to touch it, or to meet the strange look in their old captain's eyes. One made the sign of the cross over his breast. The Captain Colburn they remembered would never have turned from a fight.

Howard stared at the scimitar, too, his eyes disbelieving. He lunged across the deck to grab the knife that still lay at Sam's feet and rolled back to his feet. He scrambled back on the balls of his feet, restlessly fingering the knife in his hand.

"Not so brave now, are you, Colburn?" he taunted. "Maybe you've been walking about in that Araby dressing gown so long it feels all comfortable. Kind of like petticoats, eh, Colburn?"

Sam stood very still. He listened to the breeze thrumming in the standing rigging, to the mewing of the gulls overhead, to the steady beating of his own heart. Slowly he smiled at Howard, noting how the man rocked back and forth, low, like a crab. When finally he sprang forward, Sam was ready.

He seized Howard's wrist before he could stab upwards with the knife, and forced it back while Howard grunted and struggled to twist free. He was shorter than Sam, but heavier, and he threw his weight against Sam's hip, knocking him sideways. Sam stumbled, but kept his footing and his grip on Howard's wrist until the shorter man hooked his calf behind Sam's knee and pulled them both to the deck.

Over and over they rolled across the planking. Sam heard the others shouting, cheering them on, and then he felt the sharp edge of the railing slam into his back. Braced against it, he raised his free arm as far as he could and slammed his fist into Howard's jaw. Howard's head snapped sideways against the deck, and when he turned back to Sam, blood was running from his battered nose, but he still clasped the knife tightly in his hand.

Sam pushed his leg back against the base of the rail, searching for more leverage, and struck Howard again. This time the smaller man gasped and his whole body jerked against Sam's, his fingers relaxing long enough for Sam to seize the knife and toss it away. Breathing hard, Sam climbed to his feet, dragging Howard with him.

"You come...to Peterson..." Sam gasped, holding Howard upright against the rail, his fists knotted in the front of his bloodstained shirt. "Judge... trial...then gallows..."

Howard shook his head, his eyes unfocussed. "Hell wit' you," he said, and swung wildly at Sam. Sam ducked, and released Howard's shirt as his fist flew over Sam's bent head, over the railing. Before Sam could stop him, Howard's unsteady momentum had carried him over the railing. Sam leaned out to snatch at empty air, watching Howard flop towards the dark blue water, the soles of his boots turned up, his right hand still clenched in a fist and his mouth open in angry confusion.

Strong hands grabbed Sam and pulled him back, but not before he saw Howard rise to the surface, splashing and gasping, his bloodstained shirtfront a brilliant patch in the water. Instantly beside him came the sleek sweep of gray and paler silver of a shark's belly as it turned to seek the man's blood, the jagged row of teeth against its pink mouth, and Howard's final howl of terror and pain before he disappeared beneath the red-flecked foam.

"What's all this racketing about?" demanded Letty as she bustled up the companionway. "Amos, where've you gotten to, anyways?"

Lawson caught her arm gently and guided her back down the steps. "Hold now, lass, a word wit' you. Come below with me, there you go. Th' true cap'n's come back, an' there's been a dreadful accident...."

At the rail, Sam felt Jeremy's thick thatch of blond hair push against his arm, and he heard the boy's muffled whimper of horror. Quickly he took Jeremy's shoulders and turned his small, pale face away, into his tunic. With his hands still resting reassuringly on the boy's shaking shoulders, Sam closed his own eyes against what he'd seen. Rais bel Cossim had been wise to fear the water of Mogador Bay.

Now, he thought wearily, to find Ananiah before George Gill did.

# Chapter Nineteen

Ananiah sat perched on the edge of a damask-covered armchair in the consulate's drawing room, an untouched dish of tea on the mahogany table before her. She only half listened to Mrs. Peterson's cheerful stream of gossip about people she didn't know, and she wished Bel Mooden were here in this room with her, and not banished by Mrs. Peterson to the back courtyard. She missed the comfort of his fierce, familiar face and dramatic gestures in this genteel room, so like the ones at home, a place that now seemed oddly unreal to her.

Strange to sit on a chair after three months of camels and sand. Strange to be scrubbed clean again and smelling faintly of lavender, wearing tight little slippers and stockings with garters beneath a hastily altered gown. Strange to feel the weight of hair piled high on her head with tortoiseshell hairpins that dug into her scalp. Strange to have the luxury of sliced ham and roast fowl, and thick slabs of white bread with butter and summer-sweet blackberry jam.

Strangest of all to be here, anywhere, without Sam.

Beyond, in the hallway, she heard the front door open and shut, and men's voices that made Mrs. Peterson pat her hands together and look expectantly towards the doorway. The consul was dressed in the embroidered silk suit he had worn for calling at the pasha's palace. As he walked, smiling, towards his wife, he worked his finger into the heavy stock around his throat; his face, above it, was flushed from the heat.

Quickly Ananiah blotted the jam from the corner of her mouth and held her hand up to him. He had a kind, worn face, she decided, with a turned-up nose that belonged on a little boy, and as he took her fingers, Ananiah instantly shared his wife's confidence that he could "sort out" anything.

"I'm so glad you've come back early, my dear," Mrs. Peterson was saying, "for we've a quite, quite unexpected visitor. Allow me to present Miss—"

"Ananiah Snow." George Gill's broad shoulders were framed by the doorway, his arms crossed over his chest, and contempt was written over his face. "If you'd any decency at all, Ananiah, you would have stayed lost."

Stunned, Ananiah rose slowly to her feet, the bread and the napkin falling unnoticed to the carpet.

"Captain Gill." She swallowed back the sweet taste of blackberries that rose in her throat. "I did not expect to find you here."

But Gill ignored her, striding into the room to stand before the Petersons. "This is the very young woman I was describing to the pasha, not an hour since. A shame to her father, a disgrace to her family! I'm only thankful her parents aren't alive to hear 'traitoress' added to her list of sins."

Mrs. Peterson stared coldly at Gill, her expression an unspoken rebuke for his ill manners in her drawing room. "Mr. Gill, please, I must ask you to explain yourself."

"Better to ask the chit herself, ma'am." He turned and glared at Ananiah. "Among the papers found on my new brig I discovered a complete set in French, identifying the cargo as the property of Miss Snow's old paramour on Martinique."

Mrs. Peterson clucked her tongue. "Mr. Gill!"

"Forgive me for plain speaking, ma'am, but it's this doxy who's too foul for your presence." He jabbed righteously at the air with his thick, blunt fingers. "My shipmaster swears that when he was spoke by a French frigate, this woman beguiled the French captain, declaring her sympathy to the French cause in the most shameful and lascivious manner, regardless of the knowledge that her own country and France were at war! Treason and treachery, ma'am, there's no other way to look at it."

"By all that's holy, I swear it wasn't like that!" cried Ananiah. "False papers aren't treason, and as for the rest—it wasn't like that at all!"

Gill snorted. "I'd hardly think you'd say otherwise."

"Why are you saying these things?" Ananiah gripped the back of the armchair, clinging to any sort of reality. Where was Sam? she wondered wildly. He would tell them. He could make them understand! "What of the friendship you shared with my father?"

"It's too late to pretend to daughterly devotion now, Ananiah. I promised you I'd hunt for your poor father, and I kept my promise. I came clear to this place at my own expense, only to learn that your father perished in the desert months ago."

"That's not true, either! *I* found my father, not ten weeks ago, and he was alive!"

"Your father is alive, Miss Snow?" asked Mr. Peterson eagerly.

Ananiah's face fell. "No. He died defending me from the Arabs that held us both slaves."

"A cunning story, miss," Gill scoffed. "Where's your proof? Where's his body?"

"Where we buried him, of course."

Gill shrugged and rolled his eyes towards the ceiling with a half-muttered oath.

Ananiah rushed around the chair. "Listen to me! He told me he'd sent you five different appeals for his redemption."

"Or at least so you're saying now." Gill folded his arms again over his chest. "I received nothing."

"Then how did you know to come to Mogador? When I saw you last, at Newport, you seemed as convinced as I that my father was in a London prison, captured by the English navy. No wonder you let me believe it too." She stepped closer to him, her pale eyes flashing. "But even then you knew well enough where he was, and you ignored his pleas! You *knew*, didn't you?"

"Miss Snow's point is well taken, Gill," said Peterson thoughtfully. "When you came here, you already seemed to know that Captain Snow had been captive, and was now dead. Neither, it seems to me, you could have known before his daughter's arrival today, unless you had had some other communication directly from him. The Arabs tend to be quite efficient in sending their demands. Without the ransom, Christian captives would be useless to them."

Gill sputtered, and puffed out his chest. "You have, sir, only her word against mine!"

"Exactly." Peterson's smile echoed in the wrinkles across his face, and he turned to Ananiah. "Do you recall the name of the persons who held you?"

"Hamet was the only name the leader went by." Tears stung her eyes as she thought of how briefly she'd been reunited with her father, and she looked down so that the others wouldn't notice, down at the blotch of blackberry jam on her skirt. "I still wonder that in all the desert we were captured by the same man. Before we escaped, my father killed Hamet, and received the wound that killed him, too."

She didn't notice that Mrs. Peterson had come to stand behind her until she felt the older woman's hand rest gently on her shoulder. The simple gesture of comfort was almost too much for her fragile control, but she refused to give Gill the satisfaction of seeing her cry.

"Not such a miracle of coincidence, my dear. The same few tribesmen tend to scavenge along the beaches, and I see the same ones over and over with slaves to offer for redemption." Peterson shook his head. "Hamet was one of the poorest. He would have been content with fifty dollars for your father."

"Fifty dollars!" cried Ananiah, and she turned fiercely to face Gill, her fists clenched at her sides. "You let my father suffer for half a year for *fifty dollars?* You let him die for want of fifty dollars? God in heaven, and he believed you to be his dearest friend in Providence!"

Gill's face was mottled with anger, and the fury in his eyes was unmistakable. "Then he shouldn't have let you become that Frenchman's whore!"

Ananiah's cheeks flushed. Her shame was compounded by Mrs. Peterson's hand on her shoulder.

"Tom never wanted to marry me, any more than I did him!"

"You would have been contented enough with the fortunes involved!"

"That's quite enough, Gill!" said Mr. Peterson sharply. He took Gill by the arm, but the larger man shook him off.

"If you'll do nothing to stop her, then by God, I shall!" He grabbed Ananiah away from Mrs. Peterson, and as she stumbled off balance he roughly twisted her flat against his body, his arm like an iron band across her chest. "She's a cunning, thieving little bitch who's fooled you just like she's fooled everyone else!"

With both hands, Ananiah pulled on his arm, struggling to free herself. He seized the ivory-handled carving knife from the ham on the tea table and held the blade to her throat. With a little sob, she let her arms drop to her sides. She felt the edge of the knife against her skin and she drew back, closer to him and away from the blade, and he tightened his grip around her chest, the wool of his sleeve scratchy and smelling of snuff.

His arm was so tight that she could breathe only in tiny little gasps. Before her the white, frightened faces of the Petersons began to reel and spin, and she closed her eyes against the dizziness.

*Étienne's fingers tightened around her throat, the intaglio on his ring digging deeper into her skin. "Look at me, ma chère," he rasped, and she knew from the shudder that passed through his body to hers that he was nearly done. "Damn you, open your eyes and look at me!"*

"Let her go, Gill!" Sam thundered from the arched doorway. On either side of him stood Bel Mooden and

Rais bel Cossim, each with his scimitar drawn, and with a faint shriek, Mrs. Peterson retreated behind her husband. "Let her go *now!*"

"Colburn!" Gill's mouth worked convulsively. "Howard swore to me you were dead, too! My God, what does it take to kill you people?"

"Ask Howard, if you can find him," answered Sam his gaze intent on Ananiah. What had Gill done to her, anyway? She looked tiny and frail beneath Gill's arm, her eyelids mauve and her face ashen, and beneath the hem of her muslin gown, her slippered feet dangled as limply as a rag doll's. "Now I told you once before not to harm Ananiah, and I'm telling you again. Let her go!"

"The pasha believes me, even if you people don't!" cried Gill wildly. "He won't risk harboring a traitor just because she pretends innocence! He'll see her hung as she deserves!"

"So you can rob her fortune the same way you tried to steal my ship from me?" The man was mad, or desperate, or maybe both, and Sam knew he couldn't risk Ananiah's life to find out which. "Damnation, Gill, let her go!"

Sam inched forward, and immediately Gill responded by dragging Ananiah back with him two steps, the knife still to her throat. They blocked the only entrance to the room, and beyond the four tall windows lay only the street, two stories below. But as Gill's gaze roamed past Sam and the two Moors, searching frantically for a way to escape the room, Sam noticed how Ananiah had sunk lower in the man's grasp, her hair spilling across his bent arm. If only she could drop a little lower, or even slide free, then they could take Gill.

He'd never in his life felt so helpless with a sword in his hand. Ananiah's eyelids fluttered, and he thought he saw her stir. He remembered the times he'd called her back from Étienne's power. Maybe she was there again. Maybe, maybe, he could bring her back now.

"Ananiah, love," he said softly, almost crooning. "Ananiah, angel, it's me, Sam. Look at me, love."

*"Look at me, love." That was Sam's voice, not Étienne's. Sam, who loved her and would be her husband. Sam, the man she loved. Smiling, she opened her eyes to find him.*

She'd never seen that look in his eyes before, an awful, anxious fear, and she almost laughed to see it above the shining blade of the scimitar. What could possibly frighten Sam Colburn?

No, she thought, she'd seen him like this once before, on the beach, when she'd run away from him. Well, she'd no intention of running from him today. Today they were going to be married. She wriggled free of the man who held her and started across the six paces that separated her from Sam.

But he didn't let her. Instantly he lunged forward and threw his arms around her, crushing her to the carpet beneath his body. She heard a strange whoosh through the air that ended dully, a strangled, gurgling cry that ended before it had begun, and a woman's shrill scream.

"Don't look, Ananiah," said Sam urgently as he shielded her. "For God's sake don't look!"

But beyond his shoulder Ananiah saw Bel Mooden, standing grim-faced beside the mahogany table as the warm blood dripped from the blade of his scimitar onto Mrs. Peterson's pressed linen tea cloth. Then she remembered what had happened before Sam had come and guessed what had happened after. With a wordless little cry, she swiftly turned her face back against Sam's shoulder.

"Hush now, angel," he whispered as he held her tight. "All you must remember is how much I love you."

*Providence*
*August 1797*

The late-summer sun streamed through the tall windows of the bedchamber. The curtains were tied back and the sashes thrown open to catch the breeze from the river. A fat bumblebee, come in through the open windows, droned as it hovered near the pink roses in the vase on the mantelpiece, and the tall cherry case clock near the door chimed three times.

Ananiah stretched indolently and tugged the sheet up over her bare hip. She leaned up on one elbow, lifted Sam's hair clear of his neck, and kissed his ear, laughing softly as he growled in his sleep. Three o'clock on a Tuesday afternoon was not an ordinary time for any wedded couple to be abed, but then, as soon as they'd returned to Providence, Captain and Mrs. Samuel Colburn had made it very clear that they were not an ordinary wedded couple.

"It's after three, Sam," she said. "Letty will be shocked if she finds the door locked again."

"Hang Letty." Sam rolled onto his back and, with one arm around her waist pulled her on top of him. "Doesn't Lawson keep her busy enough?"

"He would, if you didn't keep him so busy with the *Truelove.*" She leaned forward to tease her lips across his until impatiently he pulled her down, crushing her breasts against his chest, and as they kissed she laughed with sheer contentment, deep in her throat.

His hands shoved back the sheet and slid along the curve of her bare back and hips, and her laugh changed into more of a moan as she curled her legs around his.

A little wail rose from beside the tall bed, and with a sigh, Ananiah climbed over Sam to the far side of the bed. "So soon, sweetheart? You've scarcely slept at all."

"I know the feeling well enough." Sam bent down and plucked the baby from his cradle. His tiny fists were waving with excitement. "Aye, little Jack?"

"Don't call him that, Sam. My father was always John, and no one ever *dared* call him Jack."

Sam settled back against the pillows, his son nestled contentedly in his arms. "Ah, well, when he's a great roaring shipmaster sailing off to China, then he can be Captain John, too."

Gently Ananiah stroked her baby's downy head as he looked up at her with his wide blue eyes that already reminded her of Sam's.

"Captain John Colburn," she said softly, still in awe of the little being they'd miraculously created between them. She pulled John's patchwork coverlet a little higher over his belly. "He can sail wherever he pleases as long as he comes home safe."

"I wouldn't worry about that, love," said Sam as he placed his hand over hers on the baby's coverlet, over the center patch of faded yellow paisley cashmere. "We Colburns always do."

\* \* \* \* \*

# Author's Note

North Africa was not a good place for Americans in the eighteenth and nineteenth centuries. Hundreds of American sailors were shipwrecked or captured and enslaved by Arab tribesmen and the pirates of the Barbary states. Among the captives who survived to be redeemed were some who returned home as uniquely American celebrities, visiting the White House to shake hands with the president and then sitting down to write and publish accounts of their adventures.

The best of these is *An Authentic Narrative of the Loss of the American Brig* Commerce . . . by Captain James Riley; when published in 1817, Captain Riley's book became one the earliest homegrown "bestsellers." Another "Authentic Narrative," from 1818, is by Mrs. Eliza Bradley, the wife of a shipwrecked captain. Mrs. Bradley's account is more genteel and ladylike, and among her "sufferings" are the loss of her bonnet and the destruction of her complexion beneath the Sahara sun.

Many thanks to Mary Leahy, Seymour Adelman

Rare Book Librarian of the Miriam Coffin Canaday Library, Bryn Mawr College, for making available to me both these books and others that proved equally invaluable.